Solar Fury

LOST IN THE ALPS

ST TANGIRALA

ISBN: 979-8-89694-717-2 - Ebook
ISBN: 979-8-89694-718-9 - Paperback

I dedicate this book to all the people, including friends,
family, fellow artists, entrepreneurs, creators, and people
I've met along the journey who have given me the
perspective of life and inspiration to write this book

I would also like to thank my dear friend, Michaell Margrutsche,
for sharing invaluable ideas and perspectives on Austria,
the country where the heart of this story unfolds.

CONTENTS

PROLOGUE

At the Helios Observatory, perched on a rugged cliff side off the coast of Ireland, the atmosphere was quiet, save for the soft hum of machines and the occasional gust of wind that rattled the windowpanes. Dr. Patrick Crehan hunched over the console, the dim blue glow of monitors casting lines of fatigue across his face. He rubbed his temples, eyes scanning the erratic data streaming in like a pulse gone mad.

"It doesn't make sense," he muttered.

Dr. Crehan adjusted his glasses, reran the solar flare analysis, and stared at the numbers confirmed his growing suspicion. Patterns he had memorized over a lifetime—sunspot behavior, magnetic field lines, coronal mass activity—were aligning in a way they never should.

"This can't be right," he said.

Across the room, Dr. Kazuo Tachikawa paused, his fingers hovering just above his keyboard. He didn't need to ask what Crehan had seen. He'd seen it too—long before the data had turned red.

His hands moved swiftly. Dr. Tachikawa had studied the sun like a surgeon studied anatomy. Each loop of plasma, each surge of radiation, was a known language to him. But now, that language screamed.

"A Carrington-class event," he said.

Dr. Crehan leaned back, the chair creaking beneath him. The words hung heavy between them.

"The last time Earth had struck by something like this, the world ran on steam and wine," he whispered. "Now it runs on code."

"If it hits at full strength…." Crehan said.

"We lose more than power," Tachikawa said. "Satellites. Navigation systems. Hospitals. Air traffic. Civil infrastructure. Everything."

He began compiling the data into a report, fingers gliding across the keyboard without hesitation. Every second mattered now. There was no time to warn the world gently. The report would go directly to global networks, space agencies, emergency protocols—if anyone still remembered how to prepare for something like this.

Dr. Crehan activated the emergency comm system, his hands trembling just slightly. "We've got maybe twelve hours if the velocity holds."

Dr. Tachikawa didn't reply. He was already watching the sun.

On the main screen, a visual representation of the solar surface bloomed into violence. A coronal mass ejection—bright, massive, and fast—erupted from the sun's surface, hurling a wave of radiation and magnetized plasma into space.

The instruments shrieked with warnings. The flare had breached containment.

Dr. Crehan stared, his breath caught. "There it is."

Dr. Tachikawa stood motionless, eyes fixed on the storm hurtling toward Earth. For a long moment, he said nothing.

Then, quietly, with the weight of inevitability. "It's a solar fury. Alert the governments."

Dr. Crehan grumbled. "No government has been notified of the approaching danger. This is going to go really bad. And my readings say that not just one flare. But there are multiple solar flares coming in the years ahead."

Dr. Tachikawa sighed. "It's going to be a loss for the world soon. Get ready."

The two scientists exchanged a final glance. All they could do now was watch as the storm came crashing down upon the world.

CHAPTER 1

A sunny afternoon bathed Atlanta's Hartsfield-Jackson International Airport in golden light, casting long shadows across the sprawling tarmac. The airport pulsed with energy, a constant hum of movement as thousands of travelers navigated the terminals.

Through the heavy traffic leading into the international terminal, a 2022 Volkswagen Jetta rolled up to curbside check-in before easing into a parking spot. Inside the car, Steve Turner and Lindsay Carson exchanged a long glance, their eyes wide with unspoken emotion.

"Do you want to park so we can say a proper goodbye?" Lindsay said. "I can't stand the constant whistling from the folks right in front of us."

Steve nodded. "Yeah, let's do that."

Fifteen minutes later, Steve maneuvered the car into the parking garage. His jaw dropped as he read the rates.

"It costs this much to park?" he muttered.

"Don't worry about it," Lindsay said. "Everything's expensive these days. I just hope things go back to normal soon."

Steve sighed and pulled into a spot. He stepped out of the car, adjusting the brim of his Braves World Series cap and slinging a duffel bag over his shoulder. The Georgia Bulldogs logo stretched across his chest as he shut the door with a thud. Behind him, Lindsay climbed out, tugging at the sleeve of her hoodie as her fingers brushed the silver cross at her neck—a nervous habit. Sunlight caught the threads of her ripped jeans as she glanced around, her posture a mix of anticipation and unease.

They walked in silence from the garage to the international terminal. As they entered, Lindsay let out a frustrated breath as they stepped inside.

"Can't believe we're missing our anniversary. And with the wedding coming up… this just isn't how I pictured things."

"I know," Steve said. "But the NCAA wants me to go to Finland and study the club and college sport environment. If there are opportunities to build something there, I have to be ready. I'll do whatever it takes."

Lindsay chuckled softly. "You need to stay grounded, Steve. You get caught up in chasing success too fast."

"Why not?" Steve shrugged, a flicker of pride in his voice. "I've worked my ass off to get here. It's not just about hockey or school—it's about proving I belong, you know?"

He glanced at her. "Maybe it's crazy, but one day I want to lead something bigger, the whole league, maybe. Just need to keep building."

Lindsay sighed. "I admire your ambition. It's part of why I fell for you. But I worry you're pushing too hard. Keep your feet on the ground."

Steve smirked. "And once I make it big, you won't have to work those crazy hours at the hospital."

Lindsay rolled her eyes but smiled. As they arrived at the check-in area, Steve pulled out his phone to retrieve his boarding pass.

"What airline is this again?" Lindsay asked. "Delta doesn't fly to Finland from here."

"Celestine Airlines. Just launched service," Steve said, scanning the departure board.

Lindsay frowned. "Never heard of it."

They spotted the Celestine Airlines counter tucked near the end of the concourse, partly obscured by a pillar. Steve witnessed a lone attendant standing behind it, tapping absently at a keyboard.

"Found it," Steve said.

At the counter, a check-in agent named Imani greeted them. "Welcome, sir. May I see your passport?"

Steve handed it over. "My boarding pass is on my phone. Just checking in this duffel bag."

Imani nodded. "You'll need a printed boarding pass. Celestine doesn't allow mobile boarding in case your phone dies."

Steve sighed. "Alright." He handed over his bag as she began processing.

"Final destination is Helsinki, right?" Imani asked.

"Yep," Steve said. "Not like I can go to Russia with that war going on."

Imani gave him a blank stare. Lindsay squeezed his arm. "Calm down, sweetie."

Imani handed him the boarding pass. "Gate F10. Check in starts at 5:30 pm. Don't be late."

Steve forced a chuckle. "Of course."

As they walked toward security, Lindsay crossed her arms. "What was that about? You don't have to be so passive-aggressive."

"I'm not. I just believe in efficiency," Steve said. "In business, sports, and life—speed matters."

Lindsay sighed. "Not everything is about getting ahead. You need to slow down sometimes."

Steve smiled. "Alright, Lindsay. I'll try. Like I did on that hike this summer."

Lindsay chuckled. "That wasn't just a hike. We nearly froze on that ridge in Virginia, remember? You kept us going with those survival tricks you learned way back in the Boy Scouts."

She paused, her tone softening. "Just… try to take a breath more often. Be present. Gain some perspective. I think Owen could really use that side of you."

Steve pulled her into a kiss. "I'll be back. And I won't be the same person you see now."

With a last wave, he stepped into the security line, blowing flying kisses as Lindsay watched him disappear into the crowd.

The Uber stopped at the terminal. Paul Lynds stepped out into the crisp air and pulled suitcases from the trunk.

In the backseat, Sophie nudged Oliver. "We're here."

He stirred, blinking at the gray dawn. Beside him, Amy yawned and stretched. Sophie grabbed their backpacks as the kids slid out, still half-asleep.

"Let's go," Paul called. "Bags to check, flight to catch."

"Come on, kids," Sophie coaxed in a thick British accent. "We can't miss our flight."

"Where are we, Mum?" Oliver yawned, rubbing his eyes.

"At the airport. Daddy's got our bags," Sophie said.

Paul checked his watch and exhaled sharply. "We leave in ninety minutes. Let's move."

Sophie hesitated. "Wait, the kids aren't moving."

Amy groaned, "Mummy, I'm tired."

Paul sighed and grabbed a luggage cart, stacking their suitcases. With security guards whistling at idling cars and their Uber driver shifting impatiently in his seat, Paul made a quick decision. He scooped Oliver into his arms while Sophie picked up Amy.

"Thank you for the ride, Rayshawn," Paul said hurriedly as the family rushed inside the terminal.

They navigated through the bustling crowd, making their way to the British Airways check-in counter for their flight to London Heathrow. Paul pulled out their passports and placed them on the counter.

The check-in agent, Tammy, gave them an apologetic smile. "I'm afraid today's flight to London has been cancelled because of a systemic failure."

Paul froze. "What?" His voice rose in frustration. "I never got a notification."

"We've sent several emails," Tammy said gently. "They might've gone to spam."

Paul scoffed. "I check my email every hour." He pulled out his phone, scrolling quickly. Then he opened his spam folder. His stomach dropped.

"Oh, for god's sake," he muttered.

"Yeah, that's what I'm referring to," Tammy said. "We've rebooked you on Celestine Airlines."

Paul's head snapped up. "Celestine Airlines? What the bloody hell is that?"

"It's a newer airline operating here," Tammy said. "Your new itinerary has you flying to Helsinki, Finland, then connecting you to London Heathrow. I know it's a longer route, but it's the only available option."

Paul clenched his jaw. "What about Virgin Atlantic? Delta?"

"I'm sorry, sir, but all the other flights to London have been booked. You can either take this or wait a few days."

Paul rubbed his face and turned to Sophie, frustrated. "Soph, this is ridiculous. Helsinki? That's completely out of the way."

Sophie glanced at Oliver and Amy, their eyes drooping with exhaustion. "Look at the kids, hon. They just want to go home. Ollie's been talking about spending time with your dad for weeks."

Paul let out a defeated breath. He turned back to Tammy. "Fine. Where's the check-in for Celestine Airlines?"

"Right over there, sir," Tammy said, pointing to the check-in kiosk.

Paul gave a curt nod and steered his family across the terminal.

At the counter, Imani greeted them with a practiced smile. "Morning. Suitcases on the scale, please."

Paul and Sophie placed the bags on the scale, while Oliver and Amy tried to help, but mostly got in the way.

Imani scanned the tags. "London Heathrow, with a stop in Helsinki," she said, tagging the bags.

Paul handed over the passports. "Let's just hope the connection's smooth."

"Here are your boarding passes," she said, handing them over. "Boarding starts in two hours."

Paul exhaled sharply. "Thank you."

Sophie nodded. "Let's go, kids."

As they took their shoes off at the security checkpoint, Paul muttered to Sophie, "I can't believe that British Airways had another meltdown. And now we're flying on some airline I've never heard of."

Sophie placed a reassuring hand on his arm. "Paul, we've been here two months. The kids need to see there's a world beyond Norwich."

Paul sighed. "It's just…everything feels so uncertain. The UK's future worries me, and we're still figuring out what's next."

Sophie offered a small smile. "That's why we're keeping our options open. But for now, let's just get home."

She turned to Oliver and Amy, her voice lightening. "Are you excited to see Nan?"

Both kids squealed in delight.

Paul shook his head with a small chuckle. "Well, at least someone's happy about this."

Sophie laughed, squeezing his hand. "Come on, let's go."

CHAPTER 2

Steve sank into a chair near the gate, absently scrolling through his phone as travelers rushed past—families, businesspeople, backpackers, each headed toward their own destinations. He dialed a few numbers, checking in with his friends at the NCAA, his parents, Matt and Rachel Turner, and his younger brother, Owen, a computer science student at Georgia Tech.

"Hey, just made it to the gate," he told Owen. "Looking forward to spreading the word about the NCAA in Finland."

Steve glanced up as a family slumped into the seats before him. The dad, pale and balding, dropped heavily into a chair. The mom followed, her eyes tired. Their kids, dragging backpacks, collapsed without a word. They looked like security had wrung them out. Steve nodded, recognizing the fatigue. He felt it too.

After slipping in his AirPods, Steve watched NCAA basketball highlights. Energy surged through him as he shouted, "Let's go, Dawgs!"

Several heads turned in annoyance. A Celestine Airlines agent grabbed the intercom. "Sir, we know it's a big day for the Bulldogs, but please keep it down."

Steve removed his AirPods, sheepish. "Sorry about that. I get a little carried away."

The agent nodded and moved on. Steve glanced at his phone battery–three percent.

"Damn. Gotta get this thing charged before the flight." He stood, searching for an outlet, and accidentally bumped into Paul, who was engrossed in spreadsheets on his laptop.

"Sorry about that," Steve said.

Paul looked up, smirking. "No big deal. You're fine."

Steve settled next to him, pulled out his charger. As his phone powered up, Oliver approached Paul.

"Daddy, when are we leaving?"

Paul checked the time. "In an hour, mate. Are you hungry?"

Oliver nodded.

"Go ask Mummy if you want a snack or chicken tenders," Paul said. Oliver squealed as he rushed back to Sophie.

"You've got an adorable kid."

Paul chuckled, "Thanks. Oliver and Amy are my life. We're heading back to the UK, but our direct flight got canceled. Now we're detouring through Helsinki before London. Makes no sense"

"Flying hasn't made sense since COVID," Steve said. "I'm Steve, by the way."

"Paul." They shook hands.

"Nice to meet you, Paul. I saw the spreadsheets. What do you do?"

"I run a digital marketing agency out in the UK. My wife and I have been traveling across the American South with the kids for a bit."

"Where are you guys from in the UK?" Steve asked. "I visited with family a number of times."

"Norwich."

Steve frowned. "Never been. Where's that?"

"Two hours northeast of London by train. A growing city, but most people outside the UK haven't heard of it. What about you? Atlanta?"

"Kennesaw, Georgia, but I grew up in Woodstock. My dad owns a real estate company and moonlights as a pastor. Mom works with him. I'm a junior sports exec with the NCAA, trying to expand our market. My fiancée's a nurse at Atlanta Children's Hospital."

"Sounds like a full life," Paul said.

"What about you, Paul?"

"I grew up in Aylsham, not so far from Norwich. My wife, Sophie's, a professor at the University of East Anglia, researching the environment. She's on a sabbatical, raising our two kids–Oliver, six, and Amy, four."

"You've got some adorable children," Steve laughed. "I look forward to being a dad someday."

"How old are you, mate?" Paul asked.

"Twenty-five."

"You've got plenty of time. Kids are expensive these days."

"Tell me about it," Steve sighed. "Life is just so expensive."

Paul nodded. "Inflation's brutal in the UK. Not looking forward to going back. But the kids are excited to see their grandparents."

Steve then asked, "What brought you here to the US?"

"We just wanted to take a break from everything. Sophie wanted a sabbatical from her job, and I just wanted to escape from the UK after COVID and introduce America to the kids. We've been travelling for three months with Sophie homeschooling the kids along the way."

Before Steve could respond, the intercom crackled.

"Attention, passengers for Celestine Airlines Flight 24 to Helsinki, due to technical difficulties, our flight is delayed by two hours."

"What the hell? Not again." Steve groaned.

Paul huffed. "You think you have it bad? Our first flight got canceled. Now this."

Steve got up and approached the counter. "What's the issue?"

"It looks like there is an issue with the software systems," the ticket agent said.

Steve returned to Paul, shaking his head. "Same software issue."

Paul's eyes widened. "You're kidding. That's why our last flight was cancelled."

"Hopefully, it's nothing major," Steve muttered.

Sophie approached with the kids. "The flight's delayed, and the kids are restless. I'm going to walk them around."

Paul kissed her cheek. "Go ahead, love."

Steve and Paul shared a laugh before wandering through the terminal. The atmosphere of the airport, the sheer energy of movement, made Steve feel oddly lightheaded.

When they returned, Sophie and the kids were back at the gate. Paul introduced Steve to them.

"So, this is my wife, Sophie, my son, Oliver, and my daughter, Amy," Paul said.

"Nice to meet you all," Steve said. "You've got a great family."

Oliver's eyes lit up when he saw Steve's shirt. "That's a cute little dog!"

Steve laughed, "Thanks, buddy. You have dogs in the UK, right?"

"Can you hold me?" Oliver asked. "I want to see the dog up close."

Steve glanced at Paul and Sophie, his mouth open in confusion. "Is it okay with you guys if I can put him on my lap?"

"It's fine. Ollie gets excited when he sees pictures of dogs," Paul said.

Sophie smiled. "You can hold him if you want."

Steve lifted Oliver, who examined the Georgia Bulldogs logo with wide eyes.

"What type of dog is this?" Oliver asked.

"It's a bulldog," Steve said.

Oliver turned to his parents, "Mum, can you buy me a bulldog when we get home?"

"We'll see, Ollie."

Steve set him down. "Kid's going to be a pet owner one day."

As they laughed, the intercom crackled again.

"Ladies and gentlemen for Celestine Airlines Flight 24, can I have your attention, please? We've resolved the mechanical issue. Boarding will begin shortly."

Paul exhaled. "Finally!"

Sophie smirked. "You'll be even more tired when we get home. We've got errands to run."

Paul groaned. "Of course, we do."

Steve placed his electronic devices inside his bag and joined the long line boarding the flight. He glanced at his ticket. "I'm in seat 44L. Where are you guys?"

Paul checked. "35A and 35B for me and Amy."

"I'm with Oliver in 44A and 44B," Sophie added.

"It looks like the three of us are closer by," Steve said with a grin.

Twenty minutes later, everyone was seated. The plane, half-full, buzzed with quiet anticipation. Flight attendants moved down the aisles, checking seatbelts.

From the cockpit, the captain's voice rose over the speakers. "Ladies and gentlemen, this is your Captain, Nigel Callaghan based out of Southampton in England. We'll be flying out to Helsinki in a few minutes. Flight time will be approximately eight hours and forty-three minutes, depending upon weather and traffic. Hope you all have made yourselves comfortable for this overnight flight. We would like to thank you once again for choosing Celestine Airlines."

The first officer added with an African American vernacular, "Now, this is what I call the captain–sharp and articulate." Laughter erupted through the cabin.

He continued, "I'm First Officer William Rhodes, based out of Fayetteville, Georgia, just south of the airport. We're ready to take off soon. You will enjoy a nice, smooth ride with our special relationship of British and American flying together to Finland."

"Apologies," the captain said dryly. "Our first officer likes to keep things lively."

As the safety video began its scripted monotone, Steve leaned back in his seat and dialed quickly. The plane hummed with low conversation and the occasional click of seatbelts.

Lindsay picked up on the second ring.

"I'm heading off now," Steve said, his voice low but warm. "I love you. I'll call you as soon as I land."

There was a pause on the other end, filled with the soft rustle of her breath.

"I love you too," she said, her voice gentle. "Text me when you land, even if it's late, okay?"

CHAPTER 3

At 8:30 p.m., Celestine Airlines Flight 24 lifted off from Atlanta. The engines roared beneath Steve's seat as the plane pitched upward. Runway lights streaked past, then vanished into the night.

Out the window, the city lay scattered below in gold and white, soft and distant. The skyline looked fragile from this height. Steve spotted the Chattahoochee, a silver ribbon cutting through the dark.

Lindsay would've liked that, he thought.

As the plane leveled off, the lights disappeared beneath the clouds. Moonlight skimmed the top of the overcast—a dim glow on a gray sea.

Steve leaned back. The engines hummed steadily. Somewhere behind him, someone coughed. He closed his eyes. Still hours to go.

Inside the cabin, the atmosphere had settled. The steady hum of the engines blended with the soft murmur of conversations and the occasional rustle of a magazine. Some passengers had already surrendered to sleep. Paul had reclined his seat and tilted his head back, lips slightly parted, breathing slow and even. Beside him, Amy was curled against the window, a thin airline blanket pulled to her chin. Her head dipped once, then settled still.

Across the aisle, a man tapped idly at his screen, scrolling through the movie selection. Two rows ahead, a woman chuckled softly at something on her tablet, the sound barely audible over the hush of the cabin. Screens glowed dimly, casting flickers of light across scattered faces, each caught in its own quiet world.

A chime sounded overhead.

"Ladies and gentlemen, this is your captain speaking," came the voice of Captain Callaghan. "We are now at cruising altitude. Our flight will take us over Tennessee, North Carolina, Virginia, and into the DC airspace before flying parallel to the coast. From there, we'll pass over Halifax, cross the Atlantic and enter Irish and UK airspace before arriving in Helsinki at approximately 1:00 p.m. local time."

There was a brief pause before First Officer Rhodes added dryly, "I apologize for the geography lesson. To put it simply, we'll get you there safely."

Scattered laughter rippled through the cabin, shaking a few passengers from their drowsy haze.

Steve turned back to the window. The clouds below looked like frozen waves. His reflection ghosted on the glass, lit faintly by the cabin's glow.

What if she's right about me?

Lindsay's voice echoed faintly in his mind — sharp, tired. *Arrogant. No remorse. Always angry.* Words she hadn't shouted, just dropped like stones.

He swallowed hard, a dull weight forming in his chest. He wanted to believe he was better than that. That he could be.

Something has to give, he thought. *It has to start now.*

With a sigh, Steve slid the window shade halfway down and looked at the entertainment screen. The game section caught his eye, offering a nostalgic selection–chess, sudoku, mahjong, and more.

A few rows away, Oliver stirred from his brief slumber. He rubbed his eyes and nudged Sophie's arm. "Mummy, wake up. I need to go to the bathroom."

Sophie groaned, half-conscious. "What, honey? You need to use the loo? Alright."

She unbuckled her seatbelt, helping Oliver remove his seatbelt, and guided him down the aisle. A few minutes later, they returned. Oliver's eyes drifted toward Steve's screen.

"Mummy, can I play with Steve?"

Sophie blinked at him. "Why? The games are right in front of you."

Oliver fidgeted. "I know, but I want to play with him."

Sophie sighed. "Ollie, we don't talk or play with strangers."

"He's not a stranger," Oliver insisted. "He was with Dad at the airport. They were talking. You met him before we got on the plane. There's an empty seat next to him.

Sophie released a deep breath. "Alright, go ahead."

Oliver's face lit up. He bounced in excitement before Sophie gently held caught his arm. "Keep it quiet, Ollie. People are sleeping. We don't want any trouble."

"Okay Mum," Oliver whispered.

He slipped around the back of the cabin and plopped into the empty seat next to Steve.

Steve turned, surprised to see him. His eyes were distant, pulled from some deep thought.

"Oliver? What are you doing here? Shouldn't you be with your mother?"

"Mum let me come to you," Oliver said. "I want to play *Space Invaders* with you."

Steve chuckled. "I'm not sure multiplayer works here. But let us see."

Sophie stepped up beside them.

"I'm going to be checking on Dad and Amy," Sophie said. "They should be serving dinner soon. Come back to me when you're done."

"No, Mum! I wanna sit here and eat dinner and play games!"

Sophie gave a tired but amused smile. Steve glanced up. "He'll be fine. I used to lead a Boy Scout troop before college. I know how to look after kids."

Sophie hesitated, then nodded and walked away.

Later, Sophie returned. "Did you finish eating, Ollie?"

"Yes Mum," Oliver said. "I ate the pasta. What did you, Daddy, and Amy eat?"

"Daddy had the curry. Amy and I ate the pasta," she said, smoothing his hair.

Oliver held up a small model airplane, "The flight lady gave me this."

"That's amazing. Ollie, you should go to sleep right now. I don't want you waking up exhausted when we land in Finland."

"Okay, Mum."

"Goodnight sweetheart," Sophie said.

"Goodnight, Mum. I love you."

A few minutes passed in silence, then Oliver turned to Steve.

"I think I'll go sleep next to my mum now."

Steve smiled. "Goodnight Oliver."

An hour later, the plane soared past Nova Scotia, heading east over the North Atlantic. A sudden jolt of turbulence rattled the cabin, stirring Steve from his deep sleep. Blinking groggily, he realized he had left the window shade open. As he reached to close it, something unusual caught his eye—a faint shimmer dancing across the sky.

What in the world is that?

A soft pulse stretched across the horizon—like a solar flare, golden and elusive. At first, it was barely there. Then it deepened, brushing pale light across the wings, silent and surreal.

In the cockpit, Captain Callaghan and First Officer Rhodes finished their last bites of spaghetti. The captain scanned the instrument panels, while Rhodes, posture easy on his seat, monitored the flight path.

A sudden flicker on the dashboard shattered the quiet hum of the cockpit—an amber light blinking on the dash.

"What's that?" First Officer Rhodes said.

Callaghan frowned, fingers already moving across the controls. "Not mechanical. Check the radiation levels–they're spiking."

Rhodes' eyes darted to the readings. "Is that what I think it is? A solar flare?"

"Could be," Captain Callaghan murmured. "Let's confirm."

He flipped a switch, bringing up the external camera feed. The vast darkness of the upper atmosphere filled the screen—except for a faint, undulating glow on the horizon.

"See that?" First Offer Rhodes pointed, his voice low and measured. "That's not an ordinary light show."

Captain Callaghan stared at the screen, mesmerized. The flare wasn't the violent burst that their training had anticipated. It moved like ghostly ribbons of light, elegant and eerie.

"Should we adjust our course?" First Officer Rhodes asked, his hand hovering over the controls.

Callaghan hesitated. The flare wasn't directly in their path, but its presence was unnerving.

"Not yet," he said at last. We don't want to fly into anything we're not prepared for."

He reached for the radio. "Moncton Tower, this is CS Flight 24. We're observing an unusual phenomenon ahead."

"CS 24, this is Moncton Tower. Do you require a route change?"

Callaghan studied the glow once more, his instincts nagging at him. "Yes, please."

"Do you have enough fuel for a reroute?"

"Affirmative," the captain confirmed.

"Understood, CS 24. New route approved. You'll divert toward the Azores, then through Spain, Italy, Switzerland, Austria, and Poland, before heading into Helsinki."

Callaghan exhaled. "Acknowledged. Appreciate the swift response."

As the new course data uploaded to the flight system, Callaghan and Rhodes exchanged a glance. Neither said a word—but the tension between them was unmistakable.

CHAPTER 4

Captain Callaghan's voice came over the intercom, steady but firm. "Ladies and gentlemen, this is your captain speaking. You may have noticed an unusual disturbance in the sky. To ensure your safety, we are altering our flight path. This will add approximately two hours to our journey before we land in Helsinki. We anticipate some moderate turbulence as we pass over the Alps."

A murmur spread through the cabin. Passengers exchanged uneasy glances.

Steve groaned, rubbing his eyes as he mumbled. "Not again. This airline sucks."

Moments later, a flight attendant's voice followed over the PA system.

"Before we land in Finland, ladies and gentlemen, please prepare to receive your customs and immigration forms. If you are not a citizen of Finland or another EU country, please complete these forms for landing. Use black or blue ink, and make sure to fill out the required sections. If you need any assistance, our cabin crew is here to help. Please keep the completed forms with your passport to present to immigration officers."

Steve shook his head. "Of all the times they have to make an announcement, they have to do it now? God dang it."

He glanced at the screen in front of him. The local time was 9:30 p.m. In Finland, it was already 4:30 a.m., with an estimated arrival in three hours. With a sigh, he closed his eyes, hoping for a few more hours of sleep.

As Celestine Airlines Flight 24 over the French Alps, passing through Mt. Blanc and into Swiss airspace, severe turbulence had struck the plane without warning.

"This is your captain," Callaghan announced. "We're passing through some rough turbulence."

Steve groaned, sitting upright. "Can't these guys for once fly more smoothly for once? I've got an appointment with the NCAA team."

A moment later, the flight attendant's voice cut through the intercom.

"Sir, please calm down. This is not your car. Passengers are asleep."

Steve exhaled, muttering, "My apologies." He leaned back and shut his eyes again.

What the hell was that back there?

He'd meant to stay calm, keep it light — and instead he snapped again.

You're not helping yourself, he thought. *Not anymore.*

The aircraft crossed into Austrian airspace, gliding past Innsbruck and over the mountains south of Salzburg. A faint glow appeared on the horizon—the first hint of dawn.

In the cockpit, First Officer Rhodes asked Captain Callaghan, "So, where do we make that turn towards Helsinki?"

"Here," Captain Callaghan said, pointing to the screen. "Once we pass Vienna, we turn left— seventany-five-degree angle heading straight toward Helsinki. Right now, we're over Tyrol, heading into Salzburg.

The steady hum of the engines and the quiet beeping of instruments filled the cockpit. Everything was running smoothly.

"All systems are normal, Captain," Rhodes reported. "We're right on schedule."

The captain nodded. "Let's keep it that way."

Then, the sky outside ignited in an unnatural brilliance.

The cockpit was bathed in an eerie, blinding glow–harsh and unnatural. Rhodes squinted, instinctively adjusting the glare shield.

"What the hell was that?" he said.

Before either of them could react, the plane lurched violently.

The lights in the cockpit flickered. Then came the alarms—shrill, overlapping, relentless. The instrument panel, once a serene display of greens and blues, exploded into a frenzy of flashing red and yellow warnings.

"Captain, we're losing power!" Rhodes shouted, his voice edged with panic.

Captain Callaghan gripped the yoke, his knuckles white as he fought to maintain control. The plane buckled wildly, nose dipping and rising unpredictably.

"What the hell just happened to us? Check the electrical systems!"

Rhodes scanned the displays, fingers flying. "It's not just the power–we're losing everything. I think we've been hit by another solar flare. A massive one!"

Callaghan's stomach dropped.

"Mayday, mayday, mayday!" Captain Callaghan yelled into the radio.

Only static replied.

Rhodes' voice was tight with fear. "Controls are unresponsive. We're losing altitude."

Callaghan's eyes swept the dark horizon, his mind racing for options. "We need to descend–fast. Get below the interference. And we need to find a place to land."

Outside, the jagged peaks of the Alps loomed closer.

In the cabin, screams broke through the silence.

Steve's heart slammed against his ribs. He fumbled for a napkin and pen, his hands trembling. He scribbled, "Lindsay, Mom, Dad, Owen–I love you all. God has taken me away and will soon reunite me with you all soon." He looked at Oliver and Sophie clinging together.

In the cockpit, Captain Callaghan struggled to control the aircraft, his eyes darting between the failing altimeter and the rapidly approaching ground. The once serene night sky was now a chaotic scene of flashing lights and ominous shadows.

The plane descended sharply, both Captain Callaghan and First Officer Rhodes gasping for air and slowly losing their consciousness. The engines sputtered, their usual roar reduced to a strained whine as the plane dipped lower and lower.

In the cabin, Paul scrawled a farewell note on the back of his customs form. "Mum, Dad, Alfie, thank you for looking after me. Sophie, the kids, and I will soon be departing the world. Take care, and will see you on the other side." He pulled Amy close, squeezing his eyes shut. Sophie wrapped her arms around Oliver, whispering a final prayer.

Steve braced himself, pressing his head against the tray table.

The ground was coming up too fast.

Steve's breath caught as the trees rose in the window—too close, too soon. Then, a jolt. The sickening crack of branches shearing off, a blur of limbs and leaves slamming against the fuselage. Steve's eyes closed.

A split second later, the world erupted in noise — a shriek of metal tearing against frozen earth. The cabin lurched violently, tossing him forward against the restraints.

Flames erupted from the wreckage. Silence followed.

Outside, the sky returned to its normal darkness. The solar flare had passed as swiftly as it arrived. But the damage had been done.

CHAPTER 5

At the Air Route Traffic Control Center near Zurich, Switzerland, controllers monitored flights navigating the Central European airspace. Karl, one of the controllers, noticed a plane vanish from his radar.

"CS Flight 24, do you hear me?" Karl said, his Swiss accent trembling through the microphone attached to his headphones. Static crackled in response. There was no reply from the captain or the first officer.

Karl's stomach tightened. He leaned forward, trying again. "CS 24, do you copy? Tell me your altitude." His eyes widened, and he gasped.

"Ce-les-tine Flight 24," Karl said, a lump rising in his throat. "Oh my god!" he yelled. Several of colleagues rushed his side.

"What happened?" one of the controllers asked in German.

Struggling to catch his breath, Karl said in German, "A plane just disappeared from my radar."

The room erupted into controlled chaos. Controllers scrambled to contact other aircraft and stations, desperately seeking any sign of Celestine Airlines Flight 24.

"We're not able to locate Flight 24 on radar," another controller confirmed grimly. "No contact with the pilots."

Karl immediately alerted emergency services. Search-and-rescue protocols were activated. But as the minutes ticked by, the gravity of the situation sank in.

"No response from rescue teams yet," Karl relayed in German.

Nearly an hour later, Karl finally received a word from a team based out of Innsbruck. He finally breathed a sigh of relief.

Within the hour, news networks worldwide broke the story.

"BREAKING: Plane Disappears Over Austrian Alps."

A CNN anchor relayed the report. "We just learned that Celestine Airlines Flight 24 has vanished from radar while flying over the Alps in Austria. This is a breaking story. We'll provide you with periodic updates."

This news flashed across screens from the U.S. to Europe, Asia, and beyond. Major networks pivoted to full live coverage.

Search and rescue teams mobilized from Innsbruck Airport.

At around 5:30 a.m. in the morning at their home in Kennesaw, Lindsay stirred awake, stretching lazily in bed. She rolled over and smiled.

As she dried her hair, her phone buzzed. A message from her sister, Emma, lit the screen.

"Turn on the news! Steve's plane has crashed."

Lindsay froze. Her heart stopped for a beat, then pounded against her ribs.

No. No. This isn't real.

She bolted downstairs, nearly slipping on the steps, and grabbed the remote with trembling hands, and flipped to CNN.

"BREAKING: CELESTINE AIRLINES FLIGHT 24 HAS CRASHED IN THE ALPS. NO SURVIVORS ARE FOUND."

The breath caught in her throat. The room blurred as her vision filled with tears.

Her phone vibrated again–her mom's name flashed on the screen. She answered with shaking fingers. "Hello?"

"Lindsay, sweetheart, are you there?" Sue's voice cracked.

"I'm here, Mom," Lindsay choked out. "Did they—did they find Steve?"

There was a pause, then the unmistakable sound of someone else trying to hold back tears. "Lindsay, it's Matt," came the trembling voice of Steve's father. "We don't know yet…but it's not looking good. The rescue team…they're saying they're not able to find any debris."

Lindsay's knees gave out. She collapsed onto the couch, her body trembling.

"No…no, this can't be happening," she sobbed. "I just talked to him yesterday. He said he was coming home."

A choked sob broke through the line. "We know, sweetheart," Rachel, Steve's mother whispered. "They've been searching for hours."

A heavy silence followed, each second stretching like a lifetime.

"Mom," Lindsay cried.

Sue's voice came through, broken but trying to be strong for her daughter. "We're all here, Lindsay. Your dad, Emma, we're all right here with you."

Emma, her younger sister, sniffled through the line. "Linds, we'll get through this. Together."

But the words rang hollow.

"Lindsay," Matt said, his voice steadier now. "Let's gather at our house. Cancel everything. We need to be together."

James, Lindsay's father, finally spoke, his deep voice anchoring them all. "We'll pick you up. Stay put."

Lindsay barely managed a nod. "Okay."

Lindsay sat in silence, staring at a framed photo of her and Steve taken just months ago—on a hike in the Appalachians. They had been so happy.

Now, the world felt incredibly dark.

A knock at the door startled her. She wiped her tear-streaked cheeks, trying to compose herself, but then he opened the door and saw her mother standing.

Sue pulled her into a tight embrace, holding her as she cried, her own tears mingling with her daughter's. "We're going to get through this," she whispered.

Together, they walked out of the house and drove to Steve's parents' house in Woodstock.

On top of the Alps in Austria around 6:45 a.m., a cold gust of wind howled over the wreckage. Snow whipped across the slope, stinging every exposed surface.

Steve's eyes fluttered open. Pain stabbed through his skull, his ribs, and his legs. He groaned, barely able to move. Blood trickled from a gash on his forehead, staining the snow beneath him.

Steve stepped into the snow, cold biting through his clothes. Debris crunched underfoot—shards of metal, scraps of luggage, a torn teddy bear face down in the slush.

Smoke stung his eyes as he forced himself upright. In the distance, fire flickered from the broken fuselage, casting flickering shadows over the wreckage.

Stumbling forward, Steve found a first aid kit near a shattered row of seats. He immediately plastered himself on his forehead, arms, and legs, hoping to cauterize the blood coming out of his body.

Within the next few minutes, Steve walked on the snow, searching for his bag. He witnessed fires burning, dead bodies of passengers. Due to a lack of proper protective shoes, he started to shiver and fell down several times. "Paul, Sophie, Oliver, Amy?"

"Where the hell am I?" Steve said, shivering. "I need to find my stuff." He weathered through the difficult conditions of the snow, searching through the wreckage of the plane.

Steve looked at the damaged overhead compartments. *That's right, the seating chart. Look for the one with 44L.* Several minutes later, he located the compartment. Shivering through his veins, he tried pressing the button. "Ow!" Steve said, his hands struggling to open the compartment, due to the lock being stuck.

With sheer determination, he slammed his fist against the compartment — once, twice, then a third time. The plastic panel cracked, splintering at the edges. On the fourth hit, something inside sparked.

A sudden burst of flame shot out, catching on the frayed insulation. The compartment hissed, then erupted. Plastic curled and blackened; metal warped under the heat.

Steve stumbled back as the fire consumed what was left.

"No, no," Steve squealed. "All my stuff, my clothes, laptop, and passport, are all are gone."

Steve pulled up his phone and tried turning on the screen. "No, no! Lindsay's going to be so worried. I'm screwed."

He quickly grabbed his belongings and escaped the flame throwing wreckage before hearing a faint child's cry from another side of the mountain.

CHAPTER 6

With his belongings destroyed in the wreck, Steve scoured the wreckage for anything useful. Amid the scattered debris, he found several bags and rifled through them, searching for food.

"I'm taking these," he muttered, grabbing the ones with snacks.

A child's cries rose on the wind, growing louder with each step. Steve's stomach clenched. He followed the sound and found Oliver covered in blood, his small body marred by burns and bruises. The boy knelt beside his mother's lifeless form, shaking her desperately.

"Oliver," Steve said, dropping the bags. "Are you okay? Thank goodness you're alive."

"I don't know," Oliver sobbed. "Mum won't wake up."

Steve rushed to Sophie's side and pressed two fingers to her neck. His breath caught. No pulse.

"Nothing," he murmured.

His hands moved instinctively. He laced his fingers together and placed them over her sternum. Her skin was ice cold beneath his touch, but he forced the thought aside. He leaned over, planting his hands firmly.

"What are you doing?" Oliver asked, eyes wide with fear.

"I'm trying to wake your mother up," Steve said. "It's called CPR. We don't have medical equipment, so I have to do it manually."

Steve pressed down, hard. "One, two, three, four.." Each compression was a desperate attempt to pull her back from the void. His voice was steady, counting aloud, willing for her heart to restart.

"Please Mum, come back!" Oliver sobbed.

But Sophie didn't move.

Steve exhaled sharply, his hands still on her chest. "I'm so sorry."

Oliver collapsed into Steve's arms, his cries piercing the frigid mountain air. Steve held him tightly, shielding him as best as he could.

"It's going to be okay, Ollie," he whispered. "Just like your mother said."

Oliver sniffled. "But Dad and Amy…they're here too."

Steve turned, following Oliver's gaze. Just a few feet away, Paul and Amy lay motionless, their bodies stained with blood.

Steve rushed over, his heart pounding. "Paul! Paul, wake up!"

He gripped Paul's shoulder. For a moment, nothing. Then—a flicker. Paul's eyelids fluttered. Steve and Oliver leaned in, holding their breath.

Paul's hazel eyes cracked open, unfocused. He exhaled a weak whisper. "Steve…"

"Paul, can you hear me?"

Paul shivered violently, his lips barely moving. "Amy's…dead. Sophie? Oliver?"

Steve swallowed hard. "Sophie didn't make it. But Oliver's alive. He's right here."

A faint smile flickered across Paul's face. Oliver crawled closer, resting his head against his father's chest.

"Daddy, please don't go," he pleaded. "Mum's gone. I don't want to lose you too."

Paul's gaze met Steve's. "Steve. Promise me something."

Steve wiped his eyes. "Anything."

"Take Oliver home. To my parents, his grandparents. Be there for him. He'll have no one else."

Steve gripped Paul's hand. "I promise."

A faint smile touched Paul's lips before his eyes drifted shut.

"No, please," Steve pleaded softly, tightening his grip.

Oliver wailed, burying his face in Steve's jacket. Then silence.

Dark clouds gathered overhead, heavy and slow. Steve stared up at them, barely feeling the cold anymore.

Of course it's going to snow soon.

Steve inhaled sharply. "Oliver, stay here." He scrambled through the wreckage, hands numb, until he found a first aid kit. He rushed back, tearing it open with shaking fingers.

Oliver winced as Steve gently cleaned the wounds and applied bandages where burns and cuts were worst.

"It hurts," Oliver whimpered, shivering in the snow.

"I know, buddy. I know." Steve's voice was steady, but his heart ached. "You're going to be okay. You've got first and second-degree burns, but I'll take care of you."

Within minutes, he wrapped Oliver's wounds as best as he could. Then, gripping the boy's shoulder, he said, "We have to go."

Oliver's lip trembled. "We can't leave Mum, Dad, and Amy here."

Steve's chest tightened. "Ollie. they're gone. Your dad wanted you to go home to your grandparents. That's what I promised to do."

Oliver hesitated. "Shouldn't we wait for someone to find us?"

Steve hoisted a bag onto his shoulder. "A blizzard's coming. If we stay, we'll freeze. I won't let that happen to you.

Oliver wiped off his tears. He turned toward his parents' bodies.

Steve's crouched beside him, but the words wouldn't come. *What could he possibly say? This shouldn't be his memory of them.*

"Say goodbye, Ollie," Steve whispered.

The boy sobbed, his voice cracking. "Goodbye, Mum… Dad… Amy."

Then, gripping Steve's hand, they turned away, leaving the wreckage behind as the storm rolled in.

Lindsay stepped out of the car, gravel crunching under her heels. The sky was heavy—gray and unmoving.

James adjusted his tie beside her. Sue and Emma followed in silence, their dresses shifting in the breeze.

The Turner home looked unchanged — red brick, white siding, lawn trimmed to perfection. It didn't look like a house in mourning.

Lindsay's gaze drifted to the garage. She could still picture Steve there, grease on his hands, grinning as he fixed James's bike. Now, only silence.

He should be here, she thought, throat tightening.

She took a breath and walked forward.

The front door creaked open. Matt Turner stood in the doorway, his face hollow, eyes swollen and empty.

James stepped forward. "I'm so sorry for your loss."

Matt didn't speak. He pulled James into a firm embrace, his body trembling.

Rachel appeared behind him. Lindsay rushed into her arms, and both women broke down, their sobs muffled by the cold.

"I should've stopped him from leaving," Lindsay cried. "And now he's gone."

Rachel, silent, extended a hand and motioned them inside. The TV flickered in the dim living room. Headlines scrolled across the screen.

"Some Wreckage of Celestine Flight 24 Found Scattered In The Austrian Alps." "Searching For Any Survivors Of The Crash Underway."

No one spoke. Lindsay sat rigid on the black sofa, hands knotted in her lap. The anchor's voice was a distant hum.

Please, Steve. Be out there.

Beside her, Sue gripped her hand. James leaned forward, eyes locked on the screen.

No one spoke. No one breathed.

They just watched, clinging to the hope that somehow he was still alive.

An hour after Steve and Oliver left the crash site, the distant whir of a helicopter cut through the howling wind, cutting through the dark clouds. As the massive rotor blades approached, they churned the air into a frenzy, whipping up clouds of dust and debris around the crash site.

The helicopter descended with a purposeful grace, its spotlight piercing through the gloom.

"Prepare for landing!" he barked in German.

The searchlight swept the wreckage.

"Over here!" Laura, one of the medics, called. "We've got survivors!"

Wolfgang Bach, the team leader, scanned the wreckage. "This is worse than we thought." He grabbed his radio.

"We need a larger rescue team," he said in German. "This terrain is brutal. We may have survivors on foot."

The spotlight continued to sweep across the wreckage, illuminating the empty, snow-covered ground.

CHAPTER 7

Snow had been falling relentlessly for over three hours since Steve and Oliver left the crash site. Battling injuries, Steve pressed on, trudging down the mountain with Oliver in his arms, the weight of two large backpacks and a small one strapped to his back. His breath came out in ragged puffs as he shielded Oliver's face from the swirling snow.

Oliver shivered violently. "I'm really cold. Can we stop somewhere?"

"Hold on," Steve said, squinting through the flurry. "I think I see a shack nearby."

"No," Oliver said. "I want to stop now."

"Ollie, just a few more minutes," Steve urged. But Oliver wasn't listening. He began kicking against Steve's arms, struggling against his grip.

"Hey! Stop that!" Steve snapped, rushing forward through the thick snow, desperate to reach the shelter. He stumbled inside, dropping the backpacks onto the wooden floor before turning to Oliver, his patience snapping.

"Why did you do that?" His voice rose, sharp and raw. "Don't you ever do that again!"

Oliver froze. His small chest heaved. His lower lip quivered, and tears welled in his eyes, clinging to the edges like raindrops before a storm. Then, they spilled over. Then another. He broke down, sobbing.

Shame twisted in Steve's gut. He crouched down, placing his hands gently on Oliver's shoulders. "Hey, Oliver, don't cry," he whispered. "I'm sorry. I didn't mean to yell."

Oliver recoiled, pushing Steve's hands away. "Don't hug me," he sniffled.

Steve nodded, swallowing hard. "I know. I messed up. But listen, buddy, I know you're hurting. Your mom, dad, and sister…" His voice faltered. "They're gone. But you're still here. And they are with you. You're one of the few survivors of that crash, and your dad—he told me to get you home. That's what I'm trying to do. You want to go home, right?"

Oliver wiped off tears and said, "Yes."

"I know, kid. And I'll take you there," Steve promised. "But first, we've got to make it down this mountain. And right now, we can't go anywhere until the snow stops."

Steve rifled through one backpack, pulling out a water bottle and a protein bar coated in thick chocolate.

"Oh my gosh," Steve said. "This traveler came prepared." He removed a water bottle and protein bar and gave them to Oliver. "Eat this. It's a thicker chocolate bar."

Oliver sighed in relief. "Thanks. I am hungry." He tore into the bar, gulping down water as fast as he could.

"Hey, slow down," Steve cautioned. "We don't know when we'll find more food."

Oliver chewed slower, glancing up at Steve. "How long are we going to wait here?"

"Until the blizzard clears. First, we get down the mountain. Then, we find another shack. After that, we start a fire and search for food and water," Steve said.

"That should sound like a good idea," Oliver said, rummaging for an extra jacket.

Steve shrugged off one of his and held it out. Oliver's lips were blue. His small hands trembled as he reached for the coat.

He's freezing. God, he's just a kid.

Steve knelt to help him, tucking the jacket around his shoulders. The fabric swallowed him, but it was something.

Lindsay would've known what to say right now.

Back at the Turner's house, the room was silent except for the hum of the television.

A somber CNN anchor said, her head placed down. "Search and rescue teams in Austria have located parts of the wreckage, but heavy blizzard conditions have stalled efforts."

"What?" Matt snapped. "They're just giving up? What if Steve's still out there?"

"This is bullshit," Owen said. "I could design something right now to plow through the snow and find him."

Matt turned to Rachel, his voice taut. "Do you really think anyone could have survived this?"

"Maybe," Lindsay said quietly.

"But that wreckage is so massive?" James added. "We don't even know what really happened."

"My biggest fear?" Matt muttered. "If there are survivors, they'll freeze to death before the rescue team even gets there." His fists clenched. "What the hell are the Austrians thinking?"

He turned to Rachel, his eyes burning. "And you—you've barely said a word."

Rachel swallowed hard, her voice trembling. "I-I'm scared, okay? I don't know if Steve is alive or not."

Matt exhaled sharply. "God help us."

Atop the mountain, the blizzard finally began to ease, the howling winds settling into a quiet snowfall.

Captain Müller's voice crackled over the radio, saying in German. "The blizzard has cleared. Send in more rescue helicopters."

Commander Bach responded in German. "We may need the army. The terrain is rough."

At the base of the mountain, the search and rescue camp burst into motion. Radios crackled, boots crunched on gravel, and personnel moved between tents.

Inside the Incident Command tent, responders leaned over a map covered in flags.

"Grid four has no sign yet," a man reported in German.

A woman pointed to a ridge and responded in German. "Teams here and here. We need aerial support now."

"We need to move fast," Commander Bach ordered. "There's another storm on the way." He turned to Klara, the Logistics Coordinator. "Make sure all teams have avalanche gear. We can't afford to lose anyone."

"Already on it," Klara confirmed.

As the first helicopters arrived, Captain Müller sent live footage to the command center. "The crash site is in complete disarray. The fuselage is shattered, partially buried in snow."

Rescue teams scoured the wreckage, their boots crunching over metal and ice.

A search dog named Christian sniffed through the debris.

Within several minutes, hordes of search and rescue operation personnel flew into the crash site to rescue the bodies.

The lead paramedic, Marie, summoned her team and scoured the wreckage to find any bodies that are alive.

"We're on the move," she said on the walkie talkie in German. "Hypothermia is going to be our biggest threat. Let's make this happen."

Nearby, a technician knelt beside a drone, checking the rotors.

"Battery's good. We're live," he said.

Another team member adjusted the camera angle. "We'll start with a wide sweep. Cover the full debris field."

The drone lifted, blades whining as it climbed above the treetops. Searchers moved below, marking wreckage with orange flags.

"Get a shot of that fuselage section," someone called out.

The drone hovered, camera tilting down, capturing the shattered remains now scattered across the mountain — images that, within hours, would soon circle the globe.

Marie's voice came through again. "No sign of survivors. Including the pilots. Looks like everyone is gone."

Lindsay sat stiffly on the couch, hands trembling, eyes unblinking. Owen, hunched over on the floor, stared at his phone as condolences flooded in.

Matt stood and paced around the living room back and forth, taking deep breaths in between steps.

Rachel stood in the corner, flipping through her Bible, eyes flicking between verses and the news.

Emma nibbled at the untouched cookies, desperate for any distraction.

"Steve will be alive," Matt muttered, though his voice cracked.

Then the CNN anchor's voice returned. Her voice was low, grim.

"We interrupt with breaking news. It is with a heavy heart that we report all passengers aboard Celestine Airlines Flight 24, en route from Atlanta to Helsinki, have perished. Details remain limited, but families are being offered travel assistance to the wreckage site."

Lindsay's face went pale. Her gaze fixed on the screen. "No," she whispered, her voice trembling. "That's not Steve. That can't be right."

Owen's phone buzzed relentlessly with messages: *I'm so sorry for your loss." "RIP Steve."* He looked up, eyes wide and teary. "Mom? Dad?"

Rachel's Bible slipped from her hands, thudding onto the floor. She didn't pick it up. Her hands shook as tears spilled freely. "No… no…"

Matt staggered forward. "Steve," he choked. "No…" His knees buckled, and he collapsed onto the floor, gripping his head.

Lindsay let out a scream–raw, animalistic, ripped from the depths of grief. "No!" she cried, collapsing to the floor, her face buried in her hands. "No, no, no!" She rocked back and forth, broken.

Sue and Emma rushed to her, wrapping their hands around her as they collapsed onto the floor. "My baby," Sue whispered through their tears, pressing their face into Lindsay's hair. "My baby girl…" Their voices broke as they held together tighter, all three of them sobbing in each other's arms.

James, Matt, and Owen clutched their faces, silent cries wracking their bodies. Rachel sat motionless in her chair, crying her eyes out.

The television droned on in the background, but no one heard it anymore. Their world had shattered. Matt finally lifted his head, his voice raw. "I don't care what it takes. We're going to Austria and bring Steve's body back home."

CHAPTER 8

The blizzard had softened to a light snowfall. Steve glanced outside for confirmation before turning to Oliver. "It looks like the coast is clear."

Oliver's face lit up, a wide grin spread across his cheeks. Steve knelt beside him, locking eyes. "If we hurry, we can get down the mountain before sunset."

Oliver nodded eagerly. Steve pulled out a handkerchief inside and wiped Oliver's face and long hair.

"You know," Steve mused. "You remind me of my young cousin when he was your age."

"What was his name?" Oliver asked.

"Henry Turner. He's ten years younger than me. I used to play with him, look after him when our family visited. Honestly, I treated him more like a little brother than my own brother, Owen. He lives in Houston, Texas."

Oliver tilted his head, "Where's that?"

"You remember Atlanta, where we took off from? It's several hundred—maybe a thousand—miles west of there."

Steve ruffled Oliver's hair. "Anyways, you're safe with me. Now, shall we?" He extended his hand for a high-five.

Oliver gave a tentative grin, eyes flickering with both hope and fear. He looked at Steve, clinging to that fragile trust. "Yes!"

Steve handed Oliver his backpack. "Let's see if you can walk without holding on to me."

"Okay," Oliver said.

Oliver took a step into the snow and immediately shivered. "I can't do this," he whimpered. "It's too cold."

"Come on, Ollie." Steve's voice was firm but kind. "You can't complain. If you want to grow up to be strong, you've got to push through."

Oliver shot him a sharp glare, his face scrunching up in frustration, tears brimming in his eyes.

"Alright, alright," Steve relented. "I'll carry you, but you'll have to start walking on your own soon."

Oliver rubbed his eyes and slumped against Steve's side. "I'm still tired,' he mumbled, voice soft. "And sad."

Steve scooped him up and continued down the slope until he stopped abruptly. A jagged formation of rocks blocked their path.

"What's going on?" Oliver asked.

Steve set him down and climbed the rocks to get a better view. His breath caught as he took in the view—rolling hills, sprawling valleys, emerald forests, and golden fields stretched far below. Small villages were nestled in the distance.

"What do you see?" Oliver called up.

Steve climbed back down, his expression serious. "There's no way forward here. The rocks are blocking the path, and beyond them... there's nothing. If it weren't for these boulders, we might've walked straight off the edge."

Oliver's eyes widened. "I don't want to die."

"You won't." Steve picked him up again and adjusted their bags. "We'll have to move along the ridge and find another way down. I'm pretty sure we're somewhere in Germany, Austria, Switzerland, or Italy. We'll figure it out."

❧

The morning after the crash, the rhythmic whirring of helicopter blades filled the frigid air as the wreckage came into view.

Across the snow-covered mountainside lay the scorched remains of a passenger aircraft. Twisted metal jutted out between charred trees, their blackened limbs reaching skyward. Wisps of smoke still curled into the overcast sky, carrying the sharp stench of burned fuel.

Rescue teams moved carefully through the debris, tagging bodies and marking twisted metal with bright orange flags.

Near the edge of the debris field, a group of investigators stepped from a helicopter.

Hans Friedrich, the lead investigator from the SUB, scanned the scene with a steady gaze. He adjusted his jacket and pulled out a notebook, his fingers tightening around the pen.

Sarah McCarthy from the NTSB followed close behind, her eyes narrowing at the fuselage wreckage.

Behind them, investigators from the UK's AAIB and the EASA spread out, snapping photos and taking notes.

Their faces were tight, professional, but none could hide the weight of what they witnessed.

Sarah took a deep breath, watching it mist in the cold air. Despite decades in the field, this part never got easier.

Hans gathered the team. His Austrian accent was thick, but commanding. "Alright, everyone. We've got a lot of ground to cover. Once the rescue team clears the bodies, we move in."

Sarah exhaled sharply, "Fifteen years in this job, and I've never seen a crash like this."

Hans studied her for a moment. "If you need a minute, take it. But this wreckage…it's going to take everything we've got to piece it together."

She nodded, her eyes flickering over the bodies. Her stomach tightened.

"We start by notifying the families," Hans continued. "Then we investigate."

Sarah crossed her arms. "My question is, how did a virtually unknown charter airline come out of nowhere? And what the hell caused this plane to spiral out of control?"

Gustaf, one of the team members, turned to Hans and asked in German, "Should we look for the black boxes first?"

Hans responded in English. "We wait for the rescue teams to finish. The impact wasn't strong enough to destroy them."

The next morning, Lindsay was still on the couch in yesterday's clothes, unmoving. Dark circles shadowed her swollen, red-rimmed eyes. Her lips quivered as she pressed tightly together, fighting off sobs that threatened to break free.

Sue and James sat beside her, arms wrapped around her shoulders. "We'll get through this," Sue whispered.

Matt's phone rang.

"Hello sir," a woman said in a Filipino accent. "This is the crisis line for Celestine Airlines. We're deeply sorry for your loss."

Matt stiffened. "Yes?"

"The airline is offering a compensation package and a trip for you and a loved one to retrieve your son's remains."

Matt frowned. "Wait, you're Celestine Airlines? I thought this was a European charter airline based in Finland."

"We are a global charter airline," the woman replied. "We provide budget-friendly flights worldwide."

Rachel, standing beside Matt, whispered, "Who is it?"

Matt muted the phone. "Some scam artist pretending to be the airline. You won't have someone from the Philippines dealing with crisis management."

"Send me the details," Rachel said.

Matt then found an official message from the NTSB and another from Celestine Airlines.

He read the Celestine email aloud:

We are sorry for your loss. We are offering a $100,000 compensation package and a free charter flight from Atlanta to Salzburg. The Austrian Army will escort you to the crash site via helicopter. Details are attached.

Rachel scoffed. "One hundred grand? That's all Steve's life is worth?"

James grimaced. "This airline is a damn cheapskate."

Lindsay cleared her throat. "The NCAA booked it. It was cheap and got him to Finland faster, with fewer stops."

Matt's phone rang again–this time, the NTSB.

"Mr. Turner, this is Josh from the National Transportation Safety Board. I wanted to check in regarding the email from Celestine Airlines."

Matt exhaled, "Yeah, it's a joke. One hundred grand for compensation for losing my son?"

Josh sighed. "We're looking into the airline. It was founded just last year and has raised a lot of red flags. Their crisis response has also been…problematic. Normally, airlines allow multiple family members to retrieve remains, but Celestine is limiting it to one, with a $3,000 fee per additional person."

Matt's jaw clenched. "That's outrageous."

"We agree," Josh said. "The NTSB will cover the costs for up to eight family members. We're also pushing or a fairer compensation package."

Matt's eyes widened. Everyone else stared, jaws slack. "What in the world is this?"

He let out a breath. "Thank you."

Josh continued, "A Delta charter flight departs this evening. You'll arrive in Salzburg by mid-morning. Helicopters will be waiting."

Matt turned to his family. "Alright. Let's go get Steve."

CHAPTER 9

Steve and Oliver trudged through the rough snow, their breaths fogging in the frigid air. Silence hung thick around them, broken only by the occasional groan of shifting ice or the distant crack of a glacier.

As the barren landscape gave way to the first hints of forest, Steve's eyes widened. He stopped in his tracks, taking in the view. A grin stretched across his face, and his entire body seemed to wake up. He bounced on the balls of his feet, clapping his hands with sudden energy.

"Are you serious?" Steve asked, his voice breathless. His hands flew up, fingers spread wide, as if trying to grasp the enormity of the moment.

Beside him, Oliver giggled. He squealed, his small boots stamping the snow in an erratic rhythm of excitement.

"What is it? What is it? Why are you jumping for joy?" Steve asked. Then he pointed ahead. "Look! There's a house way out there, and there's a fire burning. That means someone lives there. We might finally get something to eat."

Oliver's eyes gleamed. "I'm so hungry. We've walked way too far."

They pressed forward through the dense trees, each breath puffing out small clouds in the freezing air. Each step crunched beneath their boots, disturbing the pristine layer of snow.

Icy branches scraped Steve's jacket, leaving faint lines of frost along his sleeves. The cold bit at their faces, but through the thinning trees, Steve spotted it—soft amber light glowing through windows against the steel-blue dusk.

Steve stood outside, scanning the cabin. He approached the fire cautiously, peering closer to see what was burning.

"Ollie, come here," Steve said. Oliver ran up beside him, his eyes going wide at the sight before them.

"It's a piece of the aircraft," Steve murmured. "It's been burning this whole time."

Oliver's jaw dropped. "How do you know?"

"Trust me. I study planes. That—" he gestured toward the scorched wreckage "— is part of the wing. Either it's been smoldering since impact or reignited somehow."

Steve turned to the cabin. Snow slipped through the cracks in the shingles. Frost clung stubbornly to the shattered windows, blurring the interior.

"Let's go inside," Steve said. "Maybe we can finally get some rest after everything."

Oliver nodded. They pushed open the creaking door.

The air inside was heavy with the scent of rot. Dust coated everything—tables, shelves, even the cold stone hearth at the far end. Ashes lay scattered across the floor, disturbed by the draft slipping through the broken boards.

They dropped their bags and collapsed into dust-covered chairs. Oliver's stomach growled. "I'm hungry. Is there any more food?"

Steve rummaged through a backpack. "We've got three bags of Chex Mix."

Oliver tore open a packet and devoured it. Steve sighed. "Don't eat too much, or else you'll be starving to death."

Oliver crumpled the empty bag. "How are we going to find food?"

Steve thought for a moment. "We'll have to hunt or fish. No one's living here, so we can't count on anyone helping us."

"Do you know how to hunt and fish?"

"Yeah. I've learned from my grandfather and father. We used to fish at Lake Allatoona back home. My dad always said, 'To survive in the wild, first look for fruit, then fish, and finally hunt.'"

Oliver looked out at snow-covered trees. "No fruit here."

"Then we find a stream. First thing in the morning, we'll make fishing rod."

Oliver nodded.

"And since we can't find a bed, we'll have to sleep on the floor," Steve said. "Let me check and see if there's a furnace here, which we can heat the house."

"Yeah, I'm getting cold," Oliver said.

Steve checked around the dark cabin, his hands trailing along the rough wall to keep his balance. The faintest silver of light from the fire outside barely illuminated the space. Steve felt the thick, cold air, which carried the faint scent of rust and dampness, a telltale sign that the furnace was near.

Steve walked ever so slowly, every creak of the floorboards beneath him sounding louder in the silence. His heart pounded, his arms reached out blindly, hoping to feel the cold steel soon before the darkness overwhelmed him.

Oliver yelled in the background, "Steve, did you find it?"

"No, not yet," Steve yelled back. But moments later, his fingers brushed against cold steel. Relief flooded through him.

"I think I'm able to find it," Steve said, his heart pounded, arms reaching out blindly, hoping to feel the cold steel soon before the darkness overwhelmed them.

Within several minutes, Steve's hands finally brush against the cold metal. A surge of relief flooded through his face. With a wide grin breaking across his face, he exhaled a breath he hadn't realized he'd been holding.

"I found the furnace, Ollie," Steve said.

Oliver jumped up in joy. "Thank goodness!"

The furnace stood solid in the darkness, its presence a lifeline amid the shadows.

With a quick twist, Steve opened the door, then heard a familiar creak-like music was heard in his ears. As the glow from within spilled out, casting a soft, orange light over their face, a rush of contentment filled him. The furnace burned, heating the entire house.

Steve rushed back to Oliver. "I think we'll be sleeping well tonight here."

Oliver's eyelids dropped. He yawned, then lay down on the floor. Steve lifted him gently, carrying him to the warmth of the furnace. He wrapped his body with his two jackets and propped his head above a backpack.

Then Steve sat beside him, heart still racing from the day's chaos. He looked into the flickering light.

"Where the hell are we?" he said. "It better be Austria or Switzerland or northern Italy." Steve closed his eyes and drifted into sleep.

Within several hours, the darkness of sleep shifted violently as a nightmare took hold. In an instant, Steve was back on the plane— engines failing with a defeaning roar, the aircraft lurching as it dropped. Panic surged through his body, every muscle tensing as the cabin tilted, passengers' scream blending with the shriek of tearing metal.

Sweat beaded on his forehead as he trashed in bed, heart pounding as if it were about to burst from his chest. The smell of burning fuel, the jarring impact, the suffocating heat—it all came crashing back, vivid and real. His hands reached out instinctively, grasping for something solid, something to hold on to, but found only emptiness.

Then Steve jolted awake, gasping for breath, disoriented. The room was dark, but not the darkness of the plane's wreckage. His chest heaved as he fought to pull himself back to reality, his skin damp and clammy from sweat. Every sound, even the faintest creak of the floorboards, felt too loud, too sharp, and his hands trembled uncontrollably.

Steve glanced at Oliver, still fast asleep, with no issues. He rose briefly and went outside into the front porch of the house. He witnessed a world outside that was engulfed in a swirling sea of white, but somehow, it felt peaceful. Snowflakes danced through the air, illuminated by the soft glow of the moon, falling steadily in endless waves.

The wind whispered low through the trees, not with the fury he'd braced for, but with a stillness that felt almost intentional—like the mountain itself was holding its breath. Steve pulled his coat tighter, the quiet settling into his bones. He thought of Lindsay, of her voice on the phone, telling him to come back changed, and his family worried about his death.

The terror of his nightmare seemed to fade away as he felt a strange warmth in his chest, a sense of connection to the vast, frozen world around him.

I made it out of a plane crash—in the middle of the Alps, of all places. Just me and Oliver. Why us? Why not the others?

Shivering, Steve retreated inside and lay back down.

CHAPTER 10

In Salzburg, the Turner and Carson families arrived on a private airstrip. As they stepped off the plane, members of the Austrian Search and Rescue Team met with them.

"Are you the family of Steve Turner?" one rescuer, Lukas, asked.

"Yes," Matt said. "I'm the father."

"Please, come with me."

Clad in uniform, Lukas led the Turners and the Carson family to the Flying Hangar, located in the eastern half of the airport. The families hurriedly rushed as fast as they could.

Lindsay asked, "If Steve is dead, why are they bringing us here?"

"Let's find out," Matt replied.

Inside the hangar, Lindsay shifted in her seat, arms folded tightly across her chest. Around her, passengers avoided eye contact, their knees bouncing, fingers drumming against armrests. A man across the aisle checked his watch for the third time in a minute. The tension hung in the cabin like static—silent, but impossible to ignore. Maps covered the walls, marked with grids and red circles, indicating concentrated search areas. Radios crackled intermittently with static-laden updates, and the air smelled faintly of stale coffee and damp uniforms.

Lukas guided them into a conference room, where an elderly couple sat silently. Their hands were clasped, faces etched with lines. The woman clutched a tissue, her eyes glassy as she stared blankly at the floor. Beside her, the man sat rigid, his jaw clenched, one trembling hand gripping the armrest while the other kept smoothing the same spot on his pant leg. Neither had spoken since the announcement.

Matt approached the man and said, "Hi, my name is Matt."

The man, head lowered, responded with a British accent while shaking Matt's hand. "Hi, I'm Barry. Pleasure to meet you."

The woman, struggling to compose herself. "My name is Mary." She broke down, sobbing in tears.

Rachel moved to her side, gently taking Mary's hands.

Matt said, "I'm so sorry for your loss, whoever died in the crash."

Barry said, "Our son, Paul, his wife, Sophie, and their kids, Oliver and Amy. They were a beloved family. They lived in Norwich. We live just a few miles north, in Aylsham. The kids would come by, and we'd have fun together."

Matt offered a sympathetic smile. "I'm not great with geography. But where is Norwich?"

"Two hours northeast of London by train," Barry said. "We flew in this morning as the Austrian team organized the search aircraft."

Lindsay hugged herself, eyes downcast. Emma blinked fast, lips tight. Owen stood rigid, fists clenched. Sue and James exchanged anxious glances.

Sue checked her phone. "How long is this going to take?"

"Wait patiently," James said. "They will come."

Just then, Lukas arrived inside, joined by the two lead investigators: Hans Fredrich from the SUB and Sarah McCarthy from the NTSB. They carried several folders, along with a projector remote.

"Hi, my name is Lukas, one of the search and rescue team personnel running the base operations out of Salzburg Airport."

Lukas turned his face toward Hans. "Hello, my name is Hans Friedrich from the SUB, and the lead investigator of this crash."

Hans turned to Sarah. "I'm Sarah, with the NTSB. Since the aircraft involved was a Boeing 767, our Washington-based team is required to assist."

Hans gave a curt nod. "We're deeply sorry for your loss. The crash occurred in the mountains along the Tyrol–Carinthia border. We've just returned from the site with the cockpit voice recorder and flight data recorders."

Owen cleared his throat. "Understood. I study Aerospace Engineering and Computer Science at Georgia Tech. I'm familiar with flight data systems."

Rachel frowned, "Owen, not now. Keep it down. You don't want to cause a ruckus." She looked at Hans. "He's a wild one. My other son, Steve, was the calm one."

"No worries," Hans said. "I was like your son once, which is why I became a crash investigator."

He turned serious again. "Anyways, the reason why we wanted you here is that our search and rescue team had gathered nearly all the bodies of the deceased passengers, but they couldn't find two."

Sarah turned on the projector, showcasing the wreckage. "The team scoured every part of the crash and managed to recover all but two bodies. We verified to ensure whichever bodies matched the passenger list. We triple-checked the wreckage but couldn't find these two."

She continued. "The names missing are your son, Steve Turner," she said, pointing to the Turners. "And your grandson, Oliver Lynds," she said, pointing to Barry and Mary.

Lindsay gasped, placing her hands on her mouth.

"Are you serious?" Barry said. "Oliver survived the crash?"

"Steve also made it?" Lindsay said.

"We think so," Sarah said. "But we urge you to not get your hopes too high. They may have survived the crash, but they could still be in serious danger."

"There are two possibilities," Hans added. "Either they were thrown far from the wreckage—which is unlikely—or they were in the back seats, the safest part of the plane, which often provides the highest chance of survival."

"Two missing bodies out of 239 is a total anomaly," Sarah added.

"How do you know all this?" Owen asked.

Rachel snapped, "Quiet!"

"Most of the passengers who died were found within a two-mile radius of the crash. Preliminary analysis indicates there was no breakup of the plane prior to impact, so we know most passengers died upon impact."

Lindsay trembled as she exhaled slowly, eyes locked in on the images. Emma bit her lip, trying to hold back tears, while Rachel's jaw clenched tightly, barely daring to hope.

Sarah stepped forward and handed Barry and Mary a folded note, saying quietly, "This was recovered from your son's belongings at the crash site."

Mary unfolded the paper with trembling hands. Her voice barely above a whisper, she read aloud.

"Mum, Dad, Alfie—

Thank you for looking after me. Sophie, the kids, and I will soon be departing the world. Take care and we will see you on the other side."

Tears streamed down Mary's cheeks as the weight of the words settled in the room.

Hans asked gently, "I just need to know who's Alfie?"

"Our other son, who is no longer in contact with us," Barry said, wiping tears. "But Paul always kept tabs on him. Oliver's the last hope in our lives."

Lindsay said, "Knowing Steve, I think he found your grandson alive and is taking care of him if he's still alive. He always tries to help lost human beings or animals."

Mary raised her face and said, "Then maybe there's still hope. Oliver's all we have now."

Lukas nodded. "We have alerted the police, and they have commenced the search for Steve and Oliver. If we have any updates, we'll call you."

Matt released a deep breath. "Thank you."

Hans added, "We have commenced the investigation and will keep you informed of any updates."

"Thank you," the families echoed.

As the families exited the room, Matt asked Barry, "Do you need any support from us as you take their bodies home?"

"Yeah, that would help," Barry said. "Thank you for trying to help. I'm praying to God that Oliver is alive."

"Don't worry about it," Matt said. "My son, Steve, is an Eagle Scout. He always looks after others when they are in trouble. Your grandson is in good hands."

The next morning, the cabin door creaked open, groaning like it hadn't been moved in years. From the shadows emerged a stooped figure, his silhouette framed by the soft, fading afternoon light. His face was craggy and weathered like the Alps themselves. Thick gray brows twitched a permanent scowl.

"Was macht ihr hier?" the man barked. *What are you doing here?* His voice was rough, gravelly, like stone scraping together in a riverbed. His accent thick, unmistakably Austrian, rolled out each word with clipped precision.

Steve and Oliver rose up, with Steve towering over the old man, his eyes widened, gulping down. "Sorry, we didn't mean to stay inside. There was a blizzard yesterday."

The old man yelled, "Ich verstehe Sie nicht." *I don't understand you!*

Oliver stood frozen, his small frame trembling as if the surrounding air turned cold.

Steve said, "I'm sorry, I don't understand. We just needed somewhere to sleep. We were going to leave right now anyways."

The old man continued yelling in German, "Ihr habt hier nichts zu suchen! Verzieht euch!" *You have no business being here! Get out of here!* He spat the words. His voice rose with fury that demanded disproportionate to the situation.

Then he raised his hunting rifle, aiming it directly at them.

Oliver clung onto Steve tightly and cried to him, "I don't want to die. I want to go home."

Steve grabbed his jacket, map, and water bottle, quickly stuffing them into his duffle. Then he gathered Oliver's clothes and essentials, stuffing them in without hesitation. He zipped the bag shut and took a steady breath.

Then he raised his hands. "Oliver, raise your hands as well."

Oliver followed Steve, raising his hands. Both slowly walked their way out of the house as the old man pointed his rifle at them.

Steve and Oliver exited out of the door of the cabin, into the snow, and proceeded their way. Behind them, the old man slammed the door shut.

CHAPTER 11

Before boarding, Hans and Sarah stopped the Turners, and handed them their contact information.

"We'll be coordinating with the police to begin the search for Steve and Oliver starting today," Hans said. "We'll keep you updated with any developments."

Lindsay stepped forward, "Do you know how long or how difficult would it be to find Steve?"

Hans shook his head. "We can't say for sure. The search and rescue teams recovered Steve's iPhone. It's badly damaged, cracked and non-functional. We can't trace any location from it."

Lindsay's breath fogged in the cold air as she watched the dense forest beyond the clearing. Long shadows stretched over the snow, swallowing any sign of a path. Her heart squeezed tight. *How will he even find his way through all this?*

"Okay," she said quietly. "But… how will you find him?"

"We have every means available," Sarah said. "Don't fret too much. Just get some rest. You look like you haven't been sleeping too well."

Matt gave a weak chuckle. "At least now that we know Steve's alive, maybe we can sleep a little."

"We'll find him," Hans assured. "And we'll let you know the moment we do."

Several hours after leaving the cabin, Steve and Oliver continued their descent down the mountain. The wind howled around them, cutting at their skin. Before them lay a steep, white slope.

"Are you sure this is the only way?" Oliver asked.

Steve, panting, nodded. "Yes. We need to get to a lower altitude, so we won't freeze to death. We can find more people down the slope who can help us."

Oliver hesitated. "We should've stayed at the crash site, waited for someone."

Steve laughed, "We could've waited hours—or days. We'd have frozen to death by then. No, we've got to survive. That means moving forward."

"Have you done this kind of thing before?" Oliver asked.

"I was an Eagle Scout, where one of the activities to earn a merit badge was training junior scouts and kids like you on how to survive in the wilderness and in difficult conditions. We went to the Appalachian Mountains for that activity alone. You learn to set up camp, use the existing resources that you have to set it up. Long story short, yes, I've done plenty of these activities before."

The snow thinned, but the ground turned icy. Oliver slipped and fell. He cried out, curling into himself. His small frame trembled, tears streaking his flushed cheeks.

Steve knelt beside him, "What happened, Oliver?"

Oliver struggled to contain his tears. "I fell down and got hurt on my knee." Steve gently rolled up Oliver's pant leg and winced at the sight of blood. He rummaged through this backpack and cursed under breath.

"God, dang it. You're such a mouth breathing moron," Steve said to himself. "The one thing you forget to bring with you is the first aid kit."

Steve checked every and found a scrap of cloth. He packed the cloth with snow before pressing it against the wound.

Oliver screamed. "Ow."

"I know, I know. I'm sorry," Steve said, his voice softening. "But we've got to stop the bleeding. We'll find a town, get someone who knows what they're doing."

"I'm hungry," Oliver sniffled.

Steve released a deep sigh. "Hold on. Then we'll need to find a stream of water where we can fish. I don't seem to find any wildlife here to hunt for." He looked inside his backpack for any remaining snacks.

Steve handed Oliver a pack of Belvita biscuits, which Oliver quickly devoured. "You sure do have a big appetite for a little guy," Steve chuckled. "Let's go. I'm going to give you a piggyback ride, okay?"

Steve hoisted Oliver onto his back and trudged onward, scanning for terrain for any sign of water. The wind howled across the frozen mountainside, biting into their exposed skin like icy needles. Steve adjusted his jacket around his face, ensuring Oliver's face was covered as well.

"We should have found it now," Steve muttered through layers of wool around his mouth. His fingers, numb despite his thick gloves, trembled as he pointed ahead. "It's supposed to be just over this ridge."

Oliver struggled to hold his breath. He couldn't recognize the terrain beneath the blanket of snow, turning every landmark into a vague outline.

"The snow's covered everything," he said, pausing to catch his breath.

"Don't worry," Steve said. "I can sense that we're almost there."

They pressed forward in silence, the only sounds their labored breathing and the crunch of the snow beneath their feet. Minutes turned to hours, and still, no sign of water. The mountains loomed over them, indifferent to their struggle, their jagged peaks cutting into the sky like teeth.

Steve slipped and collapsed onto one knee, gasping.

"Are you okay?" Oliver asked.

"I'm fine," Steve said with a shrug. "I need to make sure you're okay and whatever it takes, I'll push forward and get you food." As the cold intensified, both of their muscles grew sluggish, their minds foggy.

Steve stood still, his pulse quickening. At first, all he could hear was the relentless wind, but then, there it was. Faint, but unmistakable—the sound of water. A stream, hidden beneath layers of snow and ice, but flowing, nonetheless.

"It's here, Ollie," Steve said, his voice catching in his throat. Relief flooded through both of them, and for the first time in hours, hope flickered in the frozen wilderness.

"We found it!" Oliver screamed.

Steve placed Oliver down with the bags. He quickly asked Oliver, "Are you okay? Can you walk?"

"I think I'm feeling better," Oliver said, standing up, feeling a slight amount of pain."

"The snow cauterized the wound, then," Steve said. He then told Oliver, "I'm going to go ahead and make a fishing rod and if you can, check and see if you can find any live bait. Like a piece of bread."

"Okay," Oliver said, opening the bag with shaking hands. The wind had slowly dissipated, making room for slightly sunnier skies.

Oliver yelled, "How are you creating it?"

"You'll find out," Steve yelled back. "Wait here. I need to grab a few things."

Steve scoured around for a long, flexible, and lightweight stick, strong fibrous plants like yucca, nettle, or an inner bark, a piece for a tree bone for a hook. Then he froze. *Wait, I can't leave Oliver sitting over there alone.* He returned back to Oliver who asleep and curled against the bags.

Steve gazed at Oliver, his hair growing ever longer. *Should I go ahead and take him with me?* he wondered. He lifted Oliver in his arms, shouldered the hear, and carried him to the stream.

Steve gathered all the materials needed to create the fishing rod. He used the remaining pieces of bread as live bait and then placed Oliver on the side of the stream before he inserted the fishing rod into the stream. After almost an hour, the rod began to twitch, and Steve pulled the rod as mightily as he could.

He could see it with his eyes, the movement of the fish shook the rod.

"Oliver, wake up," Steve said. "We got our lunch ready soon." Oliver slowly opened his eyes, the sheer anticipation of watching Steve trying to catch the fish.

"Is the fish here?" Oliver asked.

"Almost," Steve said.

"Mum always loved to make me fish and chips," Oliver said. "But she never ate it with us."

"Your dad told me, she doesn't like to eat meat and fish," Steve said.

Steve pulled the trout from the water. Its sleek body arched, dark spots rimmed in gold shining beneath the pale belly. The tail flicked, sending droplets scattering like jewels.

"It's a brown trout," Steve said. "We've got some essential vitamins right there inside." He placed the fish on the ground, where it thrashed wildly, fighting against the alien air. Its tail whipped back and forth in desperate, erratic motions, sending water droplets flying in all directions. The smooth, graceful movements it once exhibited in the water were gone, replaced by frantic, jerking convulsions as it tried to free itself.

Steve pulled out a knife from his pocket and took a deep breath. Oliver's eyes opened wide.

"Time to make a fire," Steve said.

"How do we do that?" Oliver said.

"Didn't they teach you in school?" Steve said. "You gather a couple of sticks and woods and then you rub those sticks against each other and set the flame off."

"I see now," Oliver said.

They gathered several sticks and created a small fireplace where they rubbed several sticks with each other, trying to get the fire started.

"We don't need a large fire," Steve said. "A small one is enough to cook this sucker."

They both struggled to rub the sticks to start off the fire when suddenly, a slight piece of the solar flare landed on top of the mini fireplace, then ignited a fire.

Steve and Oliver shook in horror, seeing the fire started for no reason. They looked around and stared at the sky.

"How did that happen?" Oliver asked. "We didn't create the fire."

"Must be that power of the sun," Steve said. "It just ignited the fire. God really wants us alive."

CHAPTER 12

The dimly lit makeshift lab at Salzburg Airport hummed with quiet intensity of focused minds. Fluorescent lights buzzed overhead. A technician adjusted a microscope. Another tapped at a laptop, eyes flicking between data streams. On the long, metal table in the center sat two black boxes, scarred from the wreckage, but intact. The flight data recorder and cockpit voice recorder were charred, scratched, and heavy with silence, their surfaces bearing the marks of catastrophe.

Lead investigator Hans Friedrich leaned over the table, his gaze fixed on the larger of two. The black casing was dulled, but the bright orange labels and stark warnings screamed of the crucial information locked inside. Beside him, Sarah alongside a technician named Stefan Hofer adjusted their headphones, fingers hovering over the control panel that would play the final moments of the flight.

"Whenever you're ready," Hans said. His voice was steady, but a faint edge of unease crept in.

Sarah nodded. "Let's do this. I've worked on countless investigations of Boeing crashes. This company's going through a hell of trouble."

Stefan nodded, his fingers tapping a series of commands into the computer. A moment later, the first sound filled the room—a low hum of static, followed by the ambient noise of the cockpit.

Hans watched the screen as data began to stream in—a series of numbers, readouts, and flight parameters flashing across the monitor in rapid succession: altitude, speed, engine performance—it was all there.

But it wasn't the data Hans was waiting for. It was the voices.

"Here it comes," Stefan whispered.

Hans and Sarah listened intently, their brows furrowed in concentration.

As they listened, the cockpit was calm at first, with the captain, Nigel Callaghan, and the first officer, William Rhodes, speaking in low-measured tones, discussing routine checks, the changes in flight plans, wind speed, along with them witnessing the first solar flare.

Then the tone shifted. "What the hell was that?" Rhodes said. The investigators witnessed the plane rapidly changing altitude and the pilots losing control of the systems.

"Captain, we're losing power," they heard Rhodes shouting.

"Check the electrical systems!" Captain Callaghan ordered.

The cockpit was no longer calm. Urgency filled the voices now, with Captain Callaghan issuing orders and First Officer Rhodes scrambling to comply. The sound of switches being flipped, and levers being pulled filled the space, but the situation only worsened. Altitude was plummeting and the cockpit filled with warning alarms and voices raising in panic.

"Mayday, mayday, mayday!" Callaghan yelled. A long stretch of silence followed. Then a sound indescribable. Metal screaming, a deafening crash, and static.

Stefan reached forward and tapped the spacebar. The recording cut off with a final burst of static. Sarah sat rigid, her fingers gripping the edge of the table, breath shallow. Hans exhaled slowly through his nose.

"They never had a chance," Sarah said, quietly, her fingers gripping the edge of the table. She closed her eyes for a moment, the image of the final seconds etched into her mind, even though she hadn't seen it.

Hans frowned, dragging the engine performance graphs back on screen. "This doesn't make any sense. It's almost as if the engine deliberately shut down due to a phenomenon. But there's no evidence of a malfunction. And nothing from the pilot or co-pilot about sabotage."

Sarah eyes flickered toward him. "What kind of phenomenon?"

"Play it again," Hans said. Stefan hit the play button, and once more, the cockpit came to life.

They stopped the tape recording when First Officer Rhodes said, "Do you see that?"

Hans leaned forward, elbows on the table, eyes fixed on the still frame of the cockpit. "That's what we need to investigate," he said, voice low. "Planes don't just fall out of the sky."

Steve trudged down the slope, Oliver just behind him. Each step sent a dull ache through his legs, but the thought of a warm bed in some distant town kept him moving. Still, his mind gnawed at the same question.

That fire… it wasn't right. Not at that altitude. Not with snow all around us. Something strange was going on—and the deeper they went, the louder that thought became.

The sun began to set, and Steve watched as Oliver ran around the grass picking dandelions and catching bugs.

"You might want to be careful there," Steve said. "You don't want to get poisoned."

"I know," Oliver said. "I'm not going to get poisoned. I'm a brave boy."

Steve chuckled. Looking at Oliver's happy face, he felt awe.

"You're lucky we're in the mountains of Central Europe," Steve said. "Back home, I'd be watching your back constantly."

"Why?" Oliver asked, hopping along the snowy trail.

"Things can get rough. Fights, shootings, disasters—it depends where you are."

Oliver didn't respond, just looked ahead, snow crunching beneath his boots.

"You're from Norwich, right?" Steve asked.

"Yeah. That's home."

"What's it like?"

Oliver shrugged. "I've got neighbors, school, sports. Fridays, we get fish and chips. Sundays, roast at Nan's. Roast beef's the best."

Steve smiled. "Sounds like a good life."

"Where are you from?"

"Just north of Atlanta. The airport we left from." A pause. "My fiancée, Lindsay... my family—they think I'm gone."

Oliver glanced at him but he stayed silent.

"I work in college sports," Steve went on. "Trying to grow the NCAA overseas. Finland, mostly." He frowned. "Not sure anyone on the other side ever really got what I was doing."

Steve and Oliver reached Hochfeld just as night fell. The village lay quiet beneath the mountains, silver light from the moon brushing the rooftops.

Steve paused at the edge of town. No lights. No voices. Just the distant rush of a river threading through the valley. The cold pressed in, sharp and still.

The cobblestone streets stretched ahead, empty. He glanced at Oliver trailing behind, his steps dragging. They were both worn down. Hungry. Cold.

Steve adjusted his pack. *We need shelter. Something. Anything.*

"Let's keep moving," he said quietly. "There has to be somewhere."

Oliver looked at Steve, his body stiffened, shoulders hunched. His hands and lips trembled.

"I'm scared," Oliver said. "Can you hold me again?"

Steve shrugged. "Not again. I've held you far too many times. We just need to find a place to eat and sleep at. There should be someone in this town who can help."

Steve spotted movement behind a curtain—a man peering through the window, arms crossed, face unreadable. A few houses down, an elderly woman stood on her stoop, broom in hand, watching them without a word. Her eyes narrowed as they passed.

Steve kept his gaze ahead, pulling Oliver a little closer. *We're not welcome here. Not yet.*

The quiet streets of Hochfeld were deserted, save for an older man standing near a fountain, his weathered face set in a frown as he watched Steve and Oliver approach him.

"Excuse me," Steve said, his voice tight. "I..I'm looking for something to eat. Can you help me?"

The man's brow furrowed deeper, his eyes narrowing as he crossed his arms. "Was? Ich verstehe nicht. Was suchen Sie?" *What? I don't understand. What are you looking for?* His voice was gruff, the accent thick and unfamiliar.

"I…the bakery. Or some place to eat," Steve said, slower this time, as if that would somehow bridge the gap. He gestured the motions of eating and sleeping. "Eat. Sleep."

The man shook his head, frustration flickering across his face as he glanced at Steve and Oliver. "Nein, nein…das ist nich richtig." *No, no… that's not right.* He gestured back toward the village, his voice rising. "Alles ist geschlossen. Closed."

"Closed?" Steve gasped. "There's nothing to eat? We're hungry."

The man threw up his hands up, shaking his head. His eyes, once merely curious, now held something darker–fear, perhaps, or something else entirely.

"Blieb hier!" *Stay here!* he snapped, his voice stern. "Lass mich jemanden finden, der dich ernähren kann." *Let me find someone who can feed you.*

Steve blinked. The tension was thick now. Though most villagers didn't understand him, the tone was enough. His and Oliver's presence sent a ripple of unease.

They stood awkwardly at the edge of the village square, their clothes damp from the long trek from the mountains. The wind carried the faint scent of woodsmoke and fresh bread, a smell that seemed out of place against the cold suspicion that hung in the air. A small group of townspeople had gathered, their eyes on the two outsiders, unblinking and unwatchful.

"Are they looking at us?" Oliver whispered, shifting uneasily beside Steve.

Steve gave a slow nod, not daring to speak. The air was thick with an unease he couldn't quite place. It was as though the entire town had been holding its breath since their arrival, waiting to see if these strangers were to be trustworthy.

An elderly woman in a heavy wool coat, her gray hair tied back in a neat bun, escorted Steve and Oliver into her home kitchen. Steve stiffened as she approached, but Oliver nudged him, his eyes flicking toward the bread.

"She's bringing us something," Oliver muttered, hope emerging in his voice.

The woman stopped a few feet away, her gaze wary but not hostile. She held out the bread, her hands trembling slightly as though unsure whether this act of kindness was a mistake. "Brot," she said, her voice low.

She handed Steve and Oliver each three pieces of bread along with milk from the locally sourced cows.

Steve exchanged a glance with Oliver, neither of them moving. "Make sure you eat plenty. We don't know where our next food will come from," Steve whispered to Oliver.

Oliver nodded.

"Dankeschön," Steve said to the woman. He turned to Oliver and said, "That's all the German I know."

Steve and Oliver devoured the bread and milk as fast as they could. Steve then asked the woman with gesticulating hand motions. "Where are we?"

"Ich verstehe nicht," the woman said. *I don't understand.*

Steve took a deep breath. "She doesn't understand me." He continued gesturing, "Where are we? What country is this?"

Oliver facepalmed, "I know some German. Mum taught me. He stepped in and asked the woman, "Welches Land ist das?" *What country is this?*

The woman responded, "Österreich."

Oliver turned to Steve. "Austria."

"Dang," Steve said. "I didn't know you could speak German. And I was right. We're in Austria." He hugged Oliver. "Thank you. You should teach me German. Why didn't you say anything when we were at the cabin earlier?"

"I was scared," Oliver said. "He was pointing a gun at us."

"Tell the woman, we need a place to sleep for the night," Steve said. "We're so tired."

Oliver said, "Zwei bedden, bitte." *Two beds, please.*

The woman escorted Steve and Oliver into the small upstairs bedroom, a perfect refuge from the harsh alpine cold outside. The walls were paneled in warm, honey-colored pine, the wood giving off a faint, earthy scent that mixed with the crisp mountain air drifting in through a slightly cracked window. Outside, there was the distant howl of the wind, but inside, it was quiet and peaceful.

CHAPTER 13

At the Turner's home, a soft, but insistent knock echoed through the quiet house.

"Who knocks instead of ringing the bell?" Matt muttered, rising to his feet, and ringing for the door.

"Jake," he said, surprised. "What are you doing here?"

Jake looked stricken. "What do you think? I was supposed to pick up Steve in Helsinki. When I found out the plane crashed in the morning, my heart sank." He bowed his head, his voice cracking. "Everyone at the NCAA is mourning. They even canceled two SEC games."

Owen appeared at the doorway. "We just got back from Austria. We saw the crash site, but Steve wasn't among the dead."

Jake's eyes widened. He raised his hands to his mouth. "Wait, you're telling me Steve made it out alive?"

"I think so," Owen said. "The rescue teams are still looking. We're hoping they'll find him soon."

"There's no way they can search all of the Alps," Jake said, shaking his head.

"They found his phone," Owen said. "It was damaged, though, so no leads yet."

He turned. "You alright, Lindsay?"

Lindsay stepped forward, visibly shaken. "I'm just jittery right now," she said, her eyes thin.

Owen gave a half-laugh. "I've got to get back to school soon. Exams are coming up, and this trip threw off everything. Maybe after Thanksgiving coming up, we can all regroup. In the meantime, spend some time at the hospital. That should take your worries off this excruciating search process."

Lindsay nodded. "Jake, you're welcome to come over for Thanksgiving."

Jake nodded. "Sure."

Night fell over Hochfeld and the winds howled through the mountains. Inside the bedroom, Steve thrashed in bed, trapped in a fever dream. In his dream, the low roar of the engines slowly crept into his mind, faint at first, but steadily growing louder.

Steve blinked and found himself sitting once again by the window, staring out at the endless stretch of the sky. The darkness felt too harsh, the colors too vivid.

Steve knew this place. The narrow seats, the stale tang of recycled air—it wasn't memory. It was a dream. His limbs wouldn't move, fused to the seat like part of the plane.

A tremor shook the cabin. Lights flickered. Faces around him blurred and faceless, shifting with panic. The plane jolted again—harder this time. Overhead bins popped open. A drop yanked the breath from his chest as the world outside the window tipped sideways—sky and mountain trading places.

Oxygen masks dropped with a mechanical snap, swinging wildly. Voices rose—screams, prayers—but distant, as if muffled by water.

Steve gripped the armrests. Useless. Powerless. The plane was falling, and all he could do was watch.

The ground surged toward them—trees and ridgelines merging into a single rushing blur.

Then, a blinding flash of white.

And silence.

Steve jolted awake, gasping for breath, his heart hammering in his chest. The dream slipped away, but the terror stuck, raw and electric. Sweat clung to his skin. His heart still pounded like the ground was rushing up to meet him.

He continued gasping as he rose, donned his shoes and jacket, and rushed outside for fresh air. He saw the rows of houses and realized, "Wait a minute, I'm not dreaming. I'm in a small town here in Austria."

Steve felt a knot in his chest, like a hand gently squeezing his heart. His vision blurred as tears gathered, teetering on the edge, though none had fallen yet.

Steve sank to the floor, his hands covered his face. Tears flowed until his body shook. In that moment, all he could do was cry and think of the number of people hurting.

"Lindsay," he whispered, brokenly. "I'm so sorry I won't be there for Thanksgiving or Christmas. I keep thinking about that ugly sweater you bought last year—the one you swore I'd wear for photos. I was supposed to propose by the tree. Now there's no tree, no you, no us."

He paused, swallowing hard.

"Jake… Helsinki should've been our launchpad. I still picture us walking into those stadium meetings, cocky as hell. You'll keep climbing, and I'll just be a question mark you carry."

He drew in a shaky breath.

"Mom, Dad, Owen—I'm sorry. I can still smell the cinnamon rolls, hear the wrapping paper tearing open. I always thought there'd be more of those mornings." He turned back, wiping his tears.

The next morning, an eerie sound caught Steve's attention, a low murmur carried on the crisp mountain air. He stood at the window, staring out into the gathering dusk, the snow-dusted peaks in the distance bathed in fading light.

A flicker of movement caught his eye. Steve put on a jacket and went to the porch of the house. At the edge of the square, shadows shifted. Figures emerged from the alleys, half-lit by a flickering lamp. A coat brushed stone. Footsteps scraped across icy cobblestones. One man glanced back, breath rising in pale wisps.

Steve observed a handful of villagers wrapped in heavy woolen coats, their faces obscured by scarves and hoods. More appeared, trickling in from every direction, gathering like storm clouds on the horizon.

The murmurs grew louder, a slow, rumbling wave of voices echoed through the narrow streets. Steve's heart quickened. He turned away from the porch and went back inside, trying to shake the feeling twisting in his gut, but it clung to him.

Outside, the figures pressed closer, no longer just isolated shadow but a crowd swelling with each passing minute. The faint glow of lanterns flickered in their hands, casting long dancing shadows on the cobblestone streets. He could see their faces now, pale in the dying light, eyes narrowed and hard. There was no mistaking the intent in their expressions.

Oliver slowly woke up. "What is it?" he asked, wiping his eyes, sensing the shift in Steve's demeanor.

"There are mobs outside, and they don't seem to be happy that we're here," Steve whispered, his voice barely audible over the growing noise. He moved toward the window, his breath fogging the glass as he peered out. Now, dozens of villagers stood in the square, all facing the house. Some were muttering to one another while others stared in silence, their gazes fixed on the door as if they were waiting for something.

A sharp crack pierced the air—a rock, small but loud, striking the front step with a thud. Steve and Oliver flinched. It was followed by another, then another, the stones bouncing off the wooden walls with hollow, menacing thuds. The noise echoed in the narrow streets, swallowed by the mountains that loomed over Hochfeld.

The murmurs rose to shouts, voices overlapping in a chaotic, angry symphony. Steve's pulse raced, his chest tight as he watched the crowd shift, their faces twisted with something darker now.

"What are they doing?" Oliver said, his voice trembling.

"I don't know," Steve said. "We were just staying here for the night and were going to leave anyways. Let me check it out for myself. You wait right here."

Steve crept to the front door and opened it. He tried to dodge the number of rocks thrown at him.

"Wait, wait," Steve yelled. "I don't speak any German. What do you guys want? Why are you throwing those rocks over here?"

The mob started shouting in German, their faces brazen with anger and suspicion.

One of the younger men from the crowd approached Steve and said in broken English, "We believe that you're a threat to our community, as we have seen a few solar flares pass by our town. It's a bad omen for all of us. And if more pass by, we fear the town will become cursed with solar flares. The town will die. I need you to leave."

CHAPTER 14

Inside a large conference room at Salzburg Airport's Hangar-7, a heavy silence settled. Rows of metal chairs faced a long table where microphones stood neatly aligned. Behind them, a banner draped over the edge bore the insignias of the Austrian Aviation Authority and the NTSB.

Fluorescent lights buzzed overhead, casting a cold, sterile glow. Everything looked slightly off—like an overexposed photograph. Hans sat motionless, spine rigid, the artificial light doing nothing to ease the knot in his chest.

He took a deep breath and leaned forward, adjusting the microphone. His voice came low and rough.

"Good afternoon. Thank you all for being here," he began. "On behalf of the investigative team and the authorities from both the SUB, NTSB, AAIB, I want to welcome you all to the press conference. I know that all of you are wanting to know what the latest updates are with the crash of Celestine Airlines Flight 24.

This has been one of the worst air disasters we've seen in recorded history, unprecedented, especially considering how safe flying has become. The odds of dying in a plane crash are significantly lower than those of a car accident, over which we have more control. I don't think Austria has seen a plane crash worse than this ever."

Hans stepped away from the podium, allowing Sarah to approach amid the flicker of cameras. She took a deep breath, her body trembling.

"Good afternoon, everyone. Thank you for being here," Sarah began. "This is not an easy update to deliver, and I've never had to address something like this before. But let's get straight to it.

After reviewing the black boxes, we've confirmed that the pilots encountered a solar flare, an intense burst of radiation from the sun, that disrupted the plane's systems and caused them to lose control.

Our focus now is on three critical questions: Why did the solar flare occur when it did? Why weren't the pilots warned? And how did the aircraft end up off course, flying over the Alps?

"Thank you."

Hans returned to the podium, his hands clasped tightly in front of him.

"I assure you that we will get to the bottom of this. I commend the search and rescue team for their efforts in recovering the bodies and returning them to their families. The captains' and the first officers' bodies have been returned to the UK and the US respectively. Now we must ask: What was Celestine Airlines' role in this? Why did they employ pilots who weren't decisive enough to navigate past these strange phenomena?"

Turning to the audience, Hans said, "We'll now take some questions from you."

A journalist spoke up. "Alina Smith from CNN. Mr. Friedrich, were you able to identify the two remaining survivors yet? Have you notified their families?"

Hans nodded. "Yes, we've notified the families. They've come to visit Salzburg. The survivors are Steve Turner, a twenty-five-year-old sports executive from Atlanta, Georgia, and Oliver Lynds, a six-year-old child from Norwich, England. It's a miracle they both survived, and our search and rescue team is working tirelessly to locate them."

Another journalist asked. "Is this any inclination of sabotage or terrorism?"

Hans' jaw clenched. "We're not ruling anything out. However, based on the black boxes, it appears that terrorism and sabotage have been ruled out. The Boeing 767 us designed with safeguards, but it's nearly thirty years old and overdue for retirement."

Sarah stepped up again. "If this were a typical crash, we'd be examining the pilots' decisions leading up to the incident. But this is a strange phenomenon that has appeared on our radars. Unfortunately, Celestine Airlines Flight 24 got caught in its path."

Commander Bach then addressed the audience in German with a translator at his side. "Thank you all. I want to say that we're still searching for the two victims, and once we find them, we'll inform you."

A murmur spread through the room.

A third reporter stood up. "Jane Simpson from the BBC News. Are you in contact with the aircraft manufacturer?"

Hans replied, "We've reached out to the airline repeatedly. So far, they haven't come forward or made a comment. This is one of their flights that crashed, and their lack of response is appalling. Despite the scandals Boeing is facing with their Max 8 and engineering problems, at least some of their people are coordinating with us. The next part of our investigation will involve looking into Celestine Airlines and understanding the cause of the holdup."

Back in Atlanta, Lindsay received a phone call.

"Hey Owen, what's up?"

"Have you been watching the press conference?"

"Yeah," Lindsay said, handing over her stomach. "It makes me sick."

"It's been ten days since we came back from Austria and so far, the search and rescue team still couldn't find Steve. I've tried calling them, emailing them, but they haven't picked up or answered any of our pleas. Dad tried once then Mom, but no luck."

"Have you tried anyone else?"

Owen continued, "We've reached out to Grandma, who lives in Switzerland to see if she could help, but she never answers the phone."

"This might be the first time I've ever heard of a grandmother living in Switzerland. Steve never told me about her," Lindsay said.

"It's a long story and one of those dark secrets of the family that many of us don't like to talk about. But to keep it short, our father grew up here in Atlanta but our grandmother, Denise, was from New York City, while our grandpa Turner was from Tennessee. It was a strange marriage. Grandma left Grandpa when Dad was young, fell in love with a Swiss man, and she took off with him. She never reached out to us and Grandpa told us to never talk about her. Grandpa practically raised Dad alone, and they never saw her again. Grandma did reach out to Dad once and gave him her number if she needed to chat."

Lindsay's eyes blinked. "I promise I won't tell anyone."

"Anyways, we tried to get everyone to do a search and rescue operation. The Austrian authorities haven't been great. The American authorities have been told to not assist the Austrians."

"It's a complete mess," Lindsay said. "At this point, we'll never be able to find Steve."

"I'm trying to figure out a way to track him myself," Owen said. "Being at Georgia Tech gives me access to a ton of resources. I just need to figure out how to use them to actually locate him."

Somewhere in the Alps, Steve and Oliver descended down the bottom of the mountain where temperatures were warmer around the 40s. The sun blazed high in the sky, casting its golden glow over the landscape.

Steve removed his jacket. "It's finally warm, Oliver. Can you believe it?"

"It's getting hot," Oliver said.

"Temperatures usually get warmer as you descend the mountain," Steve explained.

"So where are we going now?"

"I don't know," Steve said. "We need to find a town that has phone and internet access where I can let my family know where I am. This time it should be easier since you know how to speak German."

Steve further added, "You should teach me more German. I can use it to talk to people and can speak when you are afraid."

Oliver nodded. "Yes, I will. You teach me the things that you do like fishing, building homes."

As they walked, the clear, if treacherous path through the foothills became a maze of craggy outcrops and frozen ravines. The uneven ground making it difficult to tell if they were still heading toward the valley or further into the Alpine wilderness.

CHAPTER 15

"Are you sure we're going the right way?" Oliver asked, his voice wavered as he glanced up the towering peaks above them. Steve squinted into the distance, trying to make sense of their surroundings. Everything seemed distorted now. The landmarks that once guided them–the jagged rock formations, the sloping ridge in the distance—had vanished.

"I don't know," Steve admitted, his breath coming out in short, frosty puffs.

Frozen earth crunched underfoot as they picked their way through the snow-dusted foothills. Each step was a gamble—loose rocks, hidden ice, and low shrubs snagging at their legs. The wind stung their faces, and a steep drop loomed to their right, lined with jagged stone. The Alps rose in the distance, but it was the ground beneath them—the cold, uneven path—that demanded their full attention.

Steve tugged his scarf higher against the bite of the cold while carrying two heavy backpacks, his breath fogging the air in front of him. The wind felt colder to him. There were no trees this far up, no signs of life, just the cracked stone and the occasional patch of ice glittering in the weak afternoon light.

"This place has no houses," Oliver said, his voice tight, eyes scanning the wide, barren landscape. He bent down to pick up a rock and tossed it. It skittered across the frozen ground, echoing faintly in the silence. "I swear, it feels like we're walking through a dead man zone."

Steve didn't answer right away. His gaze remained fixed on the towering mass of the Alps before them, their white-capped peas casting long, cold shadows across the valley. The air was thin, and every breath felt shallow, laced with the scent of snow and stone. The emptiness of the land pressed down on both Steve and Oliver.

"We have to keep going," Steve said, his voice hoarse from the cold. He rubbed his hands together. "There's no turning back right now."

Oliver sighed, casting another glance around. "But I'm tired."

"Look around, Ollie," Steve said. "There's no place to sleep. It's barren land everywhere. No houses, no trees. We don't have materials."

Oliver's small legs stomped against the ground, the sound of his sneakers muffled by the dirt path. His little fists were balled tightly at his sides, arms swinging with extra force as if each step was a protest. He trailed behind Steve, dragging his feet just enough to show his displeasure.

"I don't want to walk anymore!" Oliver snapped, his voice high-pitched with frustration. He planted his feet firmly on the ground, refusing to take another step. His lip quivered slightly, but he masked it with a frown, crossing his arms defiantly across his chest.

Steve glanced back at him, but Oliver's scowl only deepened.

"I wanna go that way," Oliver said, jabbing his finger toward a completely different path. It led nowhere, but that didn't matter to Oliver.

Steve sighed and crouched down to Oliver's eye level. "We can't go that way, Ollie. It's not safe."

"I don't care!" Oliver snapped, stomping his foot. "You always pick the way! I never get to pick!" His voice wobbled, the tantrum building. His small body was tense, coiled up with frustration, and his brown eyes were filled with angry tears that he blinked away quickly.

Steve reached out, but Oliver stepped back, a scowl deepening on his face. "No! Don't touch me!"

"Fine!" Steve said, stomping his foot down. "I'll leave you here. Go find your own way. Ever since I've known you, you've been so stubborn. You're too young to make your own decision. Go ahead, I don't care."

Steve turned on his heel,and went his own way. *He's definitely going to come after me.*

Oliver looked past Steve and went the other direction. His heart pounded in his small chest as he looked around, his breath coming in quick shallow bursts. The vast emptiness of the mountain surrounded him, every tree looking the same, every shadow growing longer as the sun dipped behind the peaks. His eyes darted frantically searching for any sign of Steve, but there was nothing. No familiar face. No comforting voice.

A knot tightened in Oliver's throat, and his lower lip began to quiver. He blinked hard, trying to keep the tears at bay, but they were already blurring his vision. He swallowed, his little hands clenching and unclenching.

"Steve?" His voice barely a whisper at first, then louder. "Steve!" he called again, but the word echoed back to him, empty and hollow.

Fear clawed at his insides, twisted his stomach into knots. The world suddenly felt too big—too unfamiliar.

A sob escaped his lips, and then the tears came hot and fast. "Steve!" he cried again, but his voice cracked, breaking into that echoed through the empty forest.

Oliver tried to take a step forward, but his legs wobbled, refusing to move. He dropped to his knees, hugging his arms around himself, his breath coming in hiccupping sobs.

After a few minutes, someone approached Oliver slowly, crouching down a feet away. Oliver looked up at Steve's body and said, "Steve I'm sorry. I'm sorry I got mad."

Steve gave a tired smile and opened his arms. Oliver threw himself forward, burying his face in Steve's chest. Steve wrapped his arms around the boy, holding him close, feeling the warm, wet tears soak through his shirt. Steve could feel the tremors of Oliver's sobs slowly fading as the boy clung to him, his breathing still shaky but no longer so ragged.

"I was so scared," Oliver whimpered into Steve's chest, his voice muffled. "I didn't know where you were."

"I know," Steve murmured, gently stroking Oliver's back. "I'm sorry, Oliver. I'm so sorry. But you're not alone now. I'm right here, and just like I promised your dad, I will take you home."

They stayed like that for a while, the world around them quiet except for the soft rustling of the wind. Steve didn't rush him, letting Oliver take the time he needed to calm down, his body slowly relaxing as the tears finally stopped.

"Let's go, I'll carry you," Steve said. Oliver nodded, wiping his tears. Steve grabbed Oliver in his arms and carried him forward.

The sky above them had an endless stretch of pale blue, the sun sinking slowly toward the jagged peaks in the distance. Steve and Oliver trudged along the rocky path, their footsteps crunching against the dry earth, when the surrounding air seemed to hum.

Steve stopped, glancing up, his brow furrowing, "What's that sound?"

Oliver clung to his hand, his eyes wide. "It's loud..." he whispered.

Before Steve could respond, the surrounding light shifted. The sun, which had been lazily descending, flared with a blinding brilliance. The sky itself seemed to crack open, splitting apart as something enormous and fiery roared across the heavens.

A searing streak of light tore through the sky, brighter than anything Steve had ever seen.

"Get down," Steve shouted, instinctively pulling Oliver to the ground. They hit the earth hard, dust rising around them as the flare streaked past, its roar a deep rumble.

Oliver whimpered, his body trembling against Steve's side, his eyes squeezed shut as the heat from the flare seared their skin. The very air seemed to thrum with power. Steve held Oliver close, his own heart racing, every muscle tensed. He waited for something–anything–to signal that the flare had passed.

Then, just as quickly as it had happened, the light vanished. The sky snapped to its original hue, the sun now just a pale, distant orb on the horizon. The roar of the flare faded, leaving only an oppressive silence in its wake.

Steve slowly sat up, his breath coming in short, shallow bursts. He glanced down at Oliver, still huddled against him, wide-eyed and trembling, his hands gripping Steve's jacket.

"W-what was that?" Oliver stammered, his voice barely above a whisper.

Steve swallowed hard, his eyes still fixed on the empty sky where the solar flare had vanished.

"It was another solar flare that just flew by us," Steve said. "The sun up there is not relatively stable. I need to get to the bottom of this. But first, I need to get you home to your grandparents. We need to find shelter right now. Or else we'll have to build a makeshift tent out of whatever we can find here."

They both remained there for a moment longer, hearts pounding, as if waiting for the earth to settle beneath them.

After a few hours of walking westward, Steve scanned the rugged landscape of the Austrian Alps, his gaze lingering on the darkening clouds overhead. The wind had picked up, cutting through the valley, and Steve knew that he and Oliver wouldn't make it to the next village before nightfall.

"We need to make shelter here, mate," Steve said, kneeling to Oliver's level. "We're going to be okay, but we can't keep going."

Oliver nodded, though his wide eyes told Steve all he needed to know. Steve ruffled the boy's hair ever growing longer, then turned to survey their surroundings, searching for anything that might serve as a makeshift refuge.

"Stay close," Steve said, taking Oliver's hand as they moved toward the boulder. Oliver's feet crunched over patches of frost-covered grass and loose stones. "We're going to build a tent, just like we talked about before."

Oliver sniffed, his nose red from the cold. "With what?"

Steve gave him a soft smile. "With what we have around us. We'll make it work, just like always. We managed to make it to shelters so far and made it out alive. Come on, we've got an hour more to get this sucker built."

CHAPTER 16

At the Carsons' home, Sue stood at the kitchen counter, her hands covered in flour as she kneaded the dough for the bread rolls. Emma stood next to her mother, shaping the bread rolls needed to be baked. James greeted the Turners, sans Steve, inside. A familiar friend stood next to Owen as they entered and sat on the living room couch.

"Who's this fine young man?" James asked.

Owen gestured beside him. "This is Jake. This is the guy who was supposed to pick Steve up over in Helsinki. But…well, you know how that turned out."

Jake and James shook hands. "Nice to meet you," he said.

"Thank you for inviting us for dinner," Matt added. "I hope we aren't giving you guys a hard time."

"Not at all," James said. "Even though Steve may be alive, I'm sure you guys are going through a lot now. What you need is a good meal."

"Where's Lindsay?" Rachel asked.

"They called her in for an emergency shift at the children's hospital and I encouraged her to go. She's been working overtime as a way to cope. Aren't we all?"

"Yeah," Rachel said. "I've not been sleeping too well since the accident, and it's been almost a month now. This Thanksgiving was supposed to be an exciting one since Steve was about to get married."

James nodded solemnly. "The most important thing is to make sure Steve's okay. I'm sure he's fine. Lindsay's been calling the search and rescue team in Austria, along with Hans and Sarah, for constant periodic updates. But they haven't been responding."

"I've been doing the same, and they never responded," Rachel said. "They just gave us the good news that Steve is not among the 200 people who died in the crash, but they're not telling us what's going on."

Matt leaned forward. "The press conferences haven't helped either. Just vague reassurances. I believe the other survivor is that boy, Oliver, right?"

"Yeah, that's right Dad," Owen said. "Oliver Lynds."

"His grandparents are good people. You should've seen how really hurt they were that their son was gone, but their faces lit up when they found out their grandson is still alive."

"I wonder if Steve might be in Switzerland," Owen said, looking at Matt. "We're going to have to have Grandma help with the search."

"Absolutely not, Owen," Matt declared.

A few hours later, Lindsay arrived home, her facing brimming with excitement after a while. "Thank you all for coming. I'm so looking forward to this dinner."

"Yeah, we do too, as well," Rachel said.

In the dining room, the table was set with old china, each plate adorned with a carefully folded napkin and a sprig of rosemary. The oven timer dinged, and Sue wiped her hands on her apron, pulling the golden-brown turkey out and setting it on the counter. Lindsay, Rachel, and Emma helped with putting the sides on the counter. Owen and Jake joined in, asking, "Mind if we help as well?"

"Yeah," Sue said. "Get the Chardonnay and the Pinot Noir, Owen. And for you, Jake, there's a batch of apple cider in the basement. Can you bring that up?"

"It smells amazing here," Matt said as he helped Sue place the turkey on the center of the table.

Lindsay entered with a tray of mashed potatoes, her cheeks flushed from the warmth of the kitchen. The rest of the families gathered at the table, with the display of NFL games on the television screen.

Once everyone gathered, they sat down, and as they clasped hands around the table for grace, Rachel felt something shift. She began to break down and cry with Lindsay and Matt placing her hands on her.

"I just—God, I wish Steve were here," Rachel cried, pulling out a handkerchief.

"Honey don't worry," Matt said softly. "Let's try to enjoy this meal together."

"He should be here, eating this with us," Rachel said through tears. "And who knows if he's even eating at all?"

Lindsay bowed her head, tears slipping down her face. The absence of Steve settled over the table like a heavy blanket.

Later that evening, Owen gathered Lindsay, Emma, and Jake down in the basement.

"Sorry if I had to gather you guys here," Owen said. "But I don't want to be around Mom and Dad right now with these things going around. Mom just has not been eating well or sleeping well since Steve went missing. She keeps calling the investigators, and she's been so erratic. And honestly, the Austrian team's been a mess."

"What about church? Your dad's a part-time pastor there, right?" Lindsay asked.

"She stays in bed when it's time to go. She's not able to believe in, and she hasn't even been going to work."

"What can we do about it, then?" Jake asked.

Lindsay said, "The question is, what are you doing about it? How are you coping with this? Imagine how I feel. Why do you think I've been working so much?"

"You don't know my mom like I do," Owen said. "You've never seen her like this before. But what I'm trying to say is I'll have to find my own ways to find Steve."

"And how are you going to do that?" Lindsay asked.

"You'll find out," Owen said.

After landing at an empty spot covered by trees, Steve set his backpack down and began gathering materials. Fallen branches littered the ground nearby, most of them sturdy enough to form a framework.

"Here Ollie, there are the branches. Pick the strongest ones so we can build the base."

Oliver nodded, following Steve's lead. Together, they gathered an armful of branches, some long enough to lean against the boulder to form the skeleton of their shelter.

While placing down the branches, Oliver asked, "How do you know how to build this stuff?"

Steve fastened two limbs together with a strip of cloth. "I learned to do all this when I joined the Boy Scouts. Worked hard for that merit badge. But I also learned something else—life isn't fair. No one hands you the life you want. You have to build it."

Once the frame was up, Steve grabbed a thick pine branch, still bristling with needles, and placed it over the top. He layered more branches and, on top of that, creating a roof that sloped from the boulder to the ground.

"These pine needles will block off the wind and keep some heat inside," Steve said.

Oliver, clearly exhausted, asked, "Will it keep us warm?"

"It'll help," Steve replied. "But we need more. Grab some more of these branches as you can and pile them up inside."

"I want to help," Oliver said, determination in his voice.

As they worked together, Steve glanced up at the clouds, which had turned an ominous gray, heavy with the promise of snow. The winds howled through the trees, but the shelter held firm. He could see the fatigue weighing on Oliver, but the boy kept moving, digging branches over to their little makeshift home.

When the framework was thick enough, Steve added another layer of smaller, flexible branches to insulate the roof further. Then he gathered rocks to create a small windbreak around the entrance, pling them carefully to block out the worst of the chill.

"Nice work, kiddo," Steve said as he tossed the last rock into place. "We're almost there."

Oliver, his cheeks flushed, sat down inside the shelter. Steve draped his jacket over the boy's shoulders, then went back to gather pine needles and moss from the forest floor, layering it on the ground inside to create something softer than the cold earth.

Finally, Steve ducked into the shelter, sitting beside Oliver. The space was cramped, but it held the warmth they needed. Steve wrapped his arm around the boy and pulled him close, feeling Oliver lean against him.

"We're safe now," Steve said. "We made it work."

CHAPTER 17

The door swung open.

"Ah, Lukas," Hans said in German. "Any updates?"

"Please tell me you have something new," Sarah said.

Lukas shook his head, his expression unreadable. "We've done everything we can," he replied in German. "The perimeter has been searched twice over. Helicopters scanned the mountains, and we even sent drones over the ravine. There's no sign of Steve or the boy."

"What did he say?" Sarah asked.

"They couldn't find Steve or the boy," Hans translated quietly.

Sarah's chest tightened. "So that's it?" You're going to call them missing and move on?"

Lukas sighed, glancing at Hans before turning his gaze back at Sarah. He switched to English. "Sarah, the storm is coming in fast. We're talking about heavy snowfall within hours. It'll make further searching impossible."

"We don't have hours," she said, her voice cracking under the weight of her feat. "They could be injured or–"

"Or worse," Lukas finished for her, her voice firm but not unkind. "I understand. But we have to be realistic. The window to find them is closing. The government's about to pull funding for the operation."

"You're kidding," Sarah said. "The government can't just back out."

Hans rose from his chair and approached the two, stepping between them like a buffer. "What about another search team? Maybe we can request additional units from the surrounding areas."

Lukas crossed his arms, glancing at his mud-caked boots before replying. "I've called in every resource available. I have crews working double shifts. We've exhausted our equipment. The mountains are dangerous at night, and with the storm closing in, we're risking more lives by staying up there."

Sarah's shoulders slumped, but her eyes remained fierce. "We can't just stop," she said quietly.

Lukas's expression softened, his stern mask cracking for a moment. "I'm sorry Sarah. And Hans."

Hans placed a hand on Sarah's shoulder, but she brushed it off, too tense to be comforted. "Austria's budget is not the same as the United States. Maybe we can call up the United States for some funding for this operation."

"Yeah, good luck with that," Sarah said. "I've contacted everyone from the NTSB, and they have not picked up the phone. I don't know what's going on there. I'm starting to think they've put me in charge in order to get rid of me."

"Why do you think they'd get rid of you?" Hans asked. "I've seen many stories about how if it weren't for the NTSB, flight safety wouldn't be where it is today."

"In this organization, you have to follow a standard of ethics, and there might be corruption going on there," Sarah said. "The other investigative unit has not been helping out with what caused that rare solar occurrence that shut down the systems."

Lukas raised his hand and said, "There's one more option that I remember."

Both Sarah and Hans turned to him, their eyes flickering with hope.

"There's an old shepherd's hut, deep in the woods, past where we've been searching," Lukas explained, his voice steady. "It's off the mapped routes, so we didn't send teams that way initially. But if Steve and Oliver were trying to find shelter, it's possible that they could've headed there. If we can't find them there, then we'll have to end the search."

Sarah's eyes lit up. "Then why are we still standing here?" she said, already grabbing her coat.

"Sarah, wait," Hans called out, stepping forward. "It's too dangerous to go now. If the storm hits while we're out there, we'll be trapped, too."

"I don't care," she said, slipping her arms into her sleeves. "They don't have the luxury of waiting, and neither do we."

The next day, Steve scanned the edge of the alpine lake, its surface glinting in the soft afternoon sun. Surrounded by towering peaks of the Austrian Alps, the stillness felt almost deceptive. They hadn't eaten the night before, and the hunger gnawing at his stomach was a constant reminder that he needed food soon. He glanced down at Oliver, who sat cross-legged on the ground, absentmindedly playing with some pebbles, his face pale with exhaustion.

Steve looked around the rocky shoreline, eyes landing on a patch of young saplings swaying in the breeze. Thin, flexible, and strong enough for what he had in mind. He stood and made his way over, pulling out his small pocketknife as he inspected the slender branches. One sapling would work perfectly.

He wrapped his hand around the base of the branch and sawed through it with careful strokes of the blade. Once the branch snapped free, he stripped the bark, running the knife along the length of the wood until it was smooth in his hands.

Oliver watched him, his gaze lifted. "What are you doing?"

"Making a fishing rod," Steve said, trying to keep his voice steady. "We're going to catch some dinner."

Oliver scooted closer, intrigued, though the faint lines of hunger were beginning to show on his face.

Steve worked quickly, eyeing his next challenge: a fishing line. He dug through his pack and pulled out a length of paracord, the thin but strong material to deal for situations like this.

Next, Steve scanned the pebbly ground near the shore, his eyes narrowing as he spotted a sharp fragment of bone. It looked like a remnant from a bird or some small animal, likely washed ashore from the lake. Kneeling, he picked it up and turned it in his fingers–it was jagged and sharp on one side, not perfect, but it would work in a pinch.

As he turned the bone, a wave of frustration rolled through him, unexpected and unwelcome. The sharp edge dug into his palm slightly, anchoring him to a different kind of pain.

Lindsay's face flashed through his mind—her tired eyes the last time they spoke, the way she paused before saying, *"You were never really present, Steve. Not for me. Not for us."*

Steve's eyes bulged as he used the paracord to fashion the piece of bone into a crude hook, knotting it tightly and making sure it wouldn't come loose. He tugged on the line, testing its strength, then gave a satisfied nod.

Steve had always believed that climbing the ranks in the sports executive world would justify the long nights and missed birthdays. But the contracts, the politics, the endless jockeying for influence—none of it mattered now. Not here. Not with nothing. It had all slipped through his fingers like water, and all he was left with was the hollow echo of ambition unmet.

"There," he said, holding up the finished rod. "Not pretty, but it'll do the job."

Oliver tilted his head, looking from the rod to the lake. "Will it really work?"

Steve smiled faintly. "We'll find out."

They walked to the water's edge. A breeze rustled the trees. Steve cast the line out with a quick flick of the wrist, watching the ripples fan out over the surfaces of the lake. The rod bent slightly under the weight of the line, but it held firm. They stood there together, waiting, listening to the wind and the distant call of a bird echoing off the mountains.

Minutes passed. Then a sharp tug.

Steve's hands tightened on the rod, his pulse quickening. The line jerked again, and he knew something had taken the bait. He carefully pulled, guiding the fish closer to the shore, the branch bowing under the strain.

"There we go," he muttered, reeling the line in with quick, practiced motions. The fish broke the surface, its silvery scales flashing in the fading light.

He crouched and grabbed it, but the thrill was hollow. Just another small win that didn't change anything. Not the job he lost. Not Lindsay leaving nor the silence that waited when the line went slack again.

Oliver gasped, his eyes lighting up with excitement. "We caught one!"

"Yeah, we did," Steve said, hauling the small trout onto the shore.

Steve turned to Oliver. "Do you want to catch one as well? The more we catch, the less prone we are to starving to death."

Oliver nodded with glee. He grabbed the rod and within a few minutes, the line jerked again, and he enthusiastically pulled the line, bringing another fish to the shore.

"What type of fish is this?" Oliver asked.

"Trout, by the looks of it. But they've got some unusual coloring."

After several minutes of catching multiple species of fish, Steve looked around the area, his mind working quickly to come up with a way to cook their catch.

"Okay," Steve muttered to himself. "Let's get this fire going."

Steve and Oliver gathered the driest wood they could find. Beneath the pines and firs scattered around the lake, they found small twigs and branches–perfect kindling. Kneeling down, they arranged the sticks into a pyramid shape.

"You're really good at setting this up," Steve said to Oliver.

"Dad taught me this when we went out camping," Oliver said.

Steve then rubbed two sticks together. Oliver sat quietly, his eyes following every moment.

After a few minutes, a faint orange glow appeared, and Steve gently blew it until the flames caught the kindling. The fire cracked to life, the warmth instantly relieving some of the tension in Steve's chest.

"Good start," Steve said, nodding towards Oliver with a faint smile.

Steve then gathered a sharp stone, where he gutted the trout, discarding the entrails and scaling it as best as he could with his knife.

He gathered two branches and tied them together and sharped the ends of a thinner stick to act as the skewer. Once everything was ready, he impaled the fish through its mouth and out of its tail, suspending it over the fire between the two supporting branches.

The fish hung above the flames, its skin starting to sizzle as Steve rotated the spit carefully. The air was filled with the smell of roasting fish, making Oliver sit up straighter.

"How long until it's ready?" Oliver asked, his voice small but hopeful.

"Not too long," Steve said, watching the flesh of the fish turn golden and flake in the heat. "We'll have dinner soon."

They sat in silence, Steve occasionally turning the spit to ensure the fish cooked evenly. He'd managed to find some flat stones nearby, which he placed near the edges of the fire to heat up.

The fish hissed and crackled, its skin blistering in the heat, sending mouthwatering aromas into the air. After about fifteen minutes, Steve inspected it closely. The meat pulled away easily.

"It's ready," Steve announced.

He slid it off the skewer and onto a hot stone, allowing it to cool slightly before handing the larger portion to Oliver. Oliver's eyes widened as he took the first bite, his face lighting up as the rich, smoky flavor hit his tongue.

Steve dug into his half as well. The meal wasn't big, but it was enough to fill their bellies and give them the energy they needed to keep going. As the fire crackled beside them, they ate in silence, the sound of the wind and the distant calls of birds the only noise in the vast Alpine wilderness.

"This is heaven," Steve said.

CHAPTER 18

The next morning, inside the makeshift shelter, Steve gently shook Oliver awake. "Hey buddy, we need to go now."

Oliver mumbled, "A few more minutes."

"Come on, we need to move. I found a river nearby. You know what that means?"

"More fish to eat," Oliver said, smiling.

Steve chuckled. "Not just that. Following a river can lead us to a town or city. And yes, we can fish, hunt, or find berries along the way, just like our ancestors did."

"Fish and berries," Oliver said. "Those are my favorites."

"And remember, the sun rises in the east and sets in the west." Steve escorted Oliver outside, pointing to the sun. "Which direction is that?"

"The east," Oliver answered.

"Right. So, if we want to go west, which way should we go?" Steve asked.

Oliver pointed away from the sun. "That way."

"You got it. Let's head that way, and I'll show you the river."

They packed their bags and left the shelter, the sun's rays casting long shadows as they made their way to the river.

"Can we fish now?" Oliver asked. "I'm hungry."

"Let's get to a town first. They'll have better food," Steve said.

"Okay," Oliver agreed.

They trudged through rugged land, boots scraping against the uneven rocks, every step a reminder of how far they'd fallen from comfort. Beside them, the river surged with a kind of untamed purpose Steve envied it—no second-guessing, no hesitation. Just forward.

The water thundered through jagged outcroppings, foaming white as it slammed into the boulders, then slipped into calmer eddies. Steve glanced at the calm patches, where the deep turquoise mirrored the snowy peaks ahead, and thought of Lindsay. *She'd loved mountains. Said they made her feel small in a way that felt freeing.*

Steve glanced back at Oliver, who struggled to keep up, his feet slipping occasionally on the loose gravel. His face showed determination, but Steve saw the weariness his eyes. Oliver stumbled over a larger rock, catching himself before falling. Steve quickly reached out to steady him.

"Careful, buddy," Steve said softly, pulling Oliver to his side. "These rocks are tricky."

Oliver nodded, breathing heavily but not complaining. The roar of the river drowned out most other noises, save for the occasional rumble of falling pebbles or the wind cutting through a narrow pass.

After a while, Oliver sat down, exhausted. Steve turned to him as the water continued flowing.

"Are you okay?" Steve asked.

"I'm hungry," Oliver said.

Steve sighed. "Mamma mia, I have to carry this guy again. At least the bags are getting lighter." He held Oliver in his arms and proceeded further west. "We'll stop to fish when we get to the river basin."

A few hours later, they arrived at the river basin. Steve set down Oliver, who was fast asleep. Like the day before, Steve gathered materials to catch fish. He looked inside the bag and muttered, "Crap, I'm all out of bait."

Turning to Oliver, he said, "Stay here. I'm going to find some berries or something." Oliver nodded, his eyes still closed.

Steve headed into the dense forest that flanked the riverbank. The towering trees cast long shadows across the forest floor, the air cooler under the thick canopy of pines, firs, and spruces. He moved carefully, his shoes crunching over a thick layer of pine needles. The scent of evergreen resin was strong, mingling with the earthy smell of damp soil and decaying leaves.

The underbrush was tangled with low shrubs, ferns, and the occasional fallen branch blocking his path. Steve pushed forward, eyes scanning for signs of life—berries or any edible plants that might serve as bait.

The forest was alive in its own way. Birds flitted from branch to branch, calling out to one another, while faint rustles in the brush hinted at unseen deer or marmots slipping away.

Steve paused near a small clearing where sunlight broke through the canopy, illuminating a patch of wild growth. His eyes quickly landed on a cluster of low, thorny bushes adorned with small dark berries-bilberries, he realized.

"So, these are the berries commonly found in the Alps," Steve said. "They look so black." He knelt beside the bushes, carefully picking a handful, testing one by rolling it between his fingers before popping into his mouth.

"These taste pretty good," Steve said. "Tart, but sweet enough. Oliver will be enjoying these." He quickly gathered more, filling his pockets with the small berries.

As he stood, Steve picked some more berries and turned his back toward the river, where Oliver waited, and made his way through the forest with renewed determination, the taste of the berries still sharp on his tongue.

Steve approached Oliver, still fast asleep. "Wake up Ollie, try these."

Oliver's eyes fluttered open. "What is it, Steve?"

"I brought you some berries. Try them. They taste really good."

Oliver sat down beside Steve, chewing on the tart berries Steve had gathered. As the tangy sweetness hit his tongue, his movements slowed. He froze, staring at his hands. His fingers clenched tightly around the remaining berries, crushing them, until juice dripped toward his fingers.

Oliver hunched forward, hugging his knees to his chest as his head dipped low, the weight of the memory pulling him inward. His lips trembled, and he bit down hard, trying to stop the tears that were welling up in his eyes. His hands went to his face, pressing against his cheeks as if it so physically hold back the sobs. His body shook, and a quiet, shuddering cry escaped his lips.

Steve watched, noticing the way Oliver's back curled in on itself. He moved closer, sitting beside him.

"Oliver," Steve said softly, placing his hand on his back. "Hey, talk to me buddy, what's wrong?"

Oliver shook his head, his face still buried in his arms. His chest heaved with suppressed sobs, and he kept squeezing his eyes shut.

"I miss Mum and her berry pie," Oliver said as he let out a sharp, gasping sob. His fingers tightened around his knees.

Steve sat beside him, his hand never leaving Oliver's back. "It's okay man. We'll get through this together." He looked at Oliver. "Let's go grab some fish."

Upon arriving for her night shift, Lindsay's manager, Adam, approached her, noticing her once-bright eyes had dimmed, replaced by a hollow, far-off look.

"Are you okay, Lindsay?" Adam asked. "You don't look so well."

"I'm fine," Lindsay replied curtly. "I just need recognition for my hard work this year. And the children are doing fine."

Adam frowned. "You look like you haven't slept in months. Let me talk to the supervisor about sending you home to rest."

Lindsay's eyes flashed as she met Adam's gaze. "I don't need your sympathy. I'm doing absolutely fine."

"Lindsay…" Adam began.

She pulled away. "No, Adam. I'm fine. Believe me. I might be just tired."

"Or you're still in grief," Adam said cautiously.

"He's not dead," Lindsay said. "You know it, and I know it."

Suddenly, Lindsay's phone rang.

"Hello Lindsay," the agent, Milton, said. "I'm going to put Sarah on the line for you."

The line crackled as Sarah's voice broke through, distant and strained. Each word sounded hollow, as though drained of hope. "They've called off the search for Steve."

"What?" Lindsay said sharply.

"The Austrian authorities," Sarah continued, her voice heavy. "I didn't want this to end this way, but they've called off the search for Steve due to a lack of resources—or worse, corruption. We can't do anything more."

Lindsay gripped the phone and waited, hoping Sarah would say something. But they remained in silence.

Lindsay's voice rose, trembling with anger. "You mean to tell me you're just going to let my fiancée die out there in the snow?"

"They've done everything they could," Sarah's voice wavered, a fragile tremor beneath the words. "But they won't keep looking."

"Thanks a lot," Lindsay spat, her voice icy. "I knew you guys were incompetent. You really dropped the ball on this."

She ended the call and said to Adam, "I'm going to need some extended PTO."

Adam smiled gently. "I'll help you arrange that with the team. Call it bereavement leave if you need to. Go get your fiancée back."

Lindsay managed a small smile and embraced Adam. She called Rachel. "The Austrian Search and Rescue Team failed to them."

Rachel shrieked. "Oh, my god. Oh, my god. They're just going to let Steve rot out there?"

"I'm going to go see Owen first," Lindsay said firmly. "And I'm letting him know that we're going to find a way to find Steve."

"You do what you have to do," Matt said.

Lindsay ended the call and headed straight to Georgia Tech. Upon arriving at the campus, she called Owen. "Hey, where are you?"

"I'm in my room," Owen said. "What's up?"

"I'll explain when I see you," Lindsay said.

"I'm off campus. Just east of the I-75/I-85 Corridor. You'll have to go there."

"Got it. I'll be there soon."

CHAPTER 19

Lindsay stepped into Owen's apartment, immediately struck by the eclectic mix of thrifted furniture. A battered coffee table, its surface etched with forgotten homework notes and faint coffee mug rings, stood between a sagging couch and a worn armchair.

In the living room, she saw two students were engrossed in a game of *Call of Duty*. Owen emerged from his bedroom, his eyes weary, and asked, "What brings you here?"

"They're stopping the search for Steve," Lindsay replied. "The lead investigator gave me a vague excuse about budget cuts. The Austrian government slashed funding, and the NTSB is redirecting resources. They still haven't found the root cause."

"See? I told you," Owen said, frustration evident in his voice. "They're corrupt. I can't imagine them solving this crash or finding Steve and that kid. We all know the kid is with Steve, and there's no way Steve would let him die. He'll do whatever it takes to keep him alive."

He led Lindsay into his room, which consisted of a desk with large-screen computers and a bed.

"You're quite the geek, aren't you?" Lindsay said. "You like building things."

"Yeah," Owen chuckled. "While you've been pulling multiple shifts at the hospital, I've been here, trying to build a software to track and find Steve. When we were in Salzburg, I saw the outdated systems they're using. No wonder they can't get anything done."

He sat at his desk, fingers hovering uncertainly over the keyboard. The screen flickered slightly as the program loaded lines of code cascading against a black background. The interface was rudimentary, a rough skeleton of his vision. Sections remained blank, placeholders for features yet to be implemented.

Owen opened the main screen. A crude map filled the display, blurry and pixelated in places where the data hadn't fully processed. A panel on the left, intended for facial recognition matches, instead streamed error messages. The code was still riddled with bugs.

"This part's still a mess," Owen muttered, gesturing toward the blank section labeled *Activity Log*, where timestamps should've been tracking movement. "I haven't wired it to the search logs yet."

Lindsay leaned over his shoulder, squinting at the screen. "It's a solid foundation. We've only been back what—a month? And you've already built this?"

"I started last week," Owen said. "Been cramming for exams— easy stuff—and working on this. If this software can find Steve, people will recognize it for what it is: a masterpiece: cutting-edge search tech." He paused. "But none of that matters unless it works. I just need a satellite link and one reference to Steve. That's it."

Lindsay raised an eyebrow but nodded slowly. "You think they'd let you run this if they knew?"

"Not a chance," Owen said. "Don't tell anyone. If the authorities find out, they'll shut it down and slap me with interference charges."

He clicked on another window, meant to show live GPS tracking. The screen blinked, then went dark. A pop-up read: *Unable to connect to server.*

"Great," he muttered, frustration edging in. "It's supposed to track GPS through Steve's social media. Half the time it won't even connect."

"But... wasn't his phone destroyed in the crash?" Lindsay asked gently.

Owen exhaled hard. "Yeah. I know. I just…maybe there's a backup ping, a cached signal. Something. I'm stitching this thing together as best I can, but right now, it's like a glass bridge. One crack, and the whole thing goes."

After finishing their meal of berries and fish, Steve and Oliver continued westward. The river flowed lazily beside them, its clear water shimmering under the afternoon sun. The air was crisp and cool, carrying the fresh scent of pine and damp earth.

Oliver glanced at Steve, his eyes shimmering.

"You okay?" Steve asked.

"I'm sorry I cried," Oliver said softly.

"Why apologize for that?" Steve said, placing his hand on Oliver's shoulder. "You miss your mother, and it's okay to cry. Even grown men like myself would cry if their mothers were gone. There are times when it's okay to cry and times when it's not. Losing your family? That's definitely a time to cry. I see you're starting to accept what's happened, and that's a good thing."

Oliver bent down to toss a pebble into the water, giggling as it skipped once, twice, and then plopped beneath the surface with a soft splash.

Steve smiled, watching Oliver throw the pebbles, his arms spread wide like an airplane. "Careful, don't fall in," Steve called, his tone light, more amused than worried.

"I won't! Look how fast I am!" Oliver grinned, weaving between the rocks, his legs working hard as he leaped from one patch of moss to the next.

Birdsong drifted from the treetops, blending with the river's murmur and the soft crunch of footsteps. Steve followed at a steady pace behind Oliver, hands in his pockets, soothed by the simple rhythm of the moment.

Oliver stopped abruptly, crouching to examine a cluster of tiny blue flowers near the riverbank. "Look Steve! Flowers! Can we pick some?" he asked, his face bright with excitement.

Steve crouched beside him. "Sure. But let's leave a few, so they can keep growing."

Oliver carefully picked a small handful, holding them like treasure. "I'm going to keep these, forever."

"Forever's a long time, kiddo," Steve chuckled.

They continued along the river, the sun casting long shadows through the trees, warming the stones beneath their feet. As they walked, Steve felt himself relaxing in a way he hadn't in days. The weight of the journey felt lighter—as if they were just brothers, side by side, enjoying the rhythm of nature.

Oliver swung his hand into Steve's, and without a word, they walked together, the river beside them murmuring softly, as if carrying their unspoken thoughts downstream.

Hans and Sarah sat in front of the computer, listening to the cockpit voice recorder of the crash, and watched the flight data recorder. The hum of the equipment filled the dim room, broken only by the rhythmic clicking of Sarah's pen against the table. Hans hunched over the laptop.

"Speed maintained at 240 knots…altitude unchanged…no anomalies," Hans muttered, his eyes locked on the graph, displaying the plane's last moments.

"And it still went down," Sarah whispered, rubbing her temples as the stress gnawed at her. "There's something we're missing. There has to be. If it was a solar flare, the impact should've been minor. It shouldn't have caused the plane to fall from the sky."

Hans paused the playback, and leaned back. "Let's go through it again."

"No," Sarah snapped, the frustration boiling to the surface. "We've gone through it again and again. The answer isn't here. I've just had to tell the Turner and Lynds families we might never find their sons. Meanwhile, your team still can't identify the root cause, and the search is going on in circles. What kind of operation are you running?"

Hans gave her a steady look, but didn't argue. He restarted the recording. The eerie calm of the cockpit voice recorder crackled to life in their headphones. Then the panic—and finally, silence. Ten long seconds of dead air, followed by bursts of garbled shouting and alarms.

"Mayday, mayday, mayday," Captain Callaghan's voice broke through the static. A dull, metallic clunk followed. Then, the haunting, unmistakable sound of impact.

Hans paused the recording, dragging a hand down his face as though he could wipe away the weight of it. "It doesn't add up," he muttered. "No mechanical warnings before the alarms. No stall indication. Nothing. The plane just shut down."

"That's impossible!" Sarah slammed her hands against the desk, the sharp sound cutting through the stale air.

Hans glanced at his watch. "What time is it?"

Sarah checked her phone. "2:17 a.m. Holy crap. We've been at this for ten hours straight. Just listening and re-listening to the CVR."

The sharp click of the door shattered their exhausted focus flying open.

"Sarah," Timothy, her assistant, rushed in, breathless. One hand clutched his phone, the other a tablet. He looked like he'd sprinted down the hall.

Sarah jerked her head up from the graphs she'd been analyzing. "What is it, Tim?" she asked, her voice taut with exhaustion. "If it's not urgent—"

"You need to see this. Now." He tapped the screen frantically and thrust it into her hands.

"An email just came in. Someone claiming to be a disbarred scientist from Ireland. He says he's been studying extraordinary phenomena—especially solar flares. He claims a severe solar flare hit the area during the flight. So severe it disrupted the plane's avionics and communications mid-flight. But here's the kicker—" Timothy leaned in, lowering his voice. "He says it was covered up to avoid a scandal with aviation authorities and the airlines."

Sarah stared at him, the words sinking in slowly. "A solar flare?" she murmured, half in disbelief. Her eyes narrowed. "That would explain the huge electromagnetic spike we saw. But a cover up?"

Hans leaned forward, heart racing. "Let me see the email."

Sarah scrolled through the message furiously, her mind spinning. It was brief, clinical, and precise. The sender was anonymous. The subject line read:

"Celestine Airlines Flight 24: Truth Behind the Crash."

She skimmed the contents aloud: *"The plane was hit by an unexpected solar event that disrupted all avionics systems. Air traffic control was alerted to the event in real-time, but due to protocol failures, the flight crew wasn't warned. The incident was deliberately left out of official reports to avoid mass panic and liability issues."*

Hans leaned over her shoulder, his eyes scanning the message.

"There's more," Timothy added nervously, biting his lip. "The email includes attached data logs–communications between air traffic control centers–confirming the event. But..it was suppressed."

"Jesus," Hans ran a hand through his hair, pacing. "A solar flare cover-up?"

Sarah's pulse pounded in her ears. Her hands were clammy as she gripped the phone. "If this is real," she said slowly, "it explains everything. The loss of control. The alarms. The missing signals. Everything." She turned to Hans. "And they knew? They let that plane go down without warning the pilots?"

Hans sank into his chair, rubbing his temples. "This changes everything. If we can prove this, we're not just solving the crash. We're blowing the investigation wide open."

Sarah placed the phone on the desk, her eyes fixed on the attached data logs. "How do we confirm this?" she whispered.

Hans began pacing. "We'll need to cross-check these logs with satellite data from that day. If the timestamps match… we've got them."

CHAPTER 20

The river glittered in the afternoon sun as Steve stepped over a patch of loose stones, Oliver trailing behind him with a stick in hand, swinging at tall grass. Their shoes were damp from an earlier crossing, the heat now drying them with each step.

A breeze stirred the trees, and Steve tilted his face toward it, letting it cool the sweat on his forehead. Then, just ahead, rooftops broke through the treeline.

"There," he said, pointing. "Town."

Steve slowed his pace, gripping Oliver's hand a little tighter. The town's stone walls, once built for tradition, now looked more like barriers—meant to keep something out. Or maybe someone.

As they descended the hill toward the village's entrance, Oliver glanced at Steve. "Are we going to be okay here?"

Steve forced a tight-lipped smile. "Yeah, buddy. Just stay close, alright?"

The road beneath them felt uneven, the stones cracked and scattered with frost. A pair of signs, their paint peeling from years of sun and snow, marked the entrance: one naming the town in old Gothic letters—Glasdorf. Another sign read: "Aufgrund der jüngsten

Sonneneruptionen ist niemand willkommen." *Due to recent solar flares, no one is welcome.*

"Is this a common threat around every small town in Austria?" Steve muttered, but his voice came out too flat, his attempt at sarcasm buried under nerves.

As they passed the first row of houses, movement flickered at the edge of his vision—curtains twitching, a shadow shifting behind a frosted window. A woman in an apron stood frozen on her doorstep, a cigarette smoldering between her fingers, eyes narrowed at the sight of them. She didn't move. Just watched.

Steve's shoulders tensed. His breath came shallow, chest tightening under the weight of a hundred silent judgments.

On a second-floor balcony, a man leaned on the railing, arms crossed, lips tight, whispering something to someone out of view. A door slammed shut behind them. Somewhere, a dog barked.

They think we're dangerous, Steve thought. *Or worse—outsiders with no reason to be here.*

The streets were quiet, but not peaceful. Every glance felt like a held breath.

The narrow path leading into the heart of the village twisted through clusters of gnarled trees, their branches reaching like skeletal fingers toward the darkening sky. Steve kept Oliver close by his side, the boy's hand tucked tightly into his. Each step crunched on frost-covered leaves, the only sound breaking the eerie silence of the deserted outskirts.

"Are we almost there?" Oliver whispered, his voice small.

"Almost, buddy," Steve said, though he wasn't certain himself.

As they rounded the next corner, a figure emerged from the shadows of a dilapidated house–a hunched old woman, standing completely still. At first, she looked almost like a statue, her wiry hair tucked beneath a frayed wool scarf.

Steve stopped cold.

The woman clutched her axe, its blade chipped but sharp, glinting with menace in the pale light. Her sunken eyes, rimmed with exhaustion and paranoia, locked onto them with intensity.

"Zurück... oder ich werde es tun," she hissed, her voice raspy. *Get back or I'll do it.* Steve didn't understand the exact words, but her meaning was clear.

Oliver's breath hitched. "Steve?" His small hand gripped Steve's tighter, and Steve could feel him trembling.

"It's okay," Steve whispered, though he felt anything but. He slowly raised his free hand, palm outward. "We don't want any trouble. I understand that you're not accepting visitors right now."

The old woman's eyes narrowed, her grip tightening on the axe. She took a step forward, her boots scraping over the frozen ground.

"Look, all we want is some bread, cheese, and milk. This little guy needs proper food. We've just been living on fish the last couple of days."

The old woman then took a slow, deliberate step forward. She muttered something else in German—words sharp and jagged like the edge of the blade she held and glanced at Oliver.

Oliver whimpered, hiding behind Steve's leg. "Steve, she's scary."

"Stay behind me," Steve whispered. His heart pounded in his chest as he kept his body between Oliver and the woman. "Look lady, we're just passing through." He pointed down the path. "We'll leave, okay? We don't want to hurt anyone."

The woman's face twisted with rage, as if his words had been an insult. "Niemand kommt hier durch!" she spat. *No one passes through here!*

She hefted the axe, the muscles in her thin arms flexing with surprising strength. Steve tensed, ready to act.

"Run Oliver," Steve whispered urgently. "When I say go, you run."

"No!" Oliver clung to Steve's coat, crying. "I'm not leaving you!"

The woman came closer, the axe rising higher, her sunken eyes glinting with something dark and unhinged. Steve knew she wasn't bluffing. She moved through like a ghost, eyes darting, breath shallow—fear and paranoia clinging to her like a second skin.

Steve inhaled sharply. "Go!"

With a sob of fear, Oliver darted into the trees.

Steve turned just in time to catch the woman's wrist mid-swing, the axe grazing his jacket as they collided. Her breath came in ragged gasps, and her eyes—wide, glassy, terrified—met his.

For a second, neither of them moved. Then she blinked, as if waking from a dream, staring down at the axe in her hands as if surprised to see it there at all.

"I thought you were..." he whispered, trailing off.

Behind them, Oliver peeked from behind a tree, his face streaked with tears.

Steve slowly let go of the woman's wrists and stood, staggering back. She lay still for a moment, then scrambled away, muttering to herself in garbled German, her hands clawing at the ground.

"Come back here, Oliver," Steve yelled, his voice steady but urgent. Oliver ran to his side, burying his face in Steve's coat as they hurried down the path, leaving the old woman and her axe behind in the cold, desolate woods.

"We're okay, kiddo," Steve whispered, though his own hands shook. "We're okay. Just...keep moving."

The Turners and the Carsons gathered for a family Christmas Dinner.

Lindsay sat at the far end, picking at her food without appetite. *How can they do this to Steve?*

"Lindsay, are you okay?" Sue asked. "You haven't touched your ham."

"Sorry, Mom," Lindsay said. "I'm not hungry." She pushed her chair back from the dinner table, the scrape loud in the quiet room.

"Excuse me," she muttered under her breath, her voice brittle.

She walked to Steve's room, each step feeling more like a retreat than an escape.

Lindsay slipped inside and closed the door softly. With a shuddering breath, she sank onto the edge of his bed. Her hands curled into fists around the blanket, knuckles white, as she fought back the sob. She buried her face on Steve's pillow and started crying.

Several minutes later, Owen arrived inside the room alongside Emma.

"Are you okay?" Owen asked.

"Leave me alone," Lindsay said. "I'm really starting to worry that Steve might have been dead."

"We got the system working to track Steve," Owen said.

Lindsay rose her head from the bed, wiping tears. "Really?"

"Emma has helped me out on this. She found someone at her university," Owen said, pointing his face to Emma. "Tell her, Emma."

"I've got a friend from Emory who is great at fixing immediate issues on the software. Now we can get this application rolling," Emma said.

"Call Jake," Lindsay said. "He's been wanting to know whether he can help find Steve as well."

The night had been brutal, colder than they had expected. Steve and Oliver huddled beneath the makeshift tent he'd pieced together, but the mountain wind found its way through every gap, biting at their skin and rattling the branches overhead. Steve had wrapped Oliver in his coat, holding him close to keep his body warm.

By dawn, the fire was nothing but ash, and the cold gnawed at Steve's bones. His eyes cracked open at the pale light filtering through the tent walls. Oliver wasn't pressed against him anymore.

"Oliver?" Steve's voice came out hoarse. He didn't hear an answer.

Panic surged through his chest as he scrambled out from under the tarp. The sharp morning air cut through him like knives, making him suck in a breath. His eyes scanned the rocky terrain, catching sight of a small figure slumped near a low, wiry plant with pale leaves and clusters of tiny white flowers.

"Oliver!" Steve called, stumbling toward him.

Oliver lay flat on the ground, his face pale against the dark soil, his hands splayed limply at his sides. His eyes were half-lidded, glassy with exhaustion. Steve skidded to a stop, falling to his knees beside him.

"Hey! Hey, buddy," Steve shook him gently. "Oliver, wake up."

Oliver blinked up at him slowly, as if every movement took more effort than it should. His lips were faintly stained a sickly greenish yellow. Steve's stomach dropped.

"No..." Steve whispered, his gaze darting to the plant beside Oliver.

"He's eaten something poisonous," Steve muttered to himself.

His hands shook as he cupped Oliver's face. "Oliver, did you eat this?"

Oliver gave a weak nod, his eyes fluttering shut again. "I was... hungry," he said.

Panic clawed at Steve's chest.

"Buddy, stay with me," Steve said, trying to keep his voice steady. "I need you to sit up, okay? Come on, you can't lie down like this."

Oliver whimpered, curling into himself. "Just... wanna sleep..."

"No, kiddo, you have to stay awake," Steve begged, brushing the hair back from Oliver's forehead. "Look at me. Please. Just a little longer, okay? We'll get through this."

Steve held him close, feeling how light and frail he'd become. "It's okay. It's not your fault. Just stay with me, Oliver." His voice cracked, and he wiped his own tears away, forcing himself to stay calm.

Steve wrapped his coat around Oliver and stood, holding him tight against his chest. His heart pounded with fear as he scanned the barren terrain, knowing the town they'd passed wasn't far.

"Hold on, buddy," Steve whispered, starting toward the town with heavy, determined steps. Oliver sagged in his arms, and Steve tightened his grip, holding on to the boy's life with his bare hands.

CHAPTER 21

The wind howled as Hans and Sarah trudged through the dense forest, their boots crunching against the frost-covered ground. Ahead loomed scattered debris embedded in snow and jagged rock—the remnants of a once-soaring aircraft.

Sarah pulled her jacket tighter, her breath coming out in misty puffs. "He said to meet us here?" she asked, glancing at Hans.

"Yeah," Hans said, checking the coordinates on his GPS. "Right at this crash site." He scanned the tree line nervously. "But this guy better show up. I don't like being out here alone."

They moved around the perimeter, where pieces of twisted metal lay half-buried in the snow. Fragments of the cockpit jutted from the wreckage, scarred by the brutal impact. The air was sharp with the faint smell of burned fuel and melted plastic.

A movement from the trees caught Hans's attention. He nudged Sarah, pointing. "There. Someone's coming."

From the shadow of the forest emerged a man in his late forties, bundled in a long coat, his face partially obscured by a hood. He moved cautiously, glancing over his shoulder as if he'd been followed. When he reached them, he pulled back the hood, revealing deep-set eyes, grizzled hair, and a look that was equal parts fear and exhaustion.

"You must be the investigators for this crash," the man said in a low voice, his breath fogging the air. "I'm Dr. Patrick Crehan from Killarney, Ireland. I study solar flares along with my partner, Dr. Kazuo Tachikawa from Sendai, Japan."

"You're the whistleblower," Sarah said, her tone clipped. She crossed her arms. "Why bring us here? Why not meet in the city?"

Dr. Crehan's gaze darted around the crash site, his shoulders hunched. "Because people covering this up? They're watching everywhere. Here, they won't expect to see you."

Hans stepped forward. "So, what's the truth? What really happened?"

Dr. Crehan exhaled. "The plane was hit by a really bad solar storm, a flare more powerful than anything we've seen in years. It created an electromagnetic pulse that shut down the avionics. No control surfaces, no communication, no warning. The pilots were flying blind."

"Are you sure?" Sarah said, frowning. "We saw traces of the solar flare. But how could that bring a plane down?"

"Because it was covered up," Dr. Crehan said, his voice tight with frustration. "Satellite systems picked up the event, but it wasn't reported to the wider public to avoid panic. We studied the flight pattern in which the plane was flying over the Atlantic, where it was hit by the first solar flare. The control tower in Moncton redirected them from flying through Ireland and the UK to a route over the Alps, then a slight turn over Vienna. It was over Austria where the second, more severe solar flare hit. Had the controller just told them to stay the course, the flight would have safely reached Helsinki."

"How do you know the control tower made the error deliberately?" Hans asked.

"The higher ups who ordered the new route didn't account for the fact that the recent trend of solar flares has been striking the Alpine areas much more strongly, and no other plane was flying through that route.

It just doesn't make sense. Dr. Tachikawa and I have been researching why the flares are concentrating here. If we don't get to the bottom of this, the world will be in terrible danger."

Hans and Sarah exchanged a tense glance. "Do you have proof?" she asked.

Dr. Crehan nodded, looking around one last time, then reached into his coat and handed Sarah a USB stick. "Everything's on here—satellite data, internal emails—everything they tried to bury."

Sarah gripped the drive, her pulse quickening. "And what happens to you, now?"

Dr. Crehan gave her a grim smile. "I'll disappear. I've said enough already. Just make sure the truth comes out. People need to know what happened here."

Before Hans or Sarah could respond, both Dr. Crehan and Dr. Tachikawa turned and disappeared back into the forest.

Only the wind remained, threading through the wreckage like a ghostly reminder of what had been lost.

Sarah stared down at the USB drive in her hand, her mind racing. "We have it, Hans," she whispered. "The truth. Everything."

Hans stepped closer, scanning the tree line where Dr. Crehan had vanished.

"He better be right," Hans said.

With the device secure in her pocket, Sarah turned toward the forest. "Let's go."

The crash site disappeared behind them as they hurried back toward the snow, their footprints quickly swallowed by the unforgiving wilderness.

The cold bit into Steve's skin as he charged down the river, cradling Oliver in his arms. The boy's head rolled against his shoulder, breath shallow and weak. Steve's heart pounded in his chest, harder than his footsteps that stumbled across rocks and patches of frozen dirt. He refused to look down for fear of what he might see.

"Stay with me, buddy," Steve whispered, his voice ragged from fear and the sharp mountain air. "Just a little longer."

Oliver's limp body felt heavier with each step, but Steve didn't stop. His legs screamed, but he pushed through the burning ache, his mind fixed on one thing—reaching that town.

Steve crested the ridge, breathless, as the view opened before him. The town clung to the shore of the lake like a cluster of old memories stitched together—stone houses with steep wooden roofs, their shutters painted in fading blues and greens. For the first time since the crash, Steve glimpsed the pristine waters of an Alpine lake.

Steve charged straight into the heart of the town with Oliver.

"Help! Please!" His voice echoed against the cold walls, desperate and unsteady. "I need help! The boy–he's sick. He ate poison."

Curtains twitched, then snapped shut. An old man with a sack of potatoes froze mid-step, his eyes narrowing beneath bushy brows before he shuffled backwards into a doorway. A woman across the street stood still as a statue, her hand hovering in midair where she'd been sweeping. One by one, faces disappeared behind glass, shadows moving behind lace as if the town had silently agreed to watch, but not welcome.

Steve pressed on, staggering deeper into town. Remembering the smattering of German he had learned from Oliver and the townspeople, Steve forced the words out, his voice raw and cracked.

"Bitte! Jemand–irgendjemand! Er hat etwas Giftiges gegessen! *Please! Someone-anyone! He ate something poisonous!*

Steve's shout rang through the narrow street. A woman dropped her bundle of firewood. A boy clutched his mother's coat, eyes wide. At a doorway, an old man leaned on a cane, frowning. A shopkeeper paused in his doorway, wiping his hands on a stained apron.

But Steve kept moving, clutching Oliver tighter in his arms, refusing to stop. "Helft mir! Bitte!" he cried, the hoarseness in his voice betraying his fear.

"Blieb weg!" *Stay away!*

"Fremede nicht wilkommen!" someone shouted from the window. *No strangers welcome!*

Steve heard the words, but he. He cradled Oliver tighter. "I don't care what you think of me!" he shouted, his voice raw. "Help him! Please!"

A woman threw open her shutters and glared down at him. "Die Sonne har uns gewarnt!" *The sun has warned us!*

Steve's eyes darted from face to face. More villagers were gathering now, a wall of wary, mistrustful eyes. He didn't stop going further.

Oliver whimpered weakly in his arms, and Steve's panic surged. He dropped to his knees in the middle of the cobblestone square, gasping for breath. "Please," he whispered, the fight draining out of him. "He's just a kid…Help us."

And then, through the muttering, a single voice broke the tension. "Bring him inside."

An old woman stepped forward from the shadows, her eyes sharp beneath the folds of her woolen scarf. She carried a basket of herbs, and in her other hand, a battered walking stick. The crowd parted reluctantly as she approached, her expression grim.

Steve looked up at her. "You can speak English?"

The old woman responded, "Yes."

Steve sighed with relief. "Please help! He's dying. He ate a poisonous plant, and we're worried that he will die."

The woman gave him a court nod, her lips pressed into a thin line. "Follow me," she said. "Quickly."

Steve rose on shaky legs, still clutching Oliver, and followed her through the narrow streets, past suspicious glares and muttered curses. His arms ached, and his heart raced, but hope flickered inside him for the first time.

Oliver stirred weakly in his arms and Steve leaned down to whisper, "We're almost there, buddy. Hold on just a little longer."

Steve then turned and asked the woman. "What's your name?"

"Maria," she said.

"Nice to meet you, Maria," Steve replied.

CHAPTER 22

Maria led Steve to her farmhouse on the outskirts of Lichtersee, a quiet town nestled beside the lake that shared its name. The house, a traditional chalet with weathered stone walls and a sagging wooden roof, stood like a stubborn remnant of a simpler time.

Steve took it all in slowly—the barn, leaning just slightly to one side, its red paint faded to a rusty hue. Chickens scratched at the dirt, their feathers fluttering in the breeze like they had no idea anything was wrong. From the chimney, a thin line of smoke curled into the sky, carrying the scent of burning wood.

The land rolled out toward the forest, fenced off in uneven stretches, like someone had tried to keep the world at bay with what little they had. Beyond that, the jagged peaks of the Alps cut into the horizon, snow catching in the sun.

Steve absorbed the tranquil scene with weary eyes, watching the smoke curl from the chimney, scented faintly with herbs. He glanced at Oliver, telling him, "I'm sorry."

"Wait here, let me call my granddaughter, Heidi," Maria said. "She's the village doctor."

"Heidi, komm her! Wir haben einen Notfall," Maria yelled. *Heidi, come here! We have an emergency.*

A blonde woman with long hair hurried to the front porch where they stood. "Ja, was ist das Problem?" she asked. *Yes, what is the issue?*

Maria turned to Steve. "Go ahead."

Steve explained the situation to Heidi.

"Is he your son?" Heidi inquired, noting the resemblance between Steve and Oliver.

"Not exactly," Steve replied.

Heidi nodded. "You brought him here. Let's help him." She led Steve and Oliver toward her bedroom.

Steve gently laid Oliver on the bed in a small but warm bedroom, with the scent of lavender and herbs lingered in the air. Heidi draped a heavy wool blanket over Oliver, who lay pale and shivering. She moved with practiced efficiency, her steady hands administering a bitter herbal concoction into Oliver's mouth, wiping his chin when he coughed.

"Trink, Junge…just a little more," she whispered soothingly.

Steve stood by the door, tense and helpless, watching her every move.

What if he doesn't make it? He has been through a lot and his folks back home want him to be there. I should've kept a closer eye on him.

Heidi glanced at Steve and offered reassurance. "Don't worry. He'll be fine."

Steve exhaled deeply, relief washing over him. "Thank God."

Heidi remained attentive, monitoring Oliver's breathing. She turned to Steve. "You can explore Lichtersee. It's a charming town."

"I'm worried they might not welcome me," Steve admitted. "In the last few places we've been, the locals haven't been kind."

"Why is that?" Heidi raised an eyebrow.

"The solar flares have made them suspicious of outsiders. We've had to survive on berries and fish because no one would offer us food."

"I'm sorry to hear that," Heidi said. "Our town should be different. Maybe my grandmother can accompany you. It'll help people see you're not a threat. As for your friend, he just needs rest. We'll provide nourishing food to help him regain his strength," Heidi said. She then called out, "Oma! Können Sie herkommen?" *Grandma, can you come here?*

Maria hurried into the room. "Ja?"

"Können Sie ihn nach draußen bringen und ihm die Stadt zeigen?" *Can you take him outside and show him the town?*

Maria turned to Steve. "Would you like to see the town?"

"Yes, definitely," Steve replied.

Maria led Steve to a guest room, where he dropped off his bags before they headed out together to explore Lichtersee.

DECEMBER 25, 2022

Matt and Rachel sat quietly to the fireplace flipping through an old family photo album with no carols playing in the living room, no hurried whispers over the last-minute gifts, no laughter in the air.

"Look at Steve here when his team won the Little League," Rachel said, her hand covering her mouth. "He looked so adorable. And there's Owen. I wish they were here with us."

"You have to look on the bright side, honey," Matt said gently. "Steve's still alive, just missing. He can survive in the wilderness. Your dad, my dad, and the Boy Scouts taught him essential survival skills."

"What if those skills aren't enough," Rachel said. "Surviving in the Alps is not the same thing as camping in the woods."

"I know, honey," Matt said, placing his hand on Rachel's shoulder. "But we have to trust the Lord. He's watching over Steve."

Owen entered the living room, laptop on his hand, headphones resting around his neck.

"Are you still working on that app?" Rachel asked.

"Mom, I'm doing everything I can to find Steve," Owen said. "If it means working day and night on getting this ready to find him, so be it."

Owen glanced around at the room, noticing the lone string of lights. "This might be the first Christmas without any decorations, no Christmas trees."

"If we find Steve," Matt said. "We'll have the biggest celebration we've ever had."

A few minutes later, Matt opened the door.

"James, Sue, what brought you guys here?" Matt asked.

"We think we all need to go on a trip," James said. "Spending Christmas moping around isn't helping."

Matt turned to Rachel and asked, "What do you think?"

"Yeah, let's do it," Rachel agreed.

Later that day, Owen called Lindsay and Emma into his makeshift laboratory—his bedroom. Owen pushed the bed against the far wall, where it was barely visible beneath a pile of discarded clothes and half-folded blankets.

Lindsay and Emma glanced around the room, where three computer screens flickered in the dim light, casting a bluish glow that pulsed against the darkened walls.

"This looks so impressive," Emma said, sitting next to Owen and examining the monitors, which displayed central monitor displayed a series of complex code strings and data graphs, while the others showed live feeds, maps, and system diagnostics.

Lindsay watched Emma out of the corner of her eye; something about her posture capturing her attention. She noticed the way Emma leaned forward slightly whenever Owen spoke, her eyes focused intently on his face.

Looks like I'm not the only Carson who's fallen for a Turner. The realization hit her like a slow, quiet wave.

Owen then turned to the monitors, showcasing the full application. "I've gathered all the data from Steve's phone onto my system," he explained. "What I'm doing now is sending the data to satellites around the globe. These satellites should return information on the last location where the data was used. So far, it's showing the phone's last activity was in the mountains near the Austrian states of Tyrol and Carinthia."

"Except Steve's phone got destroyed in the crash," Lindsay frowned.

"You're right," Owen said. "I think what I need to do is get Steve's DNA and place it there."

The biting wind whipped across the mountain ridge as Sarah stood with her arms crossed tightly, her gaze fixed on the tree line, lips pressed into a thin line. Beside her, Hans shifted his weight from foot to foot, rubbing the back of his neck as he glanced toward the command post's radio tent. Both watched the barren landscape, each lost in their own version of hope and dread.

A group of rescuers stood by a toppled map board, arguing over conflicting coordinates. One man kicked at the snow, muttering.

"Wir haben diesen Abschnitt schon zweimal durchsucht." *We've already checked this section twice.*

Further out, a searcher waved a radio overhead, static crackling. "Kommando, hören Sie mich? Wir haben den Kontakt zu Einheit Vier verloren!" *Command, do you copy? We've lost track of Unit Four again!*

Sarah's heart sank as she scanned the area. The grid was supposed to be covered in tight formation. Now, the teams were scattered, nearly invisible in the whiteout.

"Are you serious?" Sarah snapped, yanking off her headset as the static-laden voice of the SAR team leader crackled through.

Hans' face was pale. "You've just told me you've searched the same sector twice. How do you–How's that even possible?" he demanded, his voice louder than he intended. "We're on a time crunch here."

The new SAR leader, Franz, a burly man with a thick beard, shrugged, leaning back in his chair with an infuriating lack of concern. "Well, the terrain is tricky, and the GPS has been unreliable. Also, it's almost Christmas time, and some of our people are going home to see their families. We'll resume after New Year."

Sarah's fists clenched. "Really? Even with the lives of two survivors at stake, you're all going to take the last week off?"

"We're backed by the government to take Christmas off," Franz said.

"No wonder you guys can't seem to find Steve and Oliver," Sarah said coldly.

"Look, we're doing our best. But it's the holiday season," Franz said.

"Your best is not good enough!" She turned to Hans, her eyes blazing. "Don't tell me that even you are taking the holidays off."

"I'm not," Hans said firmly. "Until this whole investigation is complete, I cannot afford to take any days off."

"Good," Sarah said. "I understand that people here like to relax, but working a little harder in exchange for a safer world would be worth it."

As they arrived back at the hangar, her assistant, Timothy met Sarah and Hans.

"We've got some good and bad news. The bad news is that Celestine Airlines is not cooperating with us, and we've found out why. The good news is that one of the engineers at Boeing has come forward with details about why the plane was vulnerable. We also did some further investigating of the Air Route Traffic Control Center in

Moncton. It turns out there was only one controller in the tower at the time, and they were slightly inexperienced, leading to a poorly planned route for the pilots."

"Sounds like this is a perfect time for a press conference," Sarah said.

CHAPTER 23

The golden light pooled in the cracks of the cobblestones as Steve walked, each step scraping over the uneven street. The air was sharp with pine and smoke, the scent tugging at a half-forgotten memory of home.

"This is the main square," Maria said warmly, gesturing toward the heart of the town, where a small fountain bubbled peacefully. Steve observed a handful of locals bustling about—an old woman picking up bread from the bakery, children in thick woolen jackets laughing as they played near a statue of a local hero.

Taking in the town's serene rhythm, so different from the chaos he'd been fleeing, Steve said, "It's quiet here. Feels like I'm in *The Sound of Music*."

Maria nodded. "It is. Lichtersee's never been a place for rush or noise. People know each other, look after each other…though they've been more cautious lately, especially with those solar flares happening. People used to come visit us from places like Salzburg and Innsbruck."

"Why is that?" Steve asked. "Every town we've been to here has been very unfriendly."

"I'm not sure," Maria replied. "But I think whenever a solar flare happens, it destroys a lot, including our ability to survive. I remember another solar flare when I was growing up. My father was a diplomat, which is why I learned English easily, living in places once devastated after World War II. There was a solar flare in France near where I was, and the towns were so devastated that people became savages, attacking other towns for food. When resources deplete, people become wild and come after others for their food, clothing, and even shelter. Because of that, whenever a solar flare occurs, townspeople become more defensive and start to attack outsiders."

"I get it now," Steve said. "We tried to reason with a lot of people, and we just couldn't make it."

Maria then asked Steve, "You're American, right?"

"Yes, I am," Steve said, looking around. "And Oliver's British."

"Oliver?" Maria said.

"Yeah, the kid your granddaughter is treating," Steve said.

"Oh right, I forgot the name," Maria said and chuckled. Her eyes flickered briefly toward the distant mountains. "I want to show you something else. Come with me."

Maria led him down a narrow path that wound behind the houses and towards the edge of the forest. The town's sounds grew distant as the trees opened up to reveal the town's namesake—Lake Lichtersee. The water shimmered in the fading light, a mirror of the deep blue sky and the jagged peaks of the Austrian Alps.

Steve stopped, stunned by the scene's beauty. "This is... incredible."

Maria smiled softly, hands tucked in the pockets of her wool coat. "It's why most of us never leave. Lichtersee has a way of pulling you in." She pointed to a small dock stretching out into the lake where a few fishing boats were moored. "My father grew up in this town and loved to fish. When he finished his diplomatic mission, he'd bring us here to this town and every weekend, we would fish. We'd sit for hours, just listening to the quiet. People here in this town want visitors to come by and enjoy the scenery. Ever since the solar flares, people have been wary of anyone they don't know."

Steve took a deep sigh of breath. "Who else in your family besides you and your granddaughter?"

Maria explained, "I have a son and two daughters who both live in Salzburg. They're coming tomorrow for Christmas dinner. My other granddaughter, Heidi's sister, is a doctor in Innsbruck, and she comes here pretty often. Still looking for someone to date. Sadly, my husband passed away a few years back."

"Right," Steve said. "You know my phone and passport got destroyed in the wreckage, so that I didn't realize that me and Oliver have been fighting for survival for a month."

"Yeah, I can see that with the beard you've grown and looking very thin that you haven't eaten much in a while. We'll make you something nice," Maria said.

"Sure, thank you," Steve nodded. "Also, I need to work on improving my German language skills."

"Before the solar flare incidents, a lot of tourists from all over Europe and even the United States used to come here and admire the place. But people have become very resistant to these things."

"I need to do some research," Steve said. "Is there a computer and internet in your house?"

"It's slow," Maria said. "But people feel happy here not being near the internet."

"After surviving the crash this past month, I've seen a world that doesn't exist on the internet. I just need to let my folks at home know I'm safe and alive."

As the sun set, Steve and Maria returned to the farmhouse. The last traces of sunlight disappeared behind the Alps' peaks, leaving the sky a deep indigo. Temperatures dropped, and the smell of damp earth and pine clung to their clothes as they approached the porch.

Steve rubbed his hands together, blowing into them to warm his chilled fingers. "Feels like the temperature has dropped ten."

"You're in Austria," Maria said. "And it's wintertime. You're lucky that there isn't much snow right now due to the solar flares happening here."

She opened the door and ushered Steve inside, the comforting warmth of the fire in the house instantly washing over them.

Inside, Steve took in the sounds and smells of dinner being prepared. Pots clanged softly, and the rich aroma of onions, herbs, and roasted meat filled the air. Heidi stood at the stove, stirring a pot with a wooden spoon, wearing a simple apron over her woolen dress.

"Heidi," Maria called, "Wir sind zurück." *We're back.*

Heidi turned, smiling when she saw them. "Just in time. Dinner will be ready soon." She wiped her hands on the apron and gestured to the table, where a basket of fresh bread sat alongside a pitcher of water. "Sit. Warm yourselves. It's too cold to be out for long."

Steve nodded his thanks and took a seat at the rustic wooden table. He asked Heidi, "Is Oliver okay?"

"I've cleared the poison from his system," Heidi said. "It should take a few days for him to recover. Luckily, you brought him here on time. One more hour, and it would've been too late."

Steve released a deep breath. "Thank goodness. He really was hungry, and no one wanted us around. The most he's eaten for a month was fish, berries, and some bread and milk."

Heidi placed her hands on her mouth. "He survived only on that?"

"Yeah," Steve said. "It's brutal out there. What did you treat him with?"

"Activated charcoal, some atropine, and naloxone," Heidi said.

Steve furrowed his brow. "Well, thanks for healing him. At least now we can go to our next place."

"Where are you headed?" Heidi asked.

"We're trying to reach the UK to take him to his grandparents," Steve said. "We survived a plane crash in the mountains to the east. The boy's parents and sister died, but he survived. Before dying, his father asked me to take him to his grandparents in the UK. We've been surviving for about a month since the crash."

"That's really sad to hear," Heidi said. "You've done well looking after him."

"Thank you," Steve said.

"But you can't leave right now for two reasons. Snow is about to fall, and most towns around here aren't safe or welcoming to outsiders due to the recent solar flare incidents. It's best you stay here for a few days." Heidi returned to the kitchen to check on her roast.

Maria joined him at the table, taking off her coat and hanging it by the door. She leaned back in her chair, her expression relaxed for the first time that evening. "Heidi's cooking is very good. I hope you're hungry."

Steve glanced at the simmering pot, his stomach grumbling in response. "Starving, actually."

Heidi's face glowed in the firelight. "Good. We'll eat soon. Tonight, it's something special—wild game from the woods and vegetables from the garden." She ladled a bit of the broth into a small bowl and tasted it, nodding approvingly. "And a little more seasoning for luck."

The house was quiet now, save for the occasional crackle of the fire and the rhythmic sounds of Heidi's cooking.

Steve looked at Maria, who gave him a reassuring smile. "You'll feel at home soon enough," she said softly.

After dinner, Steve moved quietly into Oliver's room, each step softened to avoid waking Oliver. He approached the small bed where the child lay bundled beneath a heavy wool blanket, his cheeks flushed and breath slow, his hair long. Steve's gaze softened, relief mingling with the lingering worry. He reached out, lightly brushing a loose strand of hair from the boy's forehead, his fingers light as if afraid to disturb the sleep.

Steve knelt down, his head bowed, and hands clasped tightly together, knuckled white with the weight of his gratitude. His voice was barely a whisper in the quiet of the room.

"Thank you, Lord." He closed his eyes. "Thank you for keeping Oliver safe, for bringing us through." His voice trembled. He paused, swallowing hard. "I don't know what would've happened if he passed and we never found this place and people who were willing to care for us. I thank you, Lord, for sparing us and giving us a new chance in life."

Steve sat there in silence for a long moment, taking quiet breaths, feeling the overwhelming relief wash over him. His heart steadied as he glanced over at Oliver's sleeping for with a look that held equal parts awe and love.

CHAPTER 24

In the Salzburg Hangar, the room buzzed with tense whispers as Sarah and Hans stepped up to the podium, exhaustion etched into their face. A sea of reporters sat in front of them, cameras poised and lights blinding. Everyone was waiting for answers.

Sarah cleared her throat and adjusted the microphone, glancing briefly at Hans before addressing the crowd.

"Thank you all for being here," she began, her voice steady but weary. "We're here to provide an update on the investigation into Celestine Airlines Flight 24's tragic crash and the factors that caused it."

A murmur of anticipation rippled through the audience of reporters. One reporter near the front leaned forward, pen ready.

"I can now confirm that this investigation is now over since we can now confirm that a powerful solar flare–an unforeseen and extreme event–caused a cascade of system failures on board."

She paused, letting the words sink in. "This flare was intense enough to produce an electromagnetic pulse, shutting down the plane's avionics and communication system within moments." The room held its breath as Hans stepped forward. "The pilots were flying blind—no comms, no instruments. The solar flare hit hard, and satellite systems picked it up, but that warning never reached the cockpit."

Hans hesitated. "Whether it was oversight or something deeper—maybe corruption—that failure cost lives."

Reporters' hands shot up. Sarah pointed to one.

"Are you saying this could have been prevented if the airline or authorities had acted sooner?" The reporter's voice cut through the silence.

Hans glanced at Sarah before responding. "Yes, it's possible," he said carefully. "The monitoring system detected the flare, but because of a communication breakdown, that data didn't reach the pilots. If they had known, there may have been time to take emergency precautions."

Another reporter, looking skeptical, shouted over the noise. "Who's responsible for this failure? The public deserves to know who's at fault."

Sarah's jaw tightened. "There's evidence of conflicting reports between the airline and air traffic control—someone fed false data. Either way, the result was chaos in the skies."

She glanced around the room. "Solar flares should be predictable. NASA didn't warn us. ATC didn't reroute. The airline's owner? A foreign oligarch with deep pockets and no ties to Finland except the influence he's bought."

Her voice hardened. "This isn't just miscommunication. It reeks of corruption."

Before she could continue, Hans walked over to the podium and gently took the microphone. "Solar flares of this magnitude are rare, but yes, they do pose risks on the avionics systems. This flare was far stronger than what's typically anticipated. We're working with experts in both aviation and astrophysics to ensure in the future, airlines can be better prepared."

"But people died!" another reporter shouted, her voice strained. "And now you're telling us this wasn't even considered a threat? Are there more cover-ups we should know about?"

"We're not here to justify any decisions that were made," Sarah said firmly, locking eyes with the reporter. "We're here to find the truth. And we're doing everything we can to uncover what happened and make sure it never happens again. Thank you all."

Hans and Sarah departed the podium as the room erupted in a barrage of shouted questions. Camera flashed.

Sarah and Hans stepped into the office, where the air was heavy with the scent of polished wood and leather, and the blinds were drawn, casting long shadows across the room. Behind the massive desk sat Michael Foster, the head of the NTSB. Sarah noticed his unreadable expression as he gestured for her to take a seat.

Michael said, "Hans, Sarah and I need a moment together. If you can excuse us." Hans nodded and departed the room.

Sarah had barely sat down when Foster began, his tone crisp and formal.

"Sarah, I'm going to get straight to the point," he said, folding his hands on the desk. "After a thorough review of the investigation's current direction and the reports from our oversight board, the decision has been made to remove you from your position as lead investigator on the Celestine Airlines case."

"Excuse me?" She leaned forward, her voice sharp with disbelief. "I'm the one who's been uncovering the critical leads here, Michael. I'm the one who brought the solar flare cover-up to light. You can't just take me off the case now!"

Michael's gaze was steady, almost clinical. "Sarah, you've been pushing this investigation in ways that have raised concerns, both internally and externally. The level of visibility, the media coverage—this has escalated beyond what we anticipated. Your approach has drawn far too much attention and disrupted our chain of command."

Sarah could feel her pulse pounding in her ears. "So, that's what this is about? Politics?"

Her voice shook with anger, but she fought to keep it level. "This isn't about media attention; it's about finding the truth! Yes, there are multiple parties at fault, but if you're going to make me say it's all the pilot's fault for flying through that solar flare, then I'm not going to do it. People have died, Michael. Their families deserve answers. Are you seriously going to sideline me because it's inconvenient?"

Michael sighed, leaning back in his chair, the shadows across his face hardening. "Sarah, you're a talented investigator. But this investigation has moved beyond your scope. We need someone who can de-escalate things, someone who isn't as personally invested as Hans over there."

"Personally invested?" Sarah let out a hollowed laugh. "Do you understand what we're dealing with here?" This is a cover-up of life-threatening information, Michael. And now you're telling me to just stand down and stay silent? Hans is merely doing this because the Austrian government is paying his bills. He's just doing the bare minimum work, while I've been out there pounding sand to find answers."

Michael's gaze grew colder. "I'm telling you this is no longer your fight. You'll be reassigned to another case. Your work on this one has been noted, and we appreciate it, but this is final. We don't want to damage our relationships with a lot of people whose cooperation we need."

Sarah stared at him, her mind racing, her fingers digging into the arms of the chair. The anger in her chest simmered, threatening to boil over. "This isn't right, Michael. This isn't just some case file we can close and walk away from. You know that. Deep down, you know. Don't forget Michael, we're also still searching for Steve and Oliver."

Michael's face softened for a moment. But then it was gone, replaced by the same impassive expression. "I know you're passionate, Sarah. And I respect that. But the decision's made. Please hand over all your findings to the new lead investigator by the end of the day."

Without another word, Sarah stood up, turned, and left the office, her mind reeling with anger and betrayal.

§

Steve rose from his bed and adjusted the collar of his jacket, feeling its coarse warmth against his neck. Beneath his jacket, he wore a crisp linen shirt, its collar open at the throat. He wore thick pants with woolen socks above his leather boots. The deep forest-green fabric hugged his shoulders, embroidered with subtle patterns that hinted at a history older than he could grasp.

Steve looked at Oliver, who was still asleep and recovering. He walked outside the house where Maria and Heidi sat outside drinking hot tea watching the snow fall.

"Want some tea, Steve?" Heidi asked.

"Definitely," Steve said. He sat down staring at the snow fall, sipping a cup.

"So, is any family coming for Christmas tomorrow?" Steve asked.

"Yeah," Maria said. "I think I told you my son is coming from Innsbruck with his family. I'm not sure about my other son or my oldest daughter, who's the mother of Heidi."

Steve said, "Heidi, are you married?"

"My husband is in the Austrian military. He'll join us a bit later," Heidi said. "We have to maintain this farm."

"I'm happy to help if you need to," Steve said.

"What do you plan on doing?" Maria asked.

"I need to figure everything out now that I've landed somewhere nice and Oliver is properly taken care of," Steve said. "I definitely need to call my folks back home to let them know that I'm alive."

"I assume they think you're dead," Heidi said.

Steven nodded. "God, I wonder how Lindsay has been doing with all of this going on."

"Who's Lindsay?" Heidi asked.

"My fiancée," Steve said quietly.

CHAPTER 25

As the snow thickened into a blizzard, Steve retreated indoors, settling near the crackling fire. His brows knitted furrowed, a faint line of worry etched in his forehead.

How on earth will I contact my family? Steve rose to pace the room. Moments later, Heidi and Maria entered from outside, shaking off the snow. They began preparing breakfast: an assortment of bread rolls, butter, jelly, soft-boiled eggs, and muesli.

Drawn by the aroma, Steve approached the table and eagerly tasted the muesli. "This is delicious. I've never had anything like this before."

"I'm sure you don't get muesli over there in America," Heidi said.

Steve nodded. "Back home, everything is overloaded with sugar and preservatives. Even the bread is too sweet. This tastes just right."

Heidi and Maria chuckled. Steve continued, "I need to learn these recipes before I leave. But right now, I'm exhausted from everything."

"Take plenty of rest," Maria said. "Right now, we should be getting a lot of snow today. But my son and my younger daughter and their families should be coming later this evening for dinner."

"Sure, thanks," Steve said. "Just wondering, how can I call my folks in America?"

"Our phones are limited to domestic and some European calls," Heidi explained. "For international calls, you'd need a different service. Plus, the recent solar flares have disrupted our internet and communications."

Steve's jaw tightened, the muscle ticking under his skin. "I suppose I'll have to wait until the snowfall stops and hope for no more solar events."

Maria said, "Let's wait for the family to come and maybe you can use one of their phones to contact them."

Steve nodded. "How's Oliver doing?"

"He should be fine," Heidi said. "Why don't you go sleep with him?"

"That's actually a good idea," Steve said. He rose from his chair and quietly stepped into the bedroom. Oliver was still fast asleep, his small frame curled beneath the blankets. Gently, Steve eased in beside him, the mattress dipping slightly under his weight. He pulled the covers over them both and let out a long breath, the boy's steady breathing offering a fragile sense of peace.

The day after Christmas, Sarah knocked on the front door of the Turner household in Woodstock, Georgia. Lindsay opened the door.

"Sarah, what are you doing here?" Lindsay asked.

Sarah said. "I know I'm not supposed to be here. The investigative team let me go, and I'm continuing the crash investigation on my own. Didn't you mention Owen has been tracking Steve?"

"Yes," Lindsay said. "Come on in. And our parents are out in Tennessee for vacation." She escorted Sarah into Owen's bedroom, where Owen and Emma continued tracing the steps of Steve on Owen's tracking app.

Owen looked back, his mouth wide open. "Sarah, what are you doing here?"

"I came to check on you all and see how you're doing. That application looks impressive," Sarah remarked.

Sarah leaned forward, eyes scanning the screen at the different elements of the tracking app.

"Wow. This is amazing," she murmured. "Even our agency doesn't have something this advanced. It gives us a better chance to track Steve."

"The problem is, we lack a reference point to locate him," Owen said. "All we have is the crash site."

"I have some data on my hand and using this app, we can use this as a frame of reference," Sarah said. She pulled out a hard drive containing important data and handed it to Owen.

"That's exactly what we needed," Owen said, inputting the data, which expanded the application's scope.

"Now we're making progress," he said, scanning the updated map displaying potential leads across Austria.

"Given the information, it seems they've descended the mountain and are heading west," Owen observed.

"How is it that we're closer to finding Steve than the Austrian Search and Rescue team?"

"Don't blame me," Sarah sighed. "This investigation has become a bureaucratic mess."

Then, a flicker of data appeared—an alert from a surveillance feed in a remote district. Owen's eyes sharpened as he clicked on it, the screen displaying a new window.

Sarah said, "It just looks like a passerby caught inside the camera's frame."

Owen's shoulders sagged, but he refocused his eyes. "I see the crash site here, but then the trail goes cold. Our best hope is for Steve to contact us if he's alive."

"The Austrian terrain makes finding cell service challenging," Sarah noted.

"That can't be true," Owen argued. "It's 2022, not 1982."

Owen's fingers flexed against the keyboard, concentration unwavering. "Come on, Steve. Where are you?" he whispered.

Steve jolted awake, once again gasping for breath. The echoes of screeching metal and shattering glass still ringing in his ears. His chest heaved as he clawed his way out. For a moment, he didn't know where he was; he could still the twisted wreckage, smell the smoke, feel the violent jolt reverberating through his bones.

Glancing at Oliver, who slept peacefully, Steve shut his eyes, but new terrors emerged—angry, unrecognizable faces, hands reaching out, the roughness of their grips, the pain of blows, and accusations in German: "It's your fault... because of you... the flare..."

A small hand touched Steve's shoulder, hesitant but firm. "Steve?" Oliver's voice was soft, wavering with concern.

Steve's eyes snapped open, finding Oliver beside him, clutching a worn blanket. "You were... yelling," Oliver whispered, not releasing his grip. "Are you okay?"

Steve blinked, the nightmare's fog lifting as he focused on Oliver's worried face. He steadied his breathing, easing the tension. "I'm okay, buddy. You finally woke up," he said, sitting up and ruffling Oliver's hair. "Just a bad dream. You're no longer sick."

"The last time I remembered, my eyes were closed on the dirt and now I'm on a bed. Where am I?"

Steve groaned, saying, "Lichtersee. There's a lady named Heidi over there who has treated you and healed you. Do you know what time it is?"

Oliver glanced at the grandfather clock across the room. "Looks like 6:30 p.m., but I can't tell if it's morning or evening. It's dark outside."

Steve walked to the window, observing the night blanketed in thick, steady snowfall. The Alpine mountains stood silhouetted against the dark sky. Moonlight glistened on the swirling flakes, covering rooftops, trees, and paths in shimmering white.

Pressing his hand to the cold glass, Steve's breath fogged the window. "Oliver, come here," he said. The boy joined him, gazing at the serene scene. "Isn't that pretty?" Steve said. "It looks like we won't be going anywhere anytime soon."

"I want to build a snowman."

A moment later, Heidi walked in. "It looks like both of you woke up. Our families have come, so if you want to eat dinner and meet them, you're more than welcome to."

Steve and Oliver nodded and proceeded toward the dining room where a family gathering took place. One by one, the family members greeted Steve.

"Schön, dich kennenzulernen," Maria's son, Kurt said, shaking Steve's hand.

"Well, nice to meet you," Steve chuckled.

Kurt continued in English. "I was just saying nice to meet you. My mother told me a lot about you and Oliver and how you both survived a crash."

"Yeah, about that..." Steve began, then offered a small smile. "Honestly, you're the first people we've run into in Austria who actually speak English. It's a relief."

"My mother grew up in a diplomat family. I served in the Austrian Armed forces and work with a lot of tourists in Innsbruck. Anyways, I'm sorry for the crash and I think the young kid lost his parents."

"Yes, he has," Steve said. "We need to get him back to the UK. The issue is that we can't find any internet anywhere to contact anyone. I'm surprised the search and rescue team hasn't been able to find us."

"I've seen the news of the crash and our media is reporting it as all passengers from Celestine Airlines are all dead. Austria has become very bureaucratic, and they may be compromised by a lot of factors based on what I see. And the solar flare incidents have shifted the budgets solely toward that. I think you need to make some money to be able to fly out of this country."

"How can I make money here?"

"There is a way," Kurt said.

CHAPTER 26

The next morning, after eating breakfast, Steve and Oliver stepped outside.

"That's a lot of snowfall from last night," Steve remarked. "Almost like a blizzard."

Snow stretched endlessly in every direction, muffling sound and motion. Steve's boots crunched through the thick drifts, each step slower than the last. The weight of it all—ice, silence, uncertainty—pressed on him. He glanced up at the rooftops bowed under snow, the trees hunched as if exhausted, and a bench half-swallowed by white.

Oliver dashed ahead through the fresh snow, leaving a trail of small boot prints as he laughed and scooped up handfuls of the powdery snow. His cheeks were flushed pink with excitement, breath puffing in clouds of white as he rolled the snow into a quick, uneven ball.

With a mischievous grin, he turned, squinting one eye as he took aim. "Catch, Steve!" he shouted, hurling the snowball with all the strength of his might. The snowball flew, landing a soft thud against Steve's shoulder, leaving a dusting of white on his coat.

Steve chuckled and brushed the snow off as Oliver scrambled to make another one, giggling uncontrollably. Snow flew up around Oliver as he scooped and threw at Steve, his laughter echoing through the crisp air.

Steve leaned back against a snow-dusted tree, and watched Oliver bound through the fresh snow, his laughter ringing out like a bell in the quiet winter air, his cheeks flushed pink from the cold, his eyes bright with joy. It was such a simple thing, but after days of cold, hunger, and gnawing uncertainty, it hit Steve with quiet force. He hadn't realized how much he needed this—just a flicker of normal, of lightness.

He blinked at Oliver and slightly teared up. *This kid survived death twice and he's still joyful, and happy playing around.*

"Why are you crying?" Oliver asked, cocking his head.

Steve wiped his cheek and smiled. "Cold air."

Oliver grinned and lobbed another snowball. "Let's build a snowman."

Steve laughed. "Let's do it."

They worked side by side, rolling the snow into clumsy mounds that grew heavier with each pass. Their gloves dusted with frost, they strained to stack the second ball onto the first, collapsing into laughter when it tilted slightly but held firm.

Maria poked her head out from the porch. "Hot chocolate?"

"We're okay!" Steve called back, then turned to Oliver. "Unless—"

"I'm building a snowman!" Oliver said, already chasing down the next ball of snow.

Together, they finished the snowman—stones for eyes, a crooked carrot nose, twigs sticking out like jazz hands. Steve looped a scarf around its neck.

Oliver stepped back and beamed. "He needs a name."

"Frosty?"

Oliver rolled his eyes. "We're in Austria. Let's call him *Herr Schneemann.*"

Steve chuckled, ruffling his hair. "*Herr Schneemann* it is."

Kurt trudged up the path, boots crunching in the snow. Behind him, Felix and Johann followed close, bundled in thick jackets and knit hats pulled low.

"You must be having a bit of fun," Kurt said.

"Yes," Steve said. "It's been a while."

Felix and Johann approached Steve and shook his hands speaking in German. ""Möchtest du ausgehen? *Do you want to go out?*

Steve tilted his head slightly, and Kurt said, "Excuse my sons. They don't speak English that well. They're not that interested in learning the language, and I have to remind them that they come from a family who has seen the world."

"Understandable," Steve said. "I'm picking up more German from being around here a lot." He pointed to Oliver, "The kid speaks German better than I do so, there's that."

"Really?" Kurt said. He approached Oliver and crouched down until they were eye level. A soft smile played on his lips as he murmured something in German. Oliver nodded, replying in a quiet voice, his fingers fidgeting with the hem of his coat.

Kurt stood up. "We're going to be shoveling the snow out of all the people who live here. It's the day after Christmas, so we might as well start doing the work."

"Sounds good," Steve said. "What do you think, Oliver?"

Oliver nodded. "I want to build more snowmen."

Steve's eyes lit up, and he gave a broad grin. He let out a quick breath, almost a laugh.

Steve laughed and joined Kurt at the edge of Lichtersee, where houses sat half-buried in snow. Kurt dug in with practiced strokes, barely pausing. Felix stomped the snow from his boots, cheeks flushed red, while Johann tugged his scarf higher, glancing at the heavy-laden rooftops. Oliver clutched his shovel with quiet resolve. Together, they faced the drifted street, ready to dig the town freely.

With each shovel-load of snow tossed aside, their breaths hung in clouds around them, puffing into the chilly air. Kurt knelt beside Oliver, took the boy's gloved hands, and adjusted his grip on the wooden handle.

"Du hältst es auf diese Weise." *You hold it this way.*

Steve kept an eye on Oliver, who attacked the snow with surprising determination, occasionally stopping in to exchange a smile with Steve.

Felix approached Steve and asked in German, "Bist du Amerikaner?" *Are you American?*

"Ja. Ich bin Amerikaner." *Yes. I am American.*

Felix then responded, "Amerikaner sind cool." *Americans are cool.*

"Danke schön," Steve smiled. *Thank you very much.*

House by house, they cleared paths, brushing snow from doorsteps and stacking piles by the curb. Laughter mingled with the scrape of shovels. Neighbors exchanged quick smiles and nods. Children sipped hot chocolate, cheeks flushed from the cold. When they finished, freshly lit porches cast warm glows over the cleared walkways, quiet proof of their shared effort.

Steve sighed. "The houses look even prettier now."

Kurt nodded. "Before we head in, we need to get some ice water from the lake."

"You said I was going to get some money after shoveling snow, right?" Steve asked.

"It's Christmas time," Kurt replied with a grin. "Have patience."

Back at the farmhouse, boots crunched over the packed snow as they moved with purpose. Each of them grabbed a metal bucket from the stack near the door, the handles cold and rough in their hands. Steve adjusted his grip, giving Oliver a smaller bucket, which the boy grasped with a determined expression.

Together, they made their way down the narrow, winding path that led to the lake. The trees flanked their route, branches dusted in white, the paths covered in snow as the winter sun hung low in the sky.

As they approached the lake, the group found it sealed beneath a thick layer of ice, stretching across the surface like a hard crystalline sheet.

"This can be really difficult to break through," Steve said, kneeling by the edge. He tapped the ice with his gloved hand, feeling its unyielding chill. *If we can't get through soon, it'll all be for nothing,* he thought, the weight of the moment pressing down. His eyes met Kurt's, who nodded grimly and reached for the heavy iron rod.

Kurt struck the ice with a series of forceful blows, each one sending cracks skittering across the surface like spiderwebs. Steve's breath caught—part hope, part dread—as he waited for the ice to give way.

"Welcome to winter," Kurt said. "Getting water is much more difficult than anything else."

The loud, echoing thud of metal against ice seemed to fill the silent winter air. Oliver watched with wide eyes, fascinated and a little uncertain as shards broke away, revealing silvers of dark, icy water beneath.

After several minutes, the ice gave way, splintering into chunks that floated away from the opening. Steam rose faintly from the exposed water, and they quickly dipped their buckets in, working quickly before the edges refroze. Water sloshed inside, droplets freezing on their gloves.

Oliver's eyes lit up the instant water flowed into his bucket, his small hands clapping together in excitement. "Water! I caught water."

"Great job," Steve said. "Water is important no matter where you are."

Kurt led them back to the farmhouse.

"My sister's family should be arriving later tonight," Kurt said. "She's got younger kids—Oliver will have someone to play with."

"That's good to hear," Steve said.

"But you'll have to leave before things start getting worse here."

CHAPTER 27

On the monitor, the map refreshed every few seconds, blinking with new data points–each one a possibility, a hope, and then, often, a dead end. Owen's eyes darted town to town near the crash site, scanning camera feeds, and location histories. Sweat beaded on his forehead.

"Where the hell are you, Steve?"

Behind him, Sarah paced, her arms crossed tightly over her chest.

"What about this one?" she asked, her voice strained. She pointed at a blinking red dot on the screen.

Owen shook his head. "That's from a week ago. It's old."

"God damn it," Sarah turned away. She pressed her lips into a thin line and turned away, raking a hand through her hair. "This can't be it," she muttered. "There has to be something–something we're missing."

Suddenly, Sarah's phone rang. The caller ID displayed *Dr. Patrick Crehan.*

"Dr. Crehan," she said, her voice tight. "What a surprise. Why are you calling me at this hour?"

"I hear that you've been let go from the NTSB and I'm sorry about that. Out of respect for the organization, I withheld some information when we met at the crash site."

"Do you have more details?" Sarah's eyes widened.

"Yes," Dr. Crehan said. "We need to meet private. Where are you at?"

"I'm in Atlanta, Georgia."

"All right," Dr. Crehan said. "I'll take the next flight from Ireland and arrive tomorrow or the day after. This is something only you and I can handle without public disclosure until the time is right."

"Understood, Dr. Crehan."

After the call ended, Owen asked, "Who was that?"

"A whistleblower," Sarah said. "Something we can't share with the public yet."

With Lindsay and Emma in the room, Sarah gathered everyone and lowered their voice.

"You can't share any details about this man. I've researched this guy and they say he's a dangerous scientist and a conspiracy theorist who can cause havoc worldwide. But he knows a lot about solar flares and the recent phenomena over the Atlantic and Central Europe.

She paused, scanning the room. "Every governmental aviation agency maxed out their resources during COVID-19 to keep planes flying. Now, they rely on corrupt entities like Celestine Airlines, which hasn't been cooperating with us on this accident."

"What's with Celestine Airlines?" Lindsay inquired.

Sarah nodded, prepared for the question. "Based on private research with my former assistant at the NTSB, Celestine Airlines is based in Finland and operated by a corrupt Middle Eastern billionaire. He's lived in nearly every Middle Eastern country, including Saudi Arabia, Lebanon, Syria, Jordan, Yemen, Qatar, and the UAE. The Iranians despise him because he funds anti-Iranian operations."

She continued, "He fled to Finland, and used offshore oil money to start the airline—essentially a money-laundering front. He targeted

Finland for its proximity to Russia, so oligarchs could use it as a financial channel. A former employee told me the airline was supposed to revive Finland's post-pandemic airline industry. Instead, they're destroying it."

"Ah, I see the connections now," Owen said. "Do you know when he's coming?"

"In a few days," Sarah said. "It has to be in a top-secret location. Otherwise, the US government will find him and imprison him. He has a few rich friends with private jets that could get him here. If people know about him, he's in big trouble."

"This guy seems like the Most Wanted Criminal," Owen said.

Later, Lindsay opened the door. "How was your trip to Tennessee?"

"It went fine," Matt said. "It got cold when we hiked up the mountain. I just hope no one got into trouble while we were gone—and that Steve's finally reached out."

Sarah emerged from Owen's room, leaving Matt and Rachel shocked with eyes wide open.

"Sarah," Matt said, his eyes wide open. "Good to see you again. Any updates on the latest investigation?"

"Hey Matt, Rachel. Nothing on that front. They let me go from the investigation team," Sarah said, her voice steady but edged with frustration.

Matt's expression darkened with irritation and disbelief. "That figures," he said. "Maybe they shut it down since you guys weren't able to find Steve or the second survivor."

The words hit Sarah like a slap. She took a deep breath, steadying herself to maintain her composure. 'We did everything we could, Matt. It wasn't just us–resources were limited, and the leads were almost nonexistent."

Matt rubbed his temples. "Limited resources? Come on Sarah. You guys have been on this investigation for nearly two months now.

In today's day and age, bodies can be found everywhere. How do you expect anyone to keep pushing when there's no progress?"

Sarah stepped closer, her eyes flashing with a mix of anger and hurt. "It's easy for you to say when you're not the one out there for sleepless nights, chasing shadows, hoping for a breakthrough that will never come."

Rachel looked between them, sensing the tension. Matt's jaw was tight, his hands clenched at his sides. Sarah's arms crossed, her foot tapping lightly against the floor. Rachel softly said, "Guys, calm down."

Sarah said, "I've been supporting the investigation as hard as I can. But at some point, you have to accept when something is beyond our control."

Matt's eyes bristled. "Beyond our control? Sarah, Steve is my son! I can't just accept that he's gone without exhausting every possible avenue."

"We have exhausted everything. The Austrian rescue teams have had their budgets cut. The NTSB has also cut funding for further investigations. My Austrian partner, Hans, and my replacement are in charge of wrapping this investigation up, giving their motive, and closing up shop. There's more to this investigation than just a simple plane crash."

"How are you so sure?" Matt said.

"Your other son, Owen, has developed an app to track Steve's whereabouts based on certain metrics and movements. You should be proud of him."

Sarah continued, "I know how much your son means a lot to you, but look at me. I've been away from my own family for months on end. I miss my husband and son. I've missed Thanksgiving, Christmas, and many other important days just to find Steve. It's not easy being an air crash investigator. It takes a toll on your emotional well-being. But I'm working with Owen to find Steve and solve this mystery. It's a big issue right now, and I request that you let us finish it."

Matt stared at her for a long moment, then finally nodded. "Okay, Sarah, do what you need to do." He looked at Owen. "Help her. Give her anything she needs—including the app."

JANUARY 2023

As the holidays passed and a new year began, Steve awoke to the thump of running feet overhead and bursts of laughter. Toys clattered across the floor. Oliver's voice rose in excited German, tangled with the playful shouts and squeals of the other children as they darted around the room.

"Guten Morgen!" Oliver said to Steve, as he rose.

"Man, Oliver, I think by the time we leave, you'll be able to speak German more than English."

"I'm having fun now," Oliver said, bouncing around the room.

Heidi entered and said, "Kurt and his family are leaving. If you want to say goodbye."

Steve threw on a cotton jacket and hurried to the farmhouse's front entrance. He approached Kurt and the two boys. "Thank you so much for showing me around town. I'm hoping that once I earn some money, we'll be able to leave."

Kurt chuckled. "Take your time. I'm sure the Austrian authorities don't have the resources to reach us up here, especially with all the recent budget cuts."

"No problem," he said, glancing at the half-thawed path. "I'm surprised it's gotten this warm so fast."

"It's very strange," Kurt replied, squinting at the shimmering horizon. "I used to blame climate change, but the solar flares... they're rewriting everything. We've had blizzards followed by heatwaves in a single week. It shouldn't feel like April on New Year's Day."

Branches creaked under melting ice. A distant rumble echoed across the valley — not thunder, but something slower, stranger.

"You'll need to prepare before heading to your next stop," Kurt added.

Steve exhaled, watching his breath still curl in the warming air. "Yeah. We'll see how it goes. Oliver needs a little time to just… be a kid before we move on."

CHAPTER 28

After saying goodbye to Kurt and his family, he sat down by the fireplace inside, watching Oliver run around and play with the other children. The sound of laughter filled the air, mingling the soft crackle of firewood. Through the window, he noticed the rapidly melting snow.

I should go out and tend the cows, he thought.

Maria stepped in, "Some of their bells need replacing; the cold could have damaged them."

"Sure, I don't mind," Steve said. "It's strange—just a week ago, the wind was howling, and snow buried everything. Now, the snowbanks are shrinking, muddy patches are peeking through, and icicles are dripping in the sun."

"Solar flares do disrupt the atmosphere," Maria said. "I'm going to church later today. Would you and Oliver like to join me?"

"Sure," Steve said. "Where can I get the bells?"

"In the next town, past the center of Lichtersee," Maria said. "Right by the lake. The shop is called *Schattenwald Kuhglocke*."

Steve gathered his belongings and proceeded toward the front door where Oliver ran up to him and said, "Can I come?"

"Of course," Steve said.

Just then, Simon and Theresa ran up to him and said, "Wir möchten kommen." *We would like to come.*

"They want to come with us as well," Oliver said. "They want to get to know you."

"Who are these two?" Steve asked, smiling.

Maria chuckled. "These two are my youngest grandchildren. Heidi's my oldest son's kid, while Simon and Theresa are my youngest daughter's children."

"That's quite the age gap," Steve said.

"My daughter had them very late," Maria said.

"Ah, I see," Steve said. "Let's go."

Oliver held Simon's hand, both giggling as they leaped over icy patches. Their laughter echoing in the crisp air. Theresa, taller and more confident, skipped ahead, occasionally looking back to make sure everyone was keeping up.

Theresa walked beside Steve, her words tumbling out in rapid German.

"Wie lange bleibst du hier?" she asked. "Und gefällt dir das Wetter hier?" *How long are you staying here? And do you like the weather here?*

Steve blinked—surprised, but he understood her completely.

"Ich bleibe noch zwei Wochen. Und ja, das Wetter ist überraschend angenehm," he replied without thinking. *I'm staying two more weeks. And yes, the weather is surprisingly pleasant.*

He stopped mid-step, surprised at how naturally the words had come.

Theresa paused mid-motion, her eyes narrowing in surprise. "Du sprischst Deutsch?" *You can speak German?* she asked, her tone a mix of curiosity and amusement.

Steve hesitated, his lips parting, but no sound coming. "Ja, ja, ich glaube schon," he said slowly, his voice uncertain even as the words formed perfectly. His own ears felt foreign to him, hearing himself speak the language so naturally.

Steve rubbed the back of his neck, his gaze falling to the floor. "Ich weiß nicht..ich—es ist, als ob ich gerade aufgeacht bin." *I don't know..it's like I just woke up.*

Walking alongside Simon, Oliver overheard Steve's improving language skills. "How did you get so good at German all of a sudden?"

"I don't know," Steve chuckled. "I've learned plenty from you, from Heidi, Maria, Kurt, and the time we spent with the locals over the past few days. Talking with children motivates me to understand and communicate better."

The lake lay to their right, its frozen surface slowly melting. Steve couldn't help but glance at it.

"Look at that bird," Simon said in German, pointing to a lone raven perched on a bare tree by the water's edge. Oliver tilted his head, following Simon's gaze. His eyes lit up, a grin spreading across his face.

Ahead, the outline of the bell shop appeared, its weathered wooden sign, *Schattenwald Kuhglocke,* swaying gently in the breeze. As they neared, the sound of clanging metal grew louder. Steve adjusted his scarf and glanced at Oliver.

"Almost there," Steve said, his voice soft but encouraging. Theresa turned and grinned, her cheeks pink from the cold.

"Warte, bis du die Glocken siehst! Sie sind alle unterschiedlich und sehr laut!" Theresa said. *Wait until you see the bells! They're all different and very loud!*

"Bist du schon einmal hier gewesen?" Steve asked. *Did you come here before?*

"Ja," Theresa said.

The group pushed open the heavy wooden door of the bell shop. A faint jingle welcomed them. Inside, the air was thick with the scene of polished brass and aged woods. Rows upon rows of bells lined the walls, their gleaming surfaces catching the dim light from a wrought-iron chandelier.

Oliver's eyes widened. Simon and Theresa darted ahead, their boots clunking against the uneven stone floor as they pointed out their favorite bells. Steve followed, admiring the craftsmanship.

The shopkeeper, an older man with a thick white mustache, emerged from behind the counter, his face lighting up with a warm, practiced smile.

"Wilkommen!" he said, his voice echoing in the cozy space. "Wie kann ich Ihnen helfen?" *How can I help you?*

Steve unraveled a bell he took from the farmhouse and said, "Diese Glocke wurde durch den Schneetsurm beschädigt. Haben Sie eine änliche wie diese?" *This bell has been damaged due to the snowstorm. Do you have a similar one to this?*

"Moment. Ich schaue mal nach," the shopkeeper said. *Hold on. Let me check.*

Oliver nudged Steve and said, "You're speaking better German than me."

Steve chuckled. "It's necessary. Where are Simon and Theresa?"

"They're around-- not too far from here, probably ringing every bell in sight," Oliver said.

The shopkeeper returned with several bells, moving with practiced ease. He handed Steve a small one, gleaming and light.

"Diese hier," the shopkeeper began, his voice warm and inviting. "Hat einen liechten, klaren Klang. Perfekt für einen sanften Ton." *This one has a light, crisp tone. Perfect for the gentle sound.*

Steve turned the bell over in his hand, admiring the craftsmanship. Oliver leaned closer. The shopkeeper then selected a larger, intricately carved bell adorned with Alpine flower patterns. He struck it lightly with a mallet, filling the room with a deep, resonant tone.

"Für etwas Reicheres," the shopkeeper said, his mustache twitching with a smile. "hat diese Glocke einen zeitlosen Klang." *For something richer, this bell has a timeless sound.*

Steve nodded, but hesitated, his eyes darting around the shop. Noticing this, the shopkeeper raised an eyebrow and motioned toward a display near the window.

"Oder veilleicht," he suggested, lowering his voice, "etwas Traditionelles? Diese Glocken sind denjenigen nachempfundern, die bei unseren Dorffesten verwendt werden." *Perhaps something more traditional? These bells are modeled after the ones used in our festivals.*

He picked up a bell with a worn leather strap, its surface dulled from years of handling, and extended it toward Steve.

"Probieren Sie diese," he encouraged, leaning forward with his eyes shining. *Try this one.*

"Haben Sie noch mehr von dieser Art?" Steve asked hesitantly. *Do you have more like this?*

The shopkeeper grinned. "Natürlich! Einen Moment, iche sehe nach." *Of course! One moment, I'll check.*

A few minutes later, the shopkeeper handed Steve the bell he had been seeking. Steve's eyes widened looking at the bell.

"It looks amazing," Steve said to himself. Turning to the shopkeeper, he said, "Iche nehme zwei davon." *I'll take two of these.*

"Super," the shopkeeper said. He quickly packed the bells and informed Steve. "500 Euro."

Steve reached into his pocket, searching for the money he was given to by Maria.

"Where is the money?" he said to himself. As Steve searched his pockets, the shopkeeper asked, "Sind Sie Amerikaner?" *Are you American?*

"Ja," Steve said.

"Dein Deutsch ist sehr gut," the shopkeeper said. *Your German is very good.*

"Ja. Danke," Steve chuckled. "Ich lerne Sprachen sehr schnell. *Yes. Thank you. I learn languages really quickly.*

Finally, Steve found the five 100 Euro notes Maria had provided and handed them to the shopkeeper. "Hier sind Ihre 500." *Here is your 500.*

With the bells in hand, they made their way back to the farmhouse. The gentle ringing of the bells provided a soothing soundtrack to their journey. After ensuring the children were safely home, Steve headed toward the town center in search of a phone to call home.

Entering a café, he approached one of the servers and asked, "Gibt es hier ein Telefon für internationale Anrufe?" *Is there a phone here for international calls?*

The server said, "Hier entlang am Ende der Straße." *This way, down the street.*

CHAPTER 29

As the somber New Year's Eve celebration ended, Owen walked over and opened the door.

"Jake, what are you doing here?"

"Just wanted to check in, see how the family's holding up. I heard you've created an app to help track Steve," Jake replied.

"We're heading to an undisclosed location in the Chattahoochee-Oconee Forest," Owen said. "But don't tell anyone yet."

"Oh dang," Jake said, grinning. "You're working with top-secret info now? I want in."

Owen shook his head. "No chance, man. It's only for family."

"Wait, what?" Jake said. "I'm your family, man. Steve's like a brother to me, and we've worked our way up to the NCAA."

"Look, I'll let you know when I need you, which isn't right now," Owen said. He quickly tried to close the door, but Jake held it open.

"I'm not leaving unless you tell me what's going on," Jake insisted.

Matt arrived at the door and opened it wide. "Jake, you're more than welcome to join us. We might need a helping hand."

"But Dad," Owen protested, "Sarah only wants immediate family members. The more people involved, the higher the risk of leaks."

"I promise Owen," Jake said. "For the sake of Steve, I'm not revealing anything."

"We've treated Jake like family since he and Steve were kids," Matt said. "Give him a chance. He's been with us throughout."

"Why are you in such a hurry, Owen?" Matt asked.

"I want to hear what this whistleblower has to say about the crash—and all these solar flares," Owen said.

Matt nodded. "Okay, but you need to calm down."

Owen turned to Jake. "I'll give you more info once we return from the site, okay."

Meanwhile, in Lichtersee, Steve trudged through the icy streets, his breath rising in the clouds. The town had grown colder since morning, his breath forming clouds in the frosty air. The telephone center stood at the corner of the square, a humble building with peeling paint and a single bulb above the doorway that flickered faintly in the dim light of late afternoon. *This place looks and feels pretty cozy.*

Pushing the creaky wooden door open, he stepped inside. The warmth hit him immediately, a stark contrast to the biting cold outside. The small room featured a counter at the front and three old-fashioned phone booths lining one wall. A middle-aged woman with glasses perched on her nose glanced up from her knitting behind the counter.

"Grüß Gott," she greeted, her tone neutral but polite.

Steve gave her a small nod, pulling some change from his pocket. "Ein Telefonanruf, bitte," he said hesitantly. *One phone call, please.* She nodded and gestured toward one of the booths.

Sliding into the booth, Steve closed the wooden door behind him. The scent of aged wood and faint tobacco lingered in the air. A black rotary phone sat on the small table before him, its black finish dulled.

Whom should I call first? he wondered aloud. *Owen, Mom, Dad, or Lindsay? Let's try Lindsay first. Do I still remember her number?*

"Six-seven-eight..two..something," he muttered.

The ringing tone filled the silence. Once. Twice. Three times. Steve's grip tightened on the receiver. His heart sank with each unanswered ring, the sound growing louder in his ears.

"Come on, Lindsay... pick up." Through the frosted booth door, he watched the dim street beyond, the snowy silence pressing in. Through the frosted booth door, he watched the dim street beyond, the snowy silence pressed in. "You've reached Lindsay Carson. Please leave a message after the beep."

His shoulders slumped. The weight of disappointment pressing down on him. Say something, he urged himself as the beep sounded. Then, the soft beep prompted him, and he swallowed hard, forcing himself to find the words.

"Lindsay... it's Steve." His voice cracked slightly. "I'm still here. Take care of yourself. I'll be back soon." He hung up.

He tried Owen. Then his parents. Straight to voicemail. He sat still, staring at the black cord, filling the void left by the unanswered calls. Then, with a heavy sigh, he pushed the door open and stepped back into the snowy evening, the cold biting at his feet.

Hold on, it was warm this morning, and now it's dropping. Something's really fishy here. I hope Oliver is safe.

Back in Georgia, as morning turned into afternoon, Sarah gripped the steering wheel tightly, guiding the SUV through the rugged forest trails.

"Come on," Sarah muttered under her breath. Sweat beaded on her forehead despite the heater's efforts against the cold outside.

"How far are we?" Lindsay asked.

Owen replied, checking Sarah's phone. "About three and a half miles to go."

Lindsay sighed. "Feels like we've been driving forever."

"We're almost there," Sarah said gently.

Owen looked back at Emma. "You okay, Emma?"

"It's really bumpy," Emma said, clutching her stomach. "I feel sick."

The SUV rumbled over gravel and dead leaves. Fading light filtered through the canopy, casting flickering shadows across the trail.

As they rounded a curve, Sarah slowed. Two figures stood in the clearing ahead.

Her grip tightened as the trail curved sharply, revealing a darker stretch ahead. Easing off the gas, her gaze flicked between the path and the forest beyond. Then she saw them—two figures at the edge of her vision.

"Dr. Patrick Crehan is just around the corner and looks like he brought someone with him," Sarah said.

"How well do you know him?" Lindsay asked.

"We met once in the Alps at an undisclosed location," Sarah explained. "He provided insider information about the crash."

Lindsay looked out the window. "I believe this is where Steve and I started our Appalachian Trail hike. He proposed to me halfway through."

"Nice," Owen said. "Emma, we should do that someday. Maybe when Steve comes back."

"That's wonderful to hear," Sarah added. "We're close."

The SUV came to a stop, the engine settling into a low rumble as Sarah shifted into park. The headlights cast sharp beams across the clearing, illuminating two men standing nearby: Dr. Patrick Crehan and his associate.

"Dr. Crehan," Sarah said.

"Sarah," he replied, his Irish accent catching Emma and Lindsay's attention. "This is my assistant, Dr. Kazuo Tachikawa."

"Nice to meet you," Dr. Tachikawa said, bowing slightly, his Japanese accent pronounced.

"I didn't realize he was your assistant," Sarah said.

"We met at a research conference in Italy in late 2021," Dr. Crehan explained. "We both agreed that the upcoming solar flares would be massive. The scientific community chastised us, and governments, having exhausted funds on the COVID-19 pandemic, were unprepared. We're concerned these solar flares could be catastrophic."

Dr. Tachikawa said, "We've tried to warn governments but were labeled 'conspiracy theorists.'"

Owen whispered, "I should start a thesis on the solar flare incident."

Emma nudged Lindsay. "You were right. Steve is brave; Owen is smart. They complement each other well."

Dr. Crehan stepped closer. "We've been digging into Celestine Airlines," he said, voice low. "It's worse than we thought—training is practically nonexistent. Another crash is just a matter of time."

Sarah's jaw tightened. "How did it get this bad?"

"Started in 2018. Dr Fahad Bin-Saeed launched it with Russian money—dirty money. The whole thing's a front now. Laundering cash, cutting corners. Pilots were underpaid and barely trained."

She glanced at the photos spread across the table—wreckage, flight logs, pay stubs.

"If this keeps up, families will die," he said. "And I heard the NTSB cut you loose. That means you're finally free to help us fix it."

"You want me to work with you more closely?" Sarah asked.

"Yes," Dr. Crehan said.

"But first, Steve and Oliver are still out there. We should find them first."

"We have three objectives: retrieve Steve and Oliver, expose this corrupt billionaire, and raise the alarm about imminent solar flares. A poorly operated airline won't be the only casualty; the world will be affected."

Owen interjected, "I'll join too. This isn't just about Steve anymore."

Lindsay and Emma nodded. "We're more than happy to help."

Dr. Crehan and Dr. Tachikawa nodded in approval.

The group trudged back to the clearing, their faces a mix of exhaustion and quiet frustration. As they stepped onto the gravel, expressions weary.

Then—a faint chime.

Lindsay froze. Her phone buzzed. The signal bars in the corner of the screen flickered to life, climbing higher with each passing second. Around her, others were doing the same–phones buzzing and vibrating as the notifications flooded in like water reaching a dam.

Her heart lurched when she saw the notification: *Missed Call – Unknown*. A voicemail alert pushed red.

A cold rush of adrenaline coursed through her veins. She stared at the screen for a moment, her thumb hovering over the voicemail icon for a few moments before she clicked it.

"Lindsay…it's Steve."

Her breath hitched, and her eyes welled up with tears. Then, the message cut off abruptly, leaving her staring at the phone, her heart pounding.

Lindsay cried with the group, which watched her with a mix of curiosity and concern.

"Who was it?" Sarah asked.

Lindsay swallowed hard and wiped her tears, her voice barely above a whisper. "Steve."

CHAPTER 30

The next morning, Steve glanced at Oliver. "Did you enjoy the folk music concert last night?"

"Yes, I really enjoyed it. I don't want to leave here."

"I don't want to leave either, but we need money to be able to hightail ourselves out of here. I have to go see my fiancée and you have to meet with your grandparents," Steve said. "Maybe in a few more days or so. I've been hearing weather reports that a solar flare is happening soon."

"Okay," Oliver said.

Steve smiled. "You know, we've spent nearly two months fighting for survival. Let's enjoy these moments. By the way, we're going to go to check out the local church with Maria and Heidi today."

Oliver groaned. "But I don't like churches."

Steve chuckled. "You'll definitely like it. Get dressed."

They left the farmhouse and walked down the hill, and walked through the snow-dusted cobblestone streets of Lichtersee. The church stood at the center of the town, its stone facade weathered but proud, with a spire piercing the sky.

Inside, the warmth of flickering candlelight greeted them, a soft contrast to the cold outside. The air smelled of pine, beeswax, and a faint trace of incense—sacred and still.

Steve looked down at Oliver, who clutched his hand tightly, his wide eyes taking in the vaunted ceilings and the delicate stained-glass windows.

Steve said, "Maria, I go to church back home, but I've never seen anything like this."

Maria gave a small, wry smile, while aligning her glasses. "That's funny."

As the organ's deep, haunting melody filled the church, Steve sat still, the sound pressing into his chest like a slow, steady heartbeat. Beside him, Maria and the others bowed their heads, but he kept his eyes open, staring at the stained glass as if it might speak. The music reached into him, stirring something raw—grief, maybe, or the shape of it.

Maria went up to the front of the congregants and said, "Wir haben Gäste hier, Steve und Oliver. Wenn in den nächsten Tagen etwas Seltsames passiert, sorge dafür, dass sie gut behandelt werden." *We have guests here, Steve and Oliver. As there is a strange event happening in the next couple of days, make sure they are treated well.*

When the service ended, no one rushed to leave. Oliver wandered to the front, his fingers grazing the polished wood of the altar. Steve watched him with a faint smile. *Maybe that's what I need to protect most,* he thought—not just his safety, but that spark, that light.

Steve breathed deeply, letting the calm settle inside him.

After church, Maria asked Steve and Oliver, "Do you want to go see the famous Austrian deer?"

"I want to go see the deer," Oliver said, while nodding. He looked at Simon and Theresa and asked them, "Willst du die Hirsche sehen?" *Do you want to go see the deer?*

"Ja!" Simon said.

Maria then instructed Heidi and Verena. "Mach schon mal Mittagessen. Wir kommen später wieder." *Go ahead and make lunch. We'll be back later.*

"Okay," Heidi said.

The group set out just after church, their breath visible in the crisp morning air. The snow crunched rhythmically under their boots as they made their way through a narrow trail flanked by towering pines. The scent of damp earth and evergreen needles filled the air, mingled with the faint woodsmoke drifting from distant farmhouses. Oliver clung to Steve's hand as he scanned the frost-tipped trees while Simon and Theresa whispered to each other.

Maria led the way, pointing out faint tracks in the snow. "Look here," she said in German, gesturing to hoof prints that crossed the trail. "The deer have been here recently." Her voice was low, almost reverent.

The group climbed a gentle slope, the forest thinning to reveal an open window framed by snow-covered hills. The sun hung low, casting a golden glow over the pristine white field. A small creek wound its way through the clearing, the sound of trickling water breaking the silence. Steve's gaze swept over the landscape, marveling at its untouched beauty.

"Da!" Maria said, pointing ahead. A small herd of deer stood near the creek, their sleek, tawny forms bending almost seamlessly with the surroundings. One lifted its head, ears twitching, its large, dark eyes watching the newcomers.

Oliver gasped. "Steve, look!" he said, tugging on Steve's sleeve. His cheeks flushed from the cold and wonder, and he whispered, "They're so close."

The group stood still. Even Simon, who had been cracking jokes earlier, fell silent as he watched the graceful animals.

Maria placed a gentle hand on Oliver's shoulder. "If we're quiet, they'll stay longer," she said softly. Oliver nodded eagerly as he crouched slightly to get a better view.

The group stood there, savoring the simple beauty of the scene, before the deer, sensing they had been watched long enough, bounded off into the trees. Their departure left the meadow silent once more.

Theresa smiled and looked at Oliver. "Sie bleiben nicht lange, aber genau das macht es doch besonders, oder?" *They don't stay long, but that's what makes it special, right?*

Oliver nodded, still staring at where the deer had disappeared. "That was amazing."

Then, a ripple of light shot across the heavens. Steve felt the air vibrate faintly, a barely audible hum brushing against their ears like a distant whisper. Shadows wavered unnaturally.

Maria gasped, shielding her eyes. "Eine weitere Sonneneruption?" *Another solar flare?*

Oliver, Simon, and Theresa clung onto Steve's leg, their small frames trembling as the light intensified for a brief moment.

Steve's heart thudded. "It's happening again," he said under his breath, eyes scanning the skies for any further sign of the phenomenon. The deer that had been grazing moments before darted into the forest, their white tails disappearing like specters into the shadows.

"Is…ist es gefährlick? Simon asked, his voice shuddering. *Is…is it dangerous?*

"Ja," Steve said.

The Turner and Carson families arrived separately to church in Woodstock, their presence was immediately noticed. Some of the attendees came up to them and said, "I'm sorry about Steve. May god take care of him in heaven!"

Rachel smoothed her black blazer nervously, her eyes darting toward Matt and Owen, who nodded silently and placed a hand on her back, guiding her forward.

The Carsons followed close behind. Lindsay and Emma joined their parents as Sue clung to James' arm, her lips pressed into a thin line.

They sat next to each other in the church. As the pastor took to the stage, his voice was smooth and commanding as he welcomed the congregation.

Lindsay whispered to Owen, "Have you broken the story to them?"

"No, not yet," Owen said. "I want to track Steve first based on the phone number before we can give official confirmation that he's alive."

"I really need to know where that number came from," Lindsay said.

"I'm sure it's from Austria. Where else could he go to? It's treacherous terrain," Owen said. "While we're here at church, Sarah's still working with Dr. Crehan and Dr. Tachikawa. I really want to get back to them."

Matt said, "Keep your voices down. I'm listening to something big."

"Okay, Dad."

After service, the Turners and the Carsons gathered at the Carson's home located west of Interstate 575 in Acworth, Georgia for a quick lunch before Owen received a call.

"Meet me back at your place," Sarah said. "Now that we've got the number, we're going to track that number is and then we'll be able to find Steve's whereabouts."

"Okay," Owen said. He glanced and Lindsay and Emma "We need to go back home. We're going to start tracking that phone number."

"Yeah, let's do it," Lindsay said.

Owen sank into the chair by his desk, the weight of exhaustion settling into his shoulders like a heavy cloak. The soft glow of his laptop screen cast pale light across his face, illuminating the faint lines of stress etched into his features.

"So, what are we doing here?" Sarah asked.

"We're going to use the phone number as a way to find Steve," Owen said, looking at the number in his missed calls. We've spent days, weeks trying to find Steve with no reference point. I don't think any of us can just call a random international number."

"I can," Sarah said. "One of my other phones that I have has unlimited international calling. I'll try to do that while you track Steve."

Lindsay and Emma stood next to Sarah as she called the number in Austria while Owen continued gazing at the screen as he hit Enter.

The screen went still for a moment, and then the app sprang into action. A small, pulsing dot appeared on the map, zooming in on a region marked by thick forests and winding rivers. Owen leaned forward, his heart pounding as the name of a town materialized beside the marker.

"Lichtersee."

The dot blinked steadily, its position anchored in the town's outskirts. Owen clicked on it, pulling up details the app managed to scrape—coordinates, time stamps, a faint signal trail.

"Steve, you're there," he whispered, more to himself than to anyone else.

Owen turned to Sarah, still waiting on the dial to ring on the other end, saying, "We found the town."

Lindsay and Emma rushed to the monitor where Owen said, "We found Steve."

"Lichtersee?" she whispered, her voice cracking.

Owen's shoulders eased slightly, but his brows remained drawn together. "The app traced the number. He's there."

A tear slipped down Lindsay's cheek, followed by another, the release sudden and uncontrollable. The emotions crashed over her in waves—relief, disbelief, and the aching reminder of everything they'd endured.

CHAPTER 31

"Hallo," said Chloe, the phone shop clerk in Lichtersee.

"Hallo," Sarah said. "Sprechen Sie Englisch?" *Do you speak English?*

"Not too great," Chloe said. "But I'll try."

"Great," Sarah said. "We're looking for someone who recently used this number to call us. Do you have any idea where he is?"

"Oh, yes—he was just here two days ago," she said. "Nobody in our town usually calls internationally. I'll let you know where he is."

Lindsay said, "Please tell him I want to see him. I'm his fiancée."

"Okay," Chloe said. They ended the call.

The air in the room seemed to shift as Sarah ended the call, her phone still clutched tightly in her hand. For a moment, no one spoke.

Lindsay let out a choked gasp, her hand flying to her mouth. "He's alive. He's alive."

Emma, who had been sitting silently by the window, stood abruptly, her chair scraping against the floor. She crossed the room in quick strides and wrapped Lindsay in a tight embrace. "He's alive," Emma echoed, her voice breaking as a few tears slipped her cheeks. "He's alive!"

Owen leaned back against the wall, running a hand through his hair, his head tilting toward the ceiling. His usual stoic demeanor cracked, and a faint, relieved laugh escaped him.

"I can't believe it," he murmured, shaking his head. "We've got him. We've actually got him."

Sarah, still gripping through her phone, sank into her nearest chair, her hand pressed to her chest. She closed her eyes for a moment, letting the tension seep out of her body. "It's real," she said softly, more to herself than anyone else. "We didn't lose him."

The room, which had felt so heavy with dread and uncertainty moments ago, now brimmed with cautious relief.

Lindsay pulled back from Emma, her face streaked with tears but lit with a faint smile. She turned to Owen and Sarah, her voice firm despite her trembling lips. "We have to go to him. We have to bring him home."

Sarah said, "I wouldn't be so sure. It's dangerous over there. Reports from Austria indicate that many towns have been shunning outsiders due to the solar flare incidents. We need to get Steve out of there to someplace safe. The question is, where?"

"Steve must've been through those towns a lot, so he would know," Lindsay said.

Owen pondered for a few minutes and realized. "I've got a bad idea."

"What is that?" Lindsay said.

"We'll send him to my grandmother in Switzerland, and we can meet him there."

"Wait, why?" Sarah said. "You looked at the map; Lichtersee is about 140 miles from the Swiss border, and I'm not sure he and Oliver would be able to manage that journey."

"Let me figure something out," Owen said. "First, I need to tell Mom and Dad about all of this. Let's gather together. If we get a call from the same number again, don't hesitate to pick up."

Later that evening, the family had gathered in the living room, the air thick with unspoken tension. The worn sofa and mismatched chairs sagged beneath slouched figures, every posture a portrait of fatigue. Rachel perched on the edge of her seat, fingers worrying a tissue into scraps. Matt leaned against the wall, arms crossed, eyes fixed on the floor as if the pattern in the carpet might offer answers.

Owen and Lindsay stood near the center, rigid and alert, Sarah just beside them. Owen shifted his weight, casting a glance at Lindsay. She gave him a small nod.

Clearing his throat, Owen said, "I need to tell you something. It's about Steve."

Every head turned, their eyes snapping to him. Matt straightened, his arms uncrossing, his brow furrowing deeply.

"What about Steve?" Rachel's hands stilled, the tissue falling to her lap.

Owen swallowed hard, his heart pounding in his chest. "We've found him," he said finally, the words hanging in the air like a fragile thread. "He's alive."

Rachel's gasp shattered the silence. Her hand flew to her mouth. "Alive?" she choked out.

Matt pushed off the wall, his expression shifting from disbelief to something more vulnerable—a hope he'd been too afraid to feel.

"Are you sure, Owen? This isn't a mistake?"

Sarah stepped in. "Yes. This is not a mistake. It's a miracle."

James let out a long breath, his shoulders sagging in relief. Sue clasped her hands together, a smile breaking across her face. "Thank God!"

Owen nodded, his voice steadier now. "It's real. The tracking app I've been working on pinpointed his location. He's in Lichtersee, Austria."

Matt crossed the room in a few strides, then sat beside Rachel, wrapping an arm around her trembling shoulders. His eyes glistened.

Sarah turned to Owen. "But he needs to get to safety. There's still a high risk of a major solar flare happening, and based on my intel, many towns become hostile to outsiders. We're going to get to the bottom of this soon. But, do you know anyone in Austria or Switzerland that Steve can go to quickly?"

Matt paused, his brow furrowing as he stared out the window, the faint hum of conversation fading into the background.

"I've got an idea," Rachel said.

"No, absolutely not," Matt said. "I'm not going to let him stay at my mother's in Switzerland."

"Why not?" Rachel asked. "I thought you forgave her."

"I forgave her, but I'm not interested in talking to her anymore," Matt said.

Sarah's head tilted to one side. "What happened with your mother?"

Matt sighed. "I can't tell you."

Owen stepped in and said, "Dad, I know that you're still upset with Grandma, but she's the only one who can care for Steve. Whatever happened back then—we can deal with it later. If Steve doesn't have the protection soon, he could perish from the solar flare."

"I understand, Owen, but she's not the kind of person you can trust with your life. Your grandfather loved her, but never got anything back in return."

"You know what, Dad, just give me Grandma's number and I can talk to her," Owen said. "I'm not going to let petty hatred get in the way of saving Steve's life. We can deal with everything else later."

Rachel stood up and went into the kitchen and found the slip that contained Matt's mother, Denise' name, and gave it to Owen.

He took out his phone and dialed Denise in Switzerland. After several attempts while putting the phone on speakerphone, Denise picked it up.

"Hello, who is this?" came a refined voice from a Swiss chalet.

"Hello," Owen gasped. "Hello Grandma!"

A sudden silence from Denise' end lurked on the phone.

"It's great to hear from you," Denise sobbed.

"It's Owen, Grandma!" Owen said.

"Owen, how's everyone? I'm really sorry about what happened to Steve. I've been watching the news, and I saw that Steve died. But I didn't know how to call you all," Denise said.

"Steve is still alive, Grandma," Owen said. "He's in Austria in some small town called Lichtersee in the Austrian Alps. I was thinking of sending him to you."

"Oh, goodness gracious," Denise said. "Here, it's not been a kind environment, but I'll send you my address to him."

"Sounds good, Grandma. Will do," Owen said. "Do you want to talk to Dad?"

"Yes," Denise said. Owen passed the phone over to Matt. Matt hesitated, his hand hovering over the phone.

"Do I really have to?" he muttered, his voice low, almost to himself.

"Dad, do it for Steve," Owen said. "I know you don't like to talk to Grandma, but this is important. I think even God would want you to forgive her."

"Hi Mom."

Denise sobbed as she spoke. "Hi honey, how are you doing?"I know it's been years, and I can't pretend time has erased what I did to your father. I'm not asking for forgiveness—not yet. But please know this: I'll protect your son with everything I've got. It's the only way I know how to start making things right."

Matt wiped tears off his face. "Please do. Despite the issues we've had in the past, we have to protect Steve and Oliver."

"I'll do whatever I can," Denise said

CHAPTER 32

The next morning in Austria, snow continued to fall gently. Maria approached Steve and Oliver, who were seated by the fireplace with Simon and Theresa. "I know it's cold, but would you like to go to the spa?"

"Not a bad idea," Steve said. "I need some warmth along with calling my family a second time."

As they passed the telephone shop, Chloe spotted Steve and handed him a slip of paper.

"Hi Chloe," Steve greeted her. "Was ist los?" *What's going on?*

"Deine Familie aus Amerika hat angerufen und sie möchten, dass due sie zurùckrufst," Chloe said. *Your family from America called, and they wanted you to call them back.*

Steve's eyes lit up, and a grin tugged at the corner of his mouth.

"Okay, ich komme zurück und rufe sie an," Steve said. *Okay, I will come back and call them.*

Chloe nodded and went back inside. As they walked towards the spa, Steve's felt a twisted knot in his stomach.

"My family called. Holy shit," Steve said.

"You can finally go back to America," Maria said with a gentle smile.

Upon arriving at the spa, they were greeted by warm mist hanging in the frigid air, illuminated by the soft glow of nearby lanterns.

"Wow, es ist wie Magie!" Theresa said. *Wow, it's like magic!*

"Ja," Steve agreed.

Oliver quickly removed his winter layers and jumped into the warm pool, relaxed in his demeanor.

"Hurry up, Steve!" Oliver said.

Steve smiled as he and the others began peeling off their winter clothing. One by one, they stepped into the inviting water, the heat enveloping them and melting away the cold. Steve sank deeper into the pool, sighing as the tension in his muscles dissolved.

Steve let out a breath, eyes scanning the rippling surface of the pool. "This feels... good," he said slowly, almost surprised by his own words. He leaned back against the edge, his gaze distant. "I didn't think I'd be able to feel like this again. Not yet."

Steve and Oliver watched as Maria taking her layers and keeping a T-shirt and shorts on, before joining them in the warm pool. "I know you said you weren't going to join. But you still went ahead and joined us."

"I may be eighty-three years old," Maria chuckled. "But, I enjoy the spa with my grandchildren. We come here all the time in the winter so they can have some fun."

After a few minutes, Steve and Maria emerged out of the pool while keeping an eye on the children. As they sat down on the benches next to the pool where Maria asked, "You're going to speak with your family then?"

"Yes," Steve said. "I haven't spoken to them since the plane crash. To be honest, I'm still nervous about what they would feel."

"Don't be nervous," Maria said. "Your fiancée would be happy to hear from you. Your parents will be happy that you're alive and safe here in Austria."

Steve exhaled deeply. "I know. I'm not even sure how to explain what's happened. If I want to be honest, I have survivor's guilt. Sure, my whole life was about becoming a top sports executive in the US. Now, I've spent the last two or three months surviving, looking after Oliver, trying to get him back to his grandparents in the UK. It's like I know how to survive in the wilderness but forgot what it's like being a regular person anymore.

"And when I think back to the crash, I've seen so many dead bodies, and looking at Oliver, he lost his parents and his sister. The kid cried a few times, but he seems content now because he's counting on me to be his caretaker. I don't know where to go."

Maria placed her hand on Steve's shoulder. "This is why you need to speak to your family. They can help heal you and help you get over the guilt. You saved Oliver. He's alive because of you. If he had been the only survivor, he wouldn't have made it."

She paused. "Go and tell your parents that you'll be coming back."

CHAPTER 33

Steve's breath fogged the glass door as he stared inside the phone booth. The soft hum of fluorescent lights and the faint buzz of an old radio greeted him as he stepped in.

Chloe approached Steve and said to him in English, "You can call your family."

Steve slowly but surely walked inside and held the receiver tightly to his ear, the cold plastic pressing against his temple. The phone emitted a monotonous ringtone, each tone dragging on longer than the last.

"Hello," Owen finally said. "Hello Steve!"

"Hello, Owen."

"Oh my god," Owen said, placing his hands on his mouth. The family and Sarah gathered behind him. "You're actually alive. I can't believe it."

"It's a miracle that I came out alive. My odds of surviving a crash like this were like what? Less than half a percent? The impact was brutal."

"I know," Owen said. "I'm so glad that you're alive. Do you want to speak to Mom and Dad?"

Steve swallowed hard and tightened his grip on his phone. "Yeah."

"Hello Mom, Dad," Steve said.

Rachel's shoulders sagged as tears of relief spilled down her cheeks. "My boy. You've made it alive. It's a miracle."

"I know, Mom," Steve said, wiping the last of his tears on his face. "I would've been up there in heaven by now. But there's a reason why Oliver and I survived."

"How is Oliver?" Rachel asked. "Is he okay?"

"We didn't just survive the crash. Crossing the Alps had been brutal. But it was the hunger, the flare-scarred skies, and the wary looks from strangers that wore us down. I need to understand this more."

"We've prayed a lot over the past couple of weeks. This is a miracle," Rachel said.

Rachel handed the phone to Matt. "I'm so glad you're okay. Where exactly are you calling from?"

"I'm calling from this town called Lichtersee, located on the foot of the Alps. We've been here the last few weeks resting here. I've improved my German, and grateful that Oliver and I have been shown such kindness.

"I'm not sure when I'll be leaving. I have to take Oliver back to the UK, but our passports were burned in the wreckage. I've started asking around about how to get replacements—or at least some kind of documentation. It's a slow process, but I can't afford to wait too long."

Lindsay grabbed the phone. "Hello? Hello Steve."

Steve's voice cracked. "Lindsay."

There was a pause, and then her voice came back, breathless and full of disbelief. "Steve? Steve! Oh my God, is it really you?"

"It's me," Steve managed, his voice breaking. He pressed his forehead against the cold glass, his heart pounding. "It's really me."

"Steve," her voice wavered. "Where have you been? What happened? I–I thought you were gone. I thought I'd never hear from you again."

"I know," Steve said, his voice thick with guilt. "I'm so sorry, Lindsay. I didn't mean to put you through this. I couldn't reach you. Everything fell apart after the solar flare. The plane crash, the chaos—it was like the world turned upside down. I'm determined to understand the solar flare phenomenon so that more people don't suffer as we did."

"How's Oliver?" Lindsay asked.

"Yeah, he's doing fine. I'm supposed to be taking him back to his grandparents in the UK, in a place called Norwich. But it's a rough out here in Austria."

Lindsay trembled as she glanced at Emma, who was seated beside her. "Steve, I–I don't even know what to say."

"I didn't think I'd make it," Steve admitted, his voice raw. "But I did. And I'm here now."

There was a long silence on the other end before she spoke again. "I've missed you so much."

"I missed you too. Every day I thought about you, Lindsay. I wanted to call, to find some way to let you know I was alive, but…"

"But you're calling now," she said softly. "That's all that matters. Let's chat again later. Owen wants to discuss something with you."

Before Owen took the phone from Lindsay, Sarah grabbed the phone. "Hi Steve, hope you've been well. I'm Sarah, the lead investigator for the crash of Celestine Airlines Flight 24. Thank God you and Oliver made it out alive. The Austrian team tried their best to rescue you, but the terrain is difficult for a large-scale operation."

"Seriously," Steve said. "It's 2023, and there are still problems with launching a wide scale investigation."

"We are truly sorry, Steve, for putting you through absolute hell," Sarah said. "I've been working with your brother, your fiancée, and her sister since I was removed from the NTSB. I've also been collaborating with researchers on the solar flares affecting Central Europe. You and Oliver are among the first casualties of these flares. Once you're safe, I'd like to work with you on this."

"Okay," Steve said. "I'm interested in solving the solar flare crisis—not just because of the crash, but because it's destabilizing Central Europe. Supply lines are breaking down, people are panicking, and if it keeps escalating… well, it won't stay contained for long. Someone has to step up."

Sarah nodded and handed the phone back to Owen, who put on speakerphone. "Yes, Steve, I know it's been more than forty minutes since we started talking, and you're enjoying your time in Austria."

"Of course, I am," Steve chuckled. "This is the Austrian fairytale everyone talks about,"

Owen said, "I need you to go to Grandma's home in Switzerland."

"What? Why?" Steve said. ""I don't have a passport to get there. And you know things are still rough with Grandma—I'm not sure she'd even help if I asked. But I've been thinking… maybe I can get in touch with the consulate or find someone who can help with emergency documents. I don't have it figured out yet, but I have to start somewhere.

Sarah said, "All the US Consulates in Austria are shut down at the moment based on my last intel."

"Trust me on this," Owen said. "I spoke with Grandma, and she really wants to help. Forget about the past. She'll do everything to take care of you with the impending solar flare storms. It's getting really bad out there."

Steve took a deep sigh. "Alright. If you insist. Where is she?"

"It's in this town called Dornthal, located north of Appenzell. Grandma says it's a cozy valley town surrounded by lush meadows, grazing cows, and jagged mountain peaks. We can meet there and take you back home from there."

Lindsay jumped in. "Let me come over there and see you, Steve. It's been so long."

"Of course, sweetheart. I'm really looking forward to that," Steve said.

As Steve left the phone shop, his steps grew lighter. His shoulders eased, and for once, he stood without tension. A quiet smile crossed his face—simple, unforced, real.

He rubbed his hands together briskly, more out of anticipation than the cold, his breath puffing out in visible clouds.

I'll finally get to see my family again so long. Every few steps, he let out a small laugh, shaking his head as if he still couldn't quite believe the call had happened. His pace quickened, feet crunching over the snow-covered ground, leaving behind deep, purposeful prints.

As Steve arrived at the farmhouse, Oliver rushed to him, "I'm so happy here. I want to live here."

Steve chuckled nervously, "Of course you do. But I'll be leaving soon."

"Leaving? Leaving where?" Oliver asked.

"A magical place bigger and better than this," Steve said. "You'll find out."

Steve proceeded to the bedroom, changing into his night pajamas. He sat by the fireplace, hands covering his face, listening to the kids playing.

Maria sat next to him, handing him a cup of hot milk with honey. "How was the call with your family?"

"That was the best feeling I've had in a long time. I can't wait to see them."

"Back in America?" Maria said as Heidi joined the conversation.

"No," Steve said. "My grandmother lives in Switzerland, and I'll be going there soon."

"Why?" Heidi asked. "It's a bit dangerous right now with everything going on."

"I know. But my family wants to see me there, especially my fiancée. After all, it's safer there at the moment. I've saved money from various odd jobs over the past few weeks. I asked someone about bus services to Switzerland. She mentioned going through several towns, with a bus passing through Innsbruck, then Liechtenstein, and into Switzerland."

"But you or Oliver don't have a passport," Heidi said. "You'll be illegally crossing the country."

"Don't worry about that," Steve said.

"It's not that simple," Maria said. "The Swiss border guards are very strict and if you don't have any documents, they can arrest you on the spot and deport you."

Steve pondered for a bit. "I mean I have a grandmother who's been a Swiss citizen for a very long time. She should be able to help me over there."

"The Swiss borders are closing soon," Maria said. "Solar flares are causing Central Europe to shut its borders to prevent more people from coming through. It's getting worse."

Steve nodded, stood up from the sofa, and walked into the bedroom, deep in thought. *What am I even doing?*

No passport, no real plan. Just this vague idea that I'll find someone, somewhere, who can help us get home. And even if I do… then what? Show up at Grandma's doorstep like nothing happened? She probably won't even open the door.

But I can't keep dragging Oliver through all this. He needs stability. A bed that doesn't move. A future.

Maybe the embassy's the first step. Maybe not. But I've got to try something. For his sake, not mine.

After finishing his playtime with Simon and Theresa, Oliver joined him.

Steve knelt in front of Oliver in the cozy corner of the farmhouse living room, the crackling fire casting flickering shadows on the walls. Oliver sat cross-legged on a worn rug, playing with a wooden toy horse Maria had given him, his small fingers tracing the grooves of the handmade figure. Steve placed a hand gently on Oliver's shoulder.

"Oliver," Steve began, his voice low but steady. "We can't stay here forever. In a few days, we're leaving for Switzerland."

Oliver's eyes widened. "No!" he burst out, clutching the toy horse tighter. "I don't want to go! I like it here. Maria, Heidi, Simon, Theresa are nice people, and we built a snowman! And the lake is so cool! Why do we have to leave?"

Steve sighed, sitting back on his heels. "I know, buddy. Lichtersee has been good to us. But it's not our home. We have to keep moving, to find somewhere safe, where we can really start over. Switzerland is… different. It's where we need to be right now. Your grandparents might want to see you there."

"My Nan and Grandad are in Switzerland?"

"I believe so," Steve said.

Oliver shook his head, his lips trembling. "No! What if we get lost again?" What if the bad people find us? I don't want to leave."

Steve exhaled deeply, then reached out, gently taking the toy horse from Oliver's hands. "I know it's scary, Ollie. But we can't let fear stop us from moving forward." He stood, walked to the window, and pointed toward the mountains in the distance, their snow-covered peaks glowing softly under the late afternoon light.

"You see those mountains?" Beyond them is a place where we can be safe, where you won't have to worry about anything. And I promise I'll be with you every step of the way. Just like I've been here since we crashed several hundred miles away."

Oliver frowned but didn't respond, his small hands gripping his knees tightly. Steve knelt back down, taking Oliver's hand in his. "Tell you what," he said with a smile. "Before we leave, we'll do something special. We'll go to the lake one last time and say goodbye to everything and everyone. And I'll even let you be the boss on our first day in Switzerland. Deal?"

Oliver hesitated, his bottom lip quivering. "I get to be the boss?"

Steve nodded, giving him a playful wink. "You call the shots. First meal, first place we visit–you decide."

A small, reluctant smile crept onto Oliver's face, though his eyes were still glassy with unshed tears. "Okay," he whispered, his voice barely audible. "But only I get to be the boss."

Steve grinned, ruffling Oliver's hair. "Deal, little man. You're the boss."

CHAPTER 34

The front door creaked open. Inside, a suitcase lay half-zipped on the floor, clothes spilling out. An open passport rested on the coffee table. Matt stepped in first, scanning the room. "Looks like Lindsay is about to leave."

Lindsay stood near the hallway, her back to them, stuffing a fleece jacket into her bag with quick, purposeful movements.

"You're here," she said, her voice steady but her eyes betraying a flicker of guilt. "I was just finishing up."

Rachel's gaze swept the room before landing on the packed bags. "You're leaving," she said softly, more a statement than a question.

"I have to," Lindsay replied, zipping the bag closed with a final tug. "I need to be there for Steve when he gets to Switzerland."

Matt frowned, his hands stuffed into his pockets. "And you weren't going to tell us?"

Lindsay turned to face them fully. Her hands resting on the duffel bag. "I was," she said, her voice quieter now. "I just…didn't want to argue. This is something I have to do. I haven't seen Steve for months and he needs me there."

Owen stepped closer, his brows furrowed. "You're going to Switzerland, alone?"

Lindsay nodded, her chin lifting slightly. "I've already booked the flight to Zurich. I called your grandmother, and she said she's more than happy to look after me. The sooner I leave, the sooner I can bring him back."

The room fell into a heavy silence, the weight of the situation settling over them like a thick fog.

"Are you sure you're going to be okay, Lindsay?" James asked.

"Dad, I know it's hard, but I have to be there for Steve," Lindsay said. "I'm sorry."

She wrapped her arms tightly around Rachel, whispering a tearful, "Be safe," into her ear.

"I'll bring Steve home," Lindsay promised.

She climbed onto Sarah's SUV. As they drove through the misty dawn, the headlights cutting through the muted gray as they neared Atlanta's bustling airport. The SUV hummed steadily, a stark contrast to the heavy silence that filled the house.

At the departure's terminal, Sarah pulled to the curb, the Delta Airlines sign looming above them in bold red letters. She stepped out first, retrieving Lindsay's suitcase from the trunk, her movements brisk and purposeful.

Lindsay followed, adjusting the strap of her bag over her shoulder as she glanced toward the entrance. "This is it," she said softly, her voice carrying a mix of determination and trepidation. "I'll finally be seeing Steve, and I look forward to it."

Sarah placed a steadying hand on her shoulder. "You've got this," she said firmly, her eyes searching Lindsay's face. "Just get to Switzerland and bring him home. I'll start talking with him once he arrives."

"Warum, Oliver," Theresa said. "Warum verlasst ihr uns." *Why Oliver? Why are you leaving us?*

Steve said, "Ich muss Oliver nach Hause nach Großbritannien bringen. Seine Familie braught ihn." *I have to take Oliver home to the UK. His family needs him.*

"Wir sind seine Familie," Theresa insisted. *We are his family.*

Steve's breath caught. He glanced at Oliver, whose eyes shimmered with unspoken emotion. For a moment, the world outside the little Austrian farmhouse seemed to fade away.

Steve swallowed hard, his throat tightening. He hadn't expected such a declaration, and it stuck him somewhere deep, where his resolve to leave wavered.

"Ich.." Steve rubbed the back of his neck, his usual composure crumbling under the weight of her words.

Oliver, still clutching Steve's arm, leaned into him and whispered. "Do we really have to go, Steve?" His tone nearly undid Steve entirely.

Maria turned to Theresa, her voice gentle but firm. "Theresa, es ist hier nicht mehr sicher. Es gibt zu viele Risiken." *Theresa, it's no longer safe here. There are too many risks.*

She then turned to Steve. "Look Steve, I really wished you could stay longer and have Oliver continue to play with the children. But, you're more than welcome to come back anytime."

Steve nodded, and both Steve and Oliver turned to Theresa and Simon. No words passed between them, but the connection was unmistakable—something quiet and deep forged in their time together in Lichtersee.

After finishing their breakfast of semmeln and croissants with cheese and cold cuts, Steve and Oliver grabbed their bags and stood at the front door. Tears welled in Theresa and Simon's eyes as the weight of goodbye settled in—they couldn't shake the fear that this might be the last time they saw Steve. Heidi placed her hands on the two children. "Es ist nicht das Ende. Es ist der Anfang." *It's not the end. It's the beginning.*

Maria handed Steve and Oliver a bag consisting of different home-cooked meals, including Wiener Schnitzel and Gulasch.

"I'm sure by the time you make it to Switzerland, the food will all be eaten. But it should be enough for you guys to survive," Maria said.

"Thank you, Maria," Steve said. "I'm sure we'll see each other soon. I really want to bring my fiancée here," Steve said.

"She's more than welcome to stay," Maria said.

With that, Steve and Oliver turned and left the farmhouse, making their way through Lichtersee.

As they passed the center of town, the crisp air of Lichtersee grew sharper with each passing hour, the mild chill of the day gave way to an icy stillness as evening approached. Steve and Oliver walked past the lake, which now shimmered with the first signs of ice forming at its edges.

"Where are we going?" Oliver asked.

"We're heading to the town of Struzenwald where we'll catch a bus to Innsbruck. Tomorrow, we'll take another bus to Zurich. From there, we'll proceed to Dornthal, where my grandmother lives."

But a strange tension hung in the air. The clear skies began to shift, turning a sharp, unnatural hue. The sun's rays intensified, burning brighter and harsher.

"Steve," Oliver said, shielding his eyes, his voice tinged with unease. "What's happening?"

Steve squinted upward. The glare was nearly blinding. "It's another flare. Come on—get off the road!"

He grabbed Oliver's arm and holding onto the bags, Steve pulled him toward a cluster of trees. The temperature spiked unnaturally as the solar flare unleashed its energy, an eerie hum filing the air. Static crackled around them, and Steve could feel the hair on his arms rise.

"Stay down," he ordered, crouching low behind the largest tree trunk they could find. He tossed his jacket over Oliver's head to shield him as the flare peaked. A strange, shimmering wave rippled across the horizon, lighting up the sky like a curtain of fire.

The flare subsided as suddenly as it had come, leaving an eerie silence in its wake. Steve cautiously peered out, his heart pounding. "It's over."

As they entered the outskirts of a small town, something felt off. A woman in a wool shawl yanked her child inside, bolting the door with trembling hands. Across the street, an old man peered through a lace curtain, his eyes narrow with suspicion. A teenage boy on a bike paused just long enough to spit in the street before pedaling off without a word.

"Why are they looking at us like that?" Oliver whispered, sticking close to Steve.

Steve's jaw tightened. He caught snatches of conversation as they passed—words like "outsiders", "danger', and "flare-bringers".

A man stepped into their path, his eyes hard and accusing. "Fremde sind nicht wilkommen," he spat. *Strangers are not welcome.*

"Wir wollen keinen Ärger. Wir fahren nach Struzelwald" Steve said. *We don't want any trouble. We are going to Struzenwald.*

"Sie sprechen Deutsch? Wunderbar," the man said. *You speak German? Amazing.* He patted Steve and Oliver on their shoulders and departed.

Steve thought to himself. *Is that all it takes to be respected by the locals? Knowing German?*

"Let's keep moving," Steve said, steering Oliver away, his voice low and tense.

As they hurried out of town, the sun set behind them. The warmth of Lichtersee felt like a distant memory, and Steve couldn't help but wonder how many more places they would be forced to flee before they found safety.

CHAPTER 35

Steve and Oliver arrived at the Struzenwald bus station, where a lone bus idled at the edge of the snowy lot, its engine humming softly in the crisp morning air. Steve held Oliver's hand tightly as they approached, their breath visible in the cold. The vehicle looked worn, its green paint chipped and faded—a step closer to safety.

Oliver hesitated at the bottom step, scanning the rows of frost-covered windows. Steve squeezed his hand reassuringly. "It's going to be fine. Come on, buddy."

The driver, a gruff man with a thick scarf wrapped around his neck, nodded as Steve handed over the fare.

"Innsbruck, ja?" he asked in German.

"Zwei Tickets von Innsbruck," Steve said, glancing down at Oliver, who clung to his side. *Two tickets to Innsbruck.*

They climbed aboard. The warm air inside hit them like a wave, tinged with the scent of worn leather and stale cigarettes lingered in the air. A few passengers looked up briefly, their expressions indifferent, before turning back to their own thoughts.

Steve led Oliver toward a pair of seats near the middle. He lifted Oliver onto the window seat, brushing snow off his own jacket before settling beside him. Oliver pressed his small hand against the fogged-up glass, tracing shapes absently as the town of Struzenwald stretched out in the distance.

"Do you think they'll have snow in Switzerland too?" Oliver asked softly, his voice almost lost in the steady hum of the engine.

"Maybe," Steve said, managing a smile. "I'm hoping it will be warmer there."

The bus jolted slightly as the driver shut doors with a mechanical hiss. Moments later, it pulled away, tires crunching over the icy road. Oliver turned to watch the town fade into the background, his face a mix of curiosity and sadness.

Steve leaned back, his body heavy with exhaustion, but his mind racing. He glanced at Oliver, "Can you believe that we're finally riding a vehicle after all those months of walking in the Alps?"

"I'm so tired. I want to go home," Oliver said, his voice yawning. They both closed their eyes and napped.

A few hours later, as the bus pulled into the bustling heart of Innsbruck, Steve felt a wave of relief wash over him. Buildings with pastels lined the streets, their windows glowing warmly against the pale winter light. The muffled hum of life–a blend of voices, footsteps, and distant laughter–reached their ears even through the frosted glass of the bus.

Oliver leaned forward in his seat, his wide eyes scanning the scene. "There are so many people," he whispered.

"There are," Steve said, relaxing as he took in the lively streets. "It's a large city."

When the bus came to a halt, they stepped out into the crisp air with their bags, their boots crunching against the snow-dusted pavement. Innsbruck seemed alive—groups of people bustled past, some carrying shopping bags, others laughing and chatting, their breaths visible in the cold. A group of children ran by, their scarves trailing behind them while an elderly couple huddled close, their steps slow but steady.

Steve inhaled deeply. The scent of roasted chestnuts and fresh bread drifted from a nearby street vendor.

"Doesn't feel as lonely here, does it?" Steve said, his voice light but tinged with emotion.

Oliver shook his head, a small smile spreading across his face. "No, it doesn't."

Steve looked at the timings for the next bus to Zurich. "It's 12:30 pm. Looks like we got two hours. Want to go check out the town?"

"Yes."

The plane touched down smoothly on the tarmac in Zurich, Switzerland, and Lindsay felt a mix of relief and anticipation as the announcement echoed through the cabin: "Welcome to Zurich."

She collected her belongings with steady hands, though her heart raced as she made her way through the bustling airport, weaving through travelers who spoke in a medley of languages.

Near the arrivals gate, Denise, with silver-streaked hair, stood holding a small sign that read, "Lindsay." She was poised, her expression warm but reserved, dressed in a tailored that spoke of understated wealth. When their eyes met, Denise's face softened, and she stepped forward, extending her hand before pulling Lindsay into a firm embrace.

"You must be exhausted," Denise said, her English tinged with a slight Swiss accent. "Let's get you to Dornthal. It's a bit of a drive, but the countryside is beautiful."

"Of course. Thank you."

"I'm looking forward to hearing more of your story about your relationship with Steve and how you got engaged."

Denise helped carry Lindsay's large check-in suitcase and hopped inside a Volkswagen. They departed Zurich Airport where the car ride was quiet at first, the landscape outside shifting from the bustling cityscape of Zurich to the serene, snow-dusted hills of the Swiss countryside. Lindsay watched the world blur by, her thoughts racing as Denise navigated the winding roads with practiced ease.

Denise broke her silence, her voice gentle. "I know this has been overwhelming for you. But I want you to know, Steve will soon be relieved to see you. You've done a brave thing, coming all this way. I can imagine how it must feel for him to show up and finally see you."

"I don't know, Denise," Lindsay said. "I'm kinda nervous about everything. These past few months have been some of the worst in my entire life, and dealing with the pain of uncertainty has taken a toll on me and everyone else. It really hurt when I first heard Steve was dead, a quiet relief when he was alive, and I was finally at peace when I spoke with him on the phone."

As they entered Dornthal, the picturesque village unfolded before them—quaint cottages with sloping roofs, cobblestone streets, and the faint glow of lanterns in the evening mist. Denise's home stood at the edge of the village, a charming chalet with wooden beams and flower boxes.

Denise parked the car and turned to Lindsay, her eyes kind but perceptive. "Come inside. You'll want to rest right now before you see him. There's much to prepare for."

Lindsay stepped into the cottage, the warmth enveloping her instantly as the scent of pinewood and vanilla filled the air. The wooden beams overhead were polished to a soft sheen, their natural grain glowing in the light of the crackling fireplace at the far end of the room. A thick, woven rug muffled her footsteps as she took a hesitant step forward, her eyes scanning the cozy space.

She noticed the walls adorned with framed photographs of famous Europeans and delicate tapestries, each telling a story of a life steeped in tradition and family. A small table by the window held a vase of fresh Alpine flowers, their bright colors standing out against the soft, earthy tones of the room.

Denise moved gracefully past her, hanging her coat on a brass hook by the door. "Welcome," she said softly, gesturing toward the sitting area. "Make yourself at home, dear."

Lindsay nodded, placing her suitcase down carefully near the entrance. Her hands lingered on the handle for a, then brushed the back of the plush armchair as she tried to steady herself.

The sound of the fire popping and the faint tick of a grandfather clock in the corner filled the quiet. "This place is beautiful," Lindsay said. Denise smiled, handing Lindsay a cup of hot chocolate.

"This looks really good," Lindsay said.

"It's made with some of the finest Swiss chocolates," Denise said. "You're going to really love it?"

Denise took a seat. "This home was bought by my late second husband in the 1970s. This was a historic cottage inhabited by some of the most prominent people who built Dornthal here. But, he passed away in the late '70s, and I just tended to this house ever since."

"Interesting," Lindsay said. "Steve never told me about all this. That you were living here in Switzerland."

"Well, this is where I have my fair share of regrets," Denise said.

"What do you mean?"

"What I mean to say is that I regret leaving Matt's father, Steve and Owen's grandfather, Hunter Turner." Denise said. "I was a young girl model from New York City back in the early 60s. Hunter was a struggling computer salesman, originally from Tennessee, who had moved to Atlanta. We met at a convention there, and he showed me around in his old 1955 Ford Fairlane. Atlanta was a different city back then. He was deeply religious; his father was a pastor. I came from a family of financiers, and we only went to church once in a blue moon. We fell in love and got married, much to our families' dismay.

"Hunter made some money to buy a small home in the northwest corner of Atlanta. But because he struggled so much in selling computers, I took on multiple modeling jobs to help make ends meet. One day in the '70s, a Swiss businessman named Wolf attended one of the modeling shows. He promised me the world and took me away from Hunter. The fights between Hunter and me began and escalated due to his struggles at his job, and because of that, I left him and joined Wolf.

"Hunter managed to win the custody battle for Matt and his siblings, and as a result, they never saw me or forgave me for what happened. It just so happened that when I left them, Hunter's business started taking off, and it was too late for me to come back to him. In return, the only thing I was given was this cottage, and he died suddenly in the late '70s."

"How do you feel about all of this?" Lindsay asked.

"Great shame," Denise broke down. "Great shame in everything from leaving Hunter, my kids, and I got left with a cottage and couldn't return to see my family in the States. All I can say is that God helped me stay relatively sane."

Wiping away tears, Denise continued, "Hunter was a great father who raised the kids well in my absence, even if he lost faith in love, which explains why he passed away the moment our last child got married. I'm happy that Matt and Rachel stayed close and together throughout all of this and raised Steve and Owen to be good people, and now Steve is engaged to you."

Lindsay smiled, feeling Denise's warmth.

"Never leave Steve," Denise said. "I see the good characteristics that were passed on to him by Matt and Hunter, and that's what kept him alive through this crash, the solar flares. I know Steve can be quirky, but I want you to stand by him. As someone who made a lot of mistakes, I'm giving you words of wisdom, which is the least I can do."

Lindsay nodded. "I will."

CHAPTER 36

The bus stopped at a border checkpoint just beyond the snow-covered mountains. Outside the window, Steve witnessed the bold red and white Swiss flag fluttering in the crisp Alpine breeze. Oliver's face lit up. "That flag looks so cool."

"Do you think so?" Steve said.

His stomach tightened as a group of Swiss immigration officials approached the bus, their dark coats buttoned to their chains.

Passengers murmured to one another as one officer climbed aboard, his leather boots echoing down the narrow aisle.

"Passportkontrolle, bitte," the officer announced, his voice carrying through the bus. His boots thudded heavily on the narrow aisle as he methodically moved from passenger to passenger, collecting passports and inspecting each one with a stern, practiced eye.

Steve swallowed hard. He gripped his empty pocket, where his passport should've been, but wasn't. A lump settled in his throat as he whispered to Oliver. "Stay calm, okay? We'll figure this out."

Oliver blinked at him, his face pale. "We don't have our passports, Steve."

"I know. Just trust me," Steve said softly.

The officer approached their row, his sharp gaze falling on Steve and then Oliver. "Pässe, bitte," he said, holding out a gloved hand.

Steve hesitated for half a second before meeting his eyes. "I'm sorry, officer," he said in a steady voice. "We don't have our passports with us."

The officer's brows drew together, his hand retracting. "Keine Pässe?" he repeated, his tone growing colder. A hush seemed to fall over the bus as heads turned toward them.

"No," Steve said. "They…they were lost."

The officer straightened, his posture rigid. "You're traveling without identification? That's not permitted," he replied curtly, switching to English for emphasis. "Please—both of you, we need you to leave this bus."

Oliver's hand shot up, grabbing Steve's sleeve in alarm. "Steve?"

"It's okay, kid." Steve stood and pulled Oliver to his feet. Every pair of eyes on the bus followed them as they shuffled to the front, the officer leading them down the icy metal steps.

The cold outside was biting, their breath fogging the air as Steve tightened his grip on Oliver's hand. A second officer joined them by a small, glass-windowed checkpoint booth. The two men spoke quickly in German, their voices low but firm.

"What do we do?" Oliver whispered, his teeth chattering.

Steve crouched beside him, shielding him from the wind. "We stay calm. I'll explain everything."

The first officer turned back, his brow furrowed. "Where are you traveling from?"

"Austria," Steve said. "From Lichtersee. We're trying to reach Zurich."

"And you have no documentation?" the second officer asked, his tone skeptical.

Steve shook his head. "We lost everything during a plane crash. I'm an American, and this is Oliver. He's British. I can give you names, addresses, anything you need to verify who we are. We're not here to cause trouble. We just need help."

The officers exchanged a glance. One of them muttered something under his breath before responding sharply. "No passports, no entry. That is the law."

Oliver's lip quivered, his voice breaking. "Please, we don't have anywhere else to go."

The man's expression faltered slightly as he looked at Oliver, but he held firm.

"Wait here," he said, motioning them toward a small, heated waiting area next to the checkpoint.

Steve led Oliver into the heated room, its door closing behind them with a dull thud. The room was sparse—just a few chairs and a buzzing fluorescent light overhead. But it was warm. Oliver sat down, wrapping his arms tightly around himself.

Steve dropped into the chair beside him, rubbing his face with both hands. "We'll get through this, kid."

"What if they don't let us in?" Oliver asked, his voice small.

Steve looked at him, determination hardening his gaze. "Then I'll find another way."

Minutes dragged by like hours. Through the window, Steve watched the officers on their radios, gesturing and their expressions unreadable. He exhaled sharply and offered a silent prayer.

At last, the door creaked open. The first officer stepped inside, looking stern but not unkind.

"We've contacted the authorities," he said. "You will be held here while we verify your identities. Do not leave this area."

Steve nodded, his shoulders sagging slightly in relief. "Thank you."

The officer turned, leaving them alone again. Steve leaned back in his chair, exhaustion pulling at him, but he gave Oliver a small smile. "See? It's not over yet."

The officer returned with two more uninformed guards, their boots clicking sharply against the icy pavement as they approached. Steve's heart sank when he saw the stern expressions on their faces.

"Sir," the first officer said flatly, "we cannot allow you to proceed without proper identification. You will need to come with us."

"What do you mean?" Steve's voice rose slightly as he stepped protectively against Oliver. "We told you—we lost everything. We're not criminals."

"This is procedure," the officer replied firmly, his tone brooking no argument. "You are being detained until your identities are verified."

Oliver gripped Steve's coat tightly, his eyes wide with fear. "Steve… what's happening?"

"It's okay, Oliver," Steve said quickly, his voice low and soothing. "It's just a misunderstanding."

"Follow us," one of the guards ordered, motioning toward a nearby building—a low, gray building with barred windows at its corners. The sheer sight of it sent a chill through Steve, far colder than the wind biting at its face.

They were led inside, Steve keeping one arm around Oliver, guiding him down a narrow hallway that smelled faintly of disinfectant and metal. Pale fluorescent lights buzzed overhead, casting a pale glow over the scuffed floors. The walls felt too close, like they were being funneled into something they wouldn't be allowed to leave.

He kept his expression steady, but inside, his thoughts were anything but calm. *Don't let go. Whatever happens, don't let go of him. Stay calm. He's watching you. If you panic, he will too.*

The guards stopped in front of a small, bare room with two metal chairs and a table bolted to the ground. "You'll wait here," the officer said, holding the door open. "Someone will come speak with you shortly."

Steve hesitated. "Is this really necessary?" Look at the kid. He's six years old, for god's sake."

The officer's gaze softened just slightly, but he shook his head. "This is the law."

Steve tightened his jaw, then nodded, stepping inside with Oliver. The door shut with a heavy metallic thud behind them.

The room was colder than Steve expected, its concrete walls amplifying the silence. A single bulb hung from the ceiling, emitting a weak light. Steve guided Oliver to one of the chairs and crouched beside him.

"I don't like this place," Oliver whispered, his voice trembling. He tugged at the helm of Steve's coat.

"Me neither," Steve admitted, running a hand through his disheveled hair. "But we'll be okay. They just need to figure out who we are. Once they do, we'll be out of here."

Minutes turned into hours, the silence broken only by the muffled sound of footsteps echoing in the hallway outside. Steve paced the room to keep warm, his mind racing. Every scenario played out in his head. *What if they couldn't verify his identity? What if they are stuck here indefinitely?"*

A different officer stepped inside, carrying a clipboard. "Mr. Turner," he said, his English clipped, but clear. "We have contacted your embassy. They are verifying your information. Do you want to make a phone call to someone?"

"Yes," Steve said. "Need to call my grandmother, who is here in Switzerland in the town of Dornthal."

Steve departed the room, telling Oliver, "I'll be right back. Just a few minutes." He told the officer, "Please look after the boy."

Another officer arrived and escorted Steve to the phone booth. He inhaled shakily and dialed Denise's number. As the phone rang, Steve's hand tightened around the receiver.

The line clicked. A voice came through, fragile but unmistakably clear. "Hello?"

"Grandma?" Steve's voice cracked, his composure nearly breaking into two syllables.

There was a pause on the other end. "Steve? Is that you?" Denise's voice held surprise, concern, and a hint of disbelief.

"Yeah…it's me," he stuttered. "I-I need your help. We've just got into Switzerland. We're at a detention center just at the border of

Switzerland and Austria, in this town called Grenzhausen. They stopped us and we don't have our passports due to losing them in the crash."

He rubbed a hand over his tired face, feeling the weight of the words sink in. "I need you to come. Please. I—I don't know who else to call."

Denise was silent for a moment, the kind of silence that made Steve's chest tighten. "Are you okay, dear? I heard there was a child with you—Oliver. Is he okay?"

"Yes, Grandma, he's okay," Steve said. "He went through a lot and just wants to get back home to his grandparents. His parents and sister have died in the crash. Can you come…can you talk to them?"

"Of course, Steve. Of course, I'll come," Denise said firmly, the gentle resolve in her voice like a balm on his frayed nerves. "Tell me where to find you, and I'll be there as soon as I can."

Steve exhaled deeply, the tension in his shoulders just easing a little. "Thank you, Grandma. Thank you…" His voice trailed off, thick with gratitude.

"We'll figure this out," Denise said softly. You're not alone, Steve. I'm coming. I've got a special surprise for you."

"What is it?" Steve asked.

"You'll see for yourself," Denise said.

CHAPTER 37

For several hours, Steve and Oliver sat quietly, watching officers bustle past their belongings piled near the door.

"How long will your grandmother take?" Oliver asked.

"She said a few hours," Steve said. "I borrowed a phone to check—Dornthal is about an hour or two from here. She mentioned she has a surprise."

The hum of fluorescent lights grew louder in the silence. Oliver dozed off, his head on Steve's shoulder, unaware of the turmoil within the man beside him.

Then the door creaked open.

Steve looked up, his breath catching. For a moment, he froze, questioning if she was real. But then she stepped in, brunette hair cascading over her shoulders.

"Lindsay," Steve gasped, his eyes wide opened, struggling to catch his breath.

"Steve!" Lindsay cried.

Steve stood carefully, not disturbing Oliver, and approached her. With tears welling in her eyes, Lindsay rushed forward, embracing him tightly. Steve held her close, burying his face in her should. Both teared up, sobbing in each other's arms.

"I thought. I thought you were gone," Lindsay said, her voice trembling.

"I'm here," Steve choked out, his throat raw. "I'm here. I survived so much just to see you—a plane crash, solar flares across Central Europe, the wilderness, isolated towns, and now border patrol. If none of that could keep us apart, nothing will. It's a statistical anomaly that I made it alive."

Behind them, Denise stood by the door, her worried face softening into a grateful smile.

Lindsay pulled back slightly, her hands cupping his face. Tears rimmed her eyes, but she smiled as she scanned him, reassuring herself he was whole. "You look like hell."

Steve chuckled–a weak, relieved sound that felt foreign after so long. "You should see the other guy."

Lindsay's eyes shifted to Oliver, still sleeping soundly on the bench. Her expression softened further, and she reached over, gently brushing a lock of hair from the boy's forehead. "This is him?"

Steve nodded, his voice hushed. "Oliver. He's been..everything."

"He's really cute," Lindsay said.

"I've set out on this journey just to take him home to his grandparents in the UK. I've made a promise with his father that he will be returned home safe no matter what. He's everything I could imagine a son to be."

"I know. You took great care of him bringing all the way this far," Lindsay said. "I met his grandparents during the search and rescue operation. They were overjoyed to hear both of you alive."

"Really?"

Denise approached, placing a comforting hand on Steve's shoulder. "Let's get you two and Oliver out of here. You've been through enough."

"Not yet, Grandma," Steve said. "They need to give me permission to leave first. We're scheduled for an immigration court case next week.

Oliver and I entered the country illegally; this isn't part of the Schengen Zone. That's what they told me."

The door opened quietly, and an immigration officer stepped in, his black boots tapping sharply against the tile. He held a stack of official-looking papers, edges slightly crumpled.

"Herr Turner," the officer addressed Steve, his Swiss accent thick but clear. "You and the boy are scheduled to appear in immigration court next week. And wherever you're staying, you aren't permitted to leave the town of Dornthal until the court case is complete."

"Yes, officer," Steve said. Oliver curled up on the bench beside him, sensing the shift in the room's atmosphere. The office approached the small table and set the documents down with a deliberate thud.

"You need to be present here," he tapped the top sheet with a firm finger, his gaze flicking between Steve and Oliver. "Do not miss this date–understand? It is important."

Steve nodded slowly, though his mind raced with uncertainty.

Denise told him in German, "Er bleibt bei mir in Dornthal. Ich bin seine Großmutter." *He'll stay with me in Dornthal. I'm his grandmother.* The officer nodded and departed.

Steve glanced at Denise with Oliver standing next to him. "Well Grandma, you're not the only one who can speak German. Oliver can, and I improved mine while we were in Austria."

"That's amazing. I'm proud of you," Denise said. "Let's go home. You and Oliver must be really exhausted from everything."

"Yes Grandma," Steve said, his voice gentler. "I'm holding onto the thought of having even a little time with you and Lindsay before the trial..before we have to let Oliver go."

"That sounds good," Lindsay said.

As they stepped out of the detention center, a car arrived at the front steps of the detention center. Several familiar faces have emerged from the car.

"Sarah, what are you doing here?" Lindsay said. "You came all the way here to see me and Steve?"

Behind Sarah, walking in with solemn, determined steps, were Barry and Mary Lynds–Oliver's grandparents.

Oliver, standing quietly beside Steve, gasped as his head whipped up. "Nana? Grandpa?" His voice was soft, uncertain, as if he wasn't sure whether to believe his own eyes.

Mary let out a trembling sob, her hand flying up to her mouth. "Oh Oliver!" she choked out, before rushing toward him, her arms outstretched.

Oliver broke away from Steve's side and threw himself into her embrace. "Nana!" he cried, burying his face into her shoulder as her arms wrapped around him, holding him as if she would never let go. Barry rested a steady hand on Oliver's back, his eyes glistening with unshed tears.

"There you are, son," Barry murmured, his voice low and gravelly. "You're safe now. You're home."

Oliver clung to them, his shoulders shaking. Mary pressed a kiss to his temple, her tears streaking her cheeks as she held her grandson tightly. "We missed you so much. I'm so sorry Mummy, Daddy, and Amy aren't with us."

Lindsay and Steve stood together, watching them.

"I guess we don't have to send him back to the UK. We can go back home once this trial is over," Steve said.

Barry and Mary, holding Oliver in her arms, walked up to Steve. Barry embraced him.

"Thank you," he said, voice rough. "Thank you for taking care of Oliver and bringing him back. I know it took a lot in you to be able to do it. And now, we're so grateful for you."

"Of course. It's sad that I couldn't bring back the rest of the family."

"Well, it's a tragedy. We cried over it for days," Barry said. "You're welcome to come visit us in Norwich anytime."

Steve shook Barry's hand and said. "Yeah, Lindsay and I are happy to visit. Your grandson taught me a lot and made me realize that I'm so ready to be a father myself."

Oliver stared at Steve and gave him a smile. "You saved my life. You taught me how to fish, how to build houses, fight against bad people and the solar flares."

Mary said to Steve, "He's more than happy for you to be an influence in his life."

"Well," Steve said.

Sarah said, "We have to go now. Some people are there waiting for you in Dornthal. Since Oliver is a child, he'll be returning home with his grandparents right now and won't have to face any trial."

"Wait, what?" Steve asked. "Didn't the officer just say that he has to appear at the trial?"

"One of our folks has helped convince the authorities to clear Oliver since he's a child, but you'll have to stand trial," Sarah explained.

Mary said, "Oliver, let's go home."

"Steve isn't coming with us?" Oliver asked.

"I'm afraid not, honey," Mary said. "Steve has to take care of some things."

"No," Oliver cried. "I want to be with Steve." He clung onto Steve, sobbing.

Steve knelt and gently placed his hands on Oliver's shoulders. "Ollie," he began softly, "I promise I'll come and see you. Right now, things are a bit tough here, and it's not safe for you. But as soon as everything settles down, Lindsay and I will come visit you. I promise."

"Are you sure?" Oliver said, wiping out his final tear.

"Yes. I promise. If I don't come before your seventh birthday, you will never see me ever again."

Steve said, "Promise him I'll do everything I can to come to Norwich."

Barry extended his hand, gripping Steve's firmly. "You're always welcome, Steve. You're now family to us."

As the car pulled away, Steve watched, his heart heavy yet hopeful, knowing this was just a temporary farewell, remembering the memories he had with Oliver.

CHAPTER 38

The car rolled to a gentle stop in front of Denise's home, where smoke curled lazily from the stone chimney, and warm light spilled from the windows, casting golden patches onto the snow-covered ground. Steve stepped out, his breath catching in his chest as he looked around.

He looked around the town, feeling the serenity of Dornthal, which clashed against the chaos he'd endured throughout his long journey of hunger, starvation, and survival.

Instinctively, Steve glanced toward the tree line, half-expecting someone to emerge—hostile and accusing—as they had in so many of the towns before. He shoved his hands deep into his coat pockets.

Lindsay walked up beside him, slipping her arms around his waist. "Now, this is something I've missed the past three months. "

Steve nodded. "But, I wished we could've spent the holidays together. But we made it to Switzerland and to my grandmother's. I believe Owen must've told you the whole history about Grandma Denise."

"Yeah, he did," Lindsay said. "She regrets what happened every day. Bringing the family back together is the one thing she wants to do before well, before she leaves this earth."

"She is eighty-four years old after all, just like Maria, who I stayed with in Lichtersee."

"That's her name?" Lindsay said. "Amazing."

As they reached the steps, Denise opened the door, her face lighting up with joy. "Welcome home."

Steve nodded. He stepped into the cozy warmth of the house, the scent of fresh bread and lavender drifted over him. A crackling fire beckoned from the hearth.

"This is incredible, Grandma," Steve said. "I can't imagine a better place."

He dropped his luggage next to the kitchen and sank into the plush sofa, its cushions enveloping him. He stretched his legs out, letting them rest against the worn fabric of the ottoman, and leaned back, his head sinking into the cushion.

For the first time in what felt like forever, his body began to relax.

The soft creak of the wooden floorboards pulled Steve away from his thoughts. He glanced up as Lindsay approached, carrying a tray with two mugs of hot chocolate, steam curling lazily upward, and a small plate of biscuits balanced in her hand.

"I figured you might need this." She placed the tray down on the coffee table and picked up one of the mugs, offering it to him. "Careful, it's hot."

"Thanks," he said, his voice low, almost rough from exhaustion. He watched as she settled into the armchair opposite him, tucking her legs beneath her.

For a moment, they sat in comfortable silence, sipping their drinks, letting the warmth of the fire fill the space between them.

"Where's Grandma?" Steve asked.

"She's making dinner," Lindsay said. "She's making something special for you."

Lindsay continued, her tone casual but probing. "So, what have you been up to since…everything?"

Steve let out a low laugh, shaking his head. "Where do I even start? It's been one hell of a ride. The solar flares, the plane crash, the constant need for survival—finding food and shelter, improving my German out of necessity, taking care of Oliver, ensuring his safety, facing hostility in small Austrian towns because of the solar flare incidents, almost losing Oliver until we ended up in Lichtersee. And now, we're sitting here reunited in Switzerland, of all places. I've missed Oliver sleeping on my shoulders."

"You really miss the kid," Lindsay said.

Steve released a deep breath. "He reminded me of my cousin Henry who used to fall on my shoulders and never couldn't leave me. He's a pure little innocent child who just wanted to play with his family and life dealt him a bad hand, removing him from his family."

"Yeah, I know. He was a cute child. We'll definitely try to see him."

"And now, I feel I've failed Oliver. He must hate me now."

Lindsay leaned forward, her voice firm and kind. "You didn't fail him, Steve. You brought him through all of that. You fought for him, protected him, gave him the love he needed during such a traumatic time. No child could survive a crash and make it through all that without someone like you. He'll remember you for the rest of his life. Trust me, I work with children every day at the hospital. Oliver will come around."

Steve looked at Lindsay, his eyes softening. "Thanks. Hearing you say that…it helps."

She smiled, fiddling with the edge of her mug. "You've always been stronger than you give credit for. I know that better than anyone."

"I missed this–talking with you. It feels like I haven't had a real conversation in forever."

"Well, I'm here now. And I'm not going anywhere."

"Let's go check out this town later today if you want," Steve said. "I can't go far."

Denise emerged out of the kitchen and said, "There's a music event happening in the center of town."

"Are you sure it's safe?" Steve asked.

"You'll be fine, honey," Denise said. "People here in Dornthal are very kind and don't hold the solar flares against you, and we've gotten our fair share here. We're a wealthier town which has seen people from all over Europe and it's known for its hospitality."

"I still need to figure things out," Steve said. "I believe Sarah wanted to talk to me or something, right?"

"She said she's coming over here in an hour with two VIPs," Lindsay said. "That's what she texted me."

The doorbell rang, and Denise immediately opened the front door. Sarah stepped in, followed by Dr. Kazuo Tachikawa and Dr. Patrick Crehan.

"Steve!" she called.

Behind her, Dr. Tachikawa ducked his head to fit through the doorframe, his broad shoulders bearing a large rucksack. His usual composed demeanor was softened by a faint grin.

"Great to meet you," Dr. Tachikawa said with a heavy Japanese accent, shaking Steve's hand. "My name is Dr. Kazuo Tachikawa and I'm from Japan."

Following Dr. Tachikawa, Dr. Patrick Crehan shook Steve's hand. "Dr. Patrick Crehan from Ireland. Nice to meet you, Steve."

"Nice to meet both of you," Steve said. "Turning to Sarah, he asked, "So Sarah, why did you need them here?"

"You'll find out," Dr. Crehan said.

Dr. Tachikawa sat across from Steve, notebook in hand—its pages filled with equations and notes. Dr. Crehan leaned on the coffee table, his usual laid-back demeanor replaced by a serious expression that put Steve on edge.

Steve exhaled slowly, trying to keep his voice steady.

"All right, you've been dancing around this since you got here. What's going on? Why did you track me and come all this way?"

Dr. Tachikawa adjusted his glasses, his face impassive but his tone deliberate. "Steve, the solar flares we've experienced over the past few months aren't isolated incidents. We're seeing a pattern that suggests the sun's activity is escalating far beyond what anyone initially predicted."

Steve frowned. "Escalating? How much worse are we talking?"

Dr. Crehan exchanged a quick glance with Dr. Tachikawa. "A lot worse. The last flare disrupted power grids, knocked out communication systems, and caused widespread panic. But the one we're tracking now— the next one—has the potential to be catastrophic on a global scale. It might take a year or two to finally manifest. It's not just a disruption; it could collapse the infrastructure that's barely holding together right now."

Steve ran a hand through his hair. "And what exactly do you expect me to do about it? I'm not a scientist."

Dr. Tachikawa's voice softened, but it carried weight. "You're not a scientist, but you've survived out there, Steve. You've adapted in ways most people haven't had to. We need someone who understands what's happening on the ground, someone who can help us figure out how to prepare people for what's coming."

Dr. Crehan nodded, his Irish accent more pronounced as his frustration bubbled to the surface. "This isn't just about data and predictions. We've got people out there who won't make it unless we start thinking practically about how to protect them, how to organize resources. You've seen the chaos firsthand. That experience is invaluable."

Steve's gaze flickered between the two men. "You're telling me you came all the way to Switzerland because I've been running around dodging the worst of this mess?"

Dr. Tachikawa shook his head. "We came here because you're resourceful, because you've been able to keep yourself and Oliver alive. That tells us you're someone who can help lead others through this."

Steve stood abruptly, pacing to the window. Outside, snow fell softly, blanketing the small town in a deceptive calm. He pressed his hand against the cold glass, his thoughts swirling in his head. "You think I can lead? I've barely kept my head above water. I'm not some hero in all of this. I'm just trying to survive."

Dr. Crehan's voice cut through the room, firm but not unkind. "Survival is exactly why we need you, Steve. You've already done what so many others haven't. And if we don't act now–if we don't get ahead of this–there won't be anything left to survive for."

Steve turned back to them, his expression conflicted, jaw tight.

"You think I can lead? I've barely kept my head above water." His voice cracked slightly. "I'm not some hero. I'm just trying to survive."

His chest tightened as the weight of it all settled in — the uncertainty of the case, the fragile stability he'd clawed together. One misstep, and it could all fall apart.

He glanced down, hands clenching at his sides. "So, what's the plan? You want me to what — help you brainstorm solutions? Rally people?" He let out a short, humorless laugh. "I don't even know where to start."

Dr. Tachikawa flipped to a page filled with diagrams. "We're building a model to predict and mitigate the worst flare impacts. We need someone to test those theories—see what works in the real world. And we need someone who communities will trust."

Steve stared at the notebook, the symbols and equations blurring together in his mind. "This feels too big. Too impossible."

"It is big, Steve," Dr. Crehan said. "But it's not impossible. You're not alone in this. You've got us, and you've got people who believe in you. We're not asking you to fix everything. Just help us make a start."

Steve sighed, sinking back into the armchair as he rubbed his temples. "I don't know if I can do what you're asking. But if it means giving Oliver a chance at a better future... I'll try."

CHAPTER 39

With Dr. Tachikawa and Dr. Crehan stepping out, Sarah zipped her jacket and turned to Steve. "Regarding your immigration court hearing, it's not just a standard proceeding. It's going to be a hearing about the crash, your firsthand account, and there will be cameras present. The NTSB has coordinated with the Swiss Immigration Authority to conduct your trial in this manner."

"Why?" Steve asked, with Lindsay rubbing his shoulder. "Why complicate things? I just need legal permission to leave the country."

""It's not that simple," Sarah said. "The immigration authorities would have sent you home by now, but there's a reason they've allowed you to stay in Dornthal with your grandmother. As Dr. Crehan and Dr. Tachikawa mentioned, you're the voice of the crash and have direct experience surviving solar flares—the only adult survivor. Oliver is still too young to provide such accounts."

"Look, Steve," Sarah continued, "you've been through a lot, and you're the only one who can give a full testimony about what really happened. There were no other survivors from that crash. Once you present your case, you'll be on a flight back home to Atlanta from Zurich. I'll see you in court."

Turning to Lindsay, Sarah said, "Take good care of him. He's going to need it."

"Of course," Lindsay said, squeezing Steve's arm.

After Sarah left, Denise emerged from the kitchen, asking, "What's all this about? Why do you have to appear in court?"

"I'm not entirely sure, Grandma," Steve said. "It seems I'm being recruited for something now that I'm the only adult survivor of that crash. It feels like I'm being used for something."

He glanced at the old grandfather clock near the kitchen. Steve said, "It's already 5:00 p.m.? Time has flown by. Is there anything happening in Dornthal?"

"There's a local gathering of yodelers happening near the town," Denise said. "They keep the community spirit alive. Maybe it's something you and Lindsay can enjoy, and you can explore the town more. It's a perfect opportunity for both of you to catch up on what you've missed these past few months."

"Sounds good, Grandma," Steve replied.

Denise embraced Steve tightly, tears welling up. "I want you to know, I'm truly sorry about everything."

"Grandma, don't worry," Steve said. "At least you brought me home, and that's what matters. We'll have a reunion soon. Whatever happened in the past stays in the past."

The clear evening air carried the hauntingly beautiful echoes of yodeling, reverberating off the snow-dusted peaks surrounding Dornthal. In the village square, locals gathered around a roaring bonfire, their voices rising and falling. Lanterns strung between wooden poles cast a golden glow, illuminating the cheerful faces of villagers bundled in thick coats and scarves.

Steve and Lindsay stood at the edge of the gathering, steaming mugs of mulled wine warming their hands. The rich, spiced aroma mingled with the scent of pinewood burning in the fire, creating an atmosphere that felt both festive and intimate. Steve couldn't help but glance at Lindsay, the soft light of the flames reflecting in her eyes.

"This is incredible," Steve said, his voice almost drowned out by the yodelers' chorus. "I never thought I'd experience something like this."

Lindsay turned to him with a gentle smile, her cheeks flushed—not just from the cold. "This is magical, isn't it?"

Steve nodded, his gaze lingering on her. "Yeah. Magical."

The song transitioned to a livelier tune, and some villagers began clapping along. Steve rubbed the back of his neck. "I don't think I've seen a community this connected in a long time. It makes you realize how much we've lost touch with things that really matter."

Lindsay sipped her mulled wine thoughtfully. "Maybe that's why I admire places like Switzerland. They remind you of the simplicity of it all—family, tradition, and being present in the moment."

Steve edged closer to her, his voice softening. "Speaking of being present... I've been meaning to say thank you. For everything. For being here when I needed you most."

Lindsay tilted her head, her expression tender. "You don't have to thank me, Steve. That's what we do for the people we care about."

Steve glanced down at his boots for a moment, gathering his thoughts, then looked back at her. "I didn't realize how much I've missed this. Us."

Lindsay's eyes searched his. "I've missed it too. More than I can express."

Steve hesitated, then reached for her free hand, his fingers brushing against hers before fully intertwining. "I know I've been a mess lately, and there's still a lot to figure out. But... being here with you, like this— it feels like I've found something I didn't even know I'd lost."

Lindsay squeezed his hand, her gaze steady and full of unspoken emotion. "We've both been through a lot, Steve. But maybe... maybe this is our chance to start over. To find something better together."

CHAPTER 40

As they walked back toward Denise's house, the faint echoes of the yodeling gathering still lingered in their ears, a memory they would cherish. Steve held Lindsay's hand as they climbed the steps to the porch.

"Where's the key?" Steve asked.

Lindsay pulled the key and handed to Steve. As he unlocked the door, the familiar creak of the hinges greeted them as they stepped into the entryway. He could already imagine Denise bustling about the kitchen, ready to welcome them home.

As they shrugged off their coats and stepped into the living room, Steve froze mid-step.

Sitting around the hearth, illuminated by the flickering firelight, were his parents, Matt and Rachel, his younger brother, Owen, and Lindsay's sister, Emma, all of them smiling warmly.

"Surprise!" his mother said, rising from her seat and crossing the room toward him, her arms outstretched. Steve blinked, momentarily too stunned to move, and his mouth open.

"Mom? Dad? Owen?" "What…What are you all doing here?"

His mother wrapped him in a tight hug, sobbing her embrace as comforting as it had always been. "Your grandmother called us," she said, pulling back to cup his face in her hands. "We couldn't wait any longer to see you."

His father stepped forward next and embraced him. "It's good to see you, son. I never thought I'd see you alive."

"It's great to see you all," Steve said. "Here I am. I've done everything to keep myself alive through all of this."

Owen darted forward, wrapping him in a bear hug that nearly knocked him off balance. "Steve! Man, you've been through a lot. It's so good to see you."

"Owen, buddy, I've made it alive. It's good to see you as well," Steve said. "Lindsay told me that you've built an app that tracked my whereabouts."

"Well, I did," Owen said. "That was most of my spare time when I wasn't studying for classes."

Emma walked over to hug Steve. "I've figured out that you'd need some backup too." She winked.

Steve looked at Lindsay, whose face mirrored the surprise and emotions.

Denise appeared in the doorway, her hands clasped and her expression warm. "I thought you could use a little reunion," she said softly. "You've been through enough. It's time you had your family close."

Steve turned back to his parents, overwhelmed by the sight of them.

"Thank you," he said. "I..I didn't realize how much I needed this."

They gathered around the fireplace, familiar voices filling the space like music. Steve sat beside Lindsay, their hands brushing.

"So," he said. "What brought you guys here?"

"What were you thinking?" Rachel said. "And Sarah told me that you were going to be testifying for a trial in Zurich."

"Well, I got detained by the Swiss authorities," Steve said. "Sarah told me that this is going to be not just an immigration trial, but also the trial of the crash of Celestine Airlines Flight 24."

Denise said, "She's going to be here tomorrow to give you briefings on how to present yourself at the trial."

"Shouldn't I be getting a lawyer or something?"

"I'm not sure. You'll have to ask Sarah tomorrow," Denise said.

Within a few minutes, the family gathered at the dining room, which was filled with a warm, savory aroma of melted cheese fondue pot bubbling gently in the center of the table. Denise placed platters of freshly baked bread, tender potatoes, crisp vegetables, and slices of cured meat, inviting everyone to dig in. The rich aroma of melted Gruyère and Emmental filled the air, blending with the faint woodsy scent from the nearby fireplace.

Steve sat close to Lindsay as he speared a chunk of bread and swirled it in the creamy cheese.

"Once again, it's so good that everyone's here," Steve said. "Where's James and Sue?"

"Well," Emma said, "Dad got stuck with legal stuff again, and Mom's not feeling well enough to travel. But look around — your parents, your grandmother, your fiancée, your brother — we're all here for you. That's what matters."

Lindsay said, "I hope Oliver is safe with his grandparents."

"Oliver is doing fine now," Steve said. "His grandparents will take good care of him. But, I really miss our time together."

"I've been thinking," Lindsay said softly. "We should make sure he knows he's part of our family, too."

Steve looked at her, puzzled. "What do you mean?"

"I mean…" She hesitated, searching for the right words. "Not just visits or birthdays. I'm talking about being there for him — really there. Like unofficial guardians, or something even more."

Steve frowned. "But his grandparents are already raising him. They're doing a good job."

"They are," Lindsay agreed. "But that's exactly why we should step in, too. Not to take over — just so he knows he has more people who love him, who are in his corner for life."

Lindsay continued, "What if they die tomorrow? Who will take care of him? The last time I checked, he has no close knit family over there. I saw them in Salzburg. Barry and Mary are not in contact with their second son, and Sophie's family... they're out of the picture. Who will look after him? The only people who even bothered to show up at the crash site were Barry and Mary."

Rachel said, "You took good care of Oliver when he was with you. You connected with him in a way no one else did. Barry and Mary might not be able to keep up with Oliver due to their age. You have to be there for him."

"Your Mom's right," Matt said. "We'll be there for you in every step. We prayed about it and it's the best thing you can do."

Then, a blinding flash of light filled the room, overpowering the soft glow of the candles and fireplace. The hum of conversation ceased as the windows rattled violently, and a deep vibration resonated through the walls.

"What was that?" Lindsay gasped, her fork clattering onto her plate.

Steve was already on his feet. A sharp, crackling sound erupted outside, followed by a brief but defeaning silence. Then came the distant but unmistakable hum of electronics failing–lights flickered, the faint whir of appliances faded, and the dining room plunged into an uneasy quiet, illuminated only by the flickering light of the fireplace.

"Everyone, get down!" Steve shouted, his voice commanded but laced with urgency.

Lindsay grabbed Steve's arm, pulling him down just as another tremor rattled the room, sending a stack of dishes toppling to the floor. Emma grabbed Owen's arm as they ducked underneath the table.

The fire in the hearth sputtered briefly before dimming. The air felt charged, almost electric, and the faint sound of crackling static could be heard somewhere outside.

"What's happening?" Rachel whimpered as she turned to Matt.

"It's okay, sweetheart," Matt said. He turned to Denise and said, "Mom, are you okay?"

"I'm fine," Denise said.

Moments stretched into what felt like hours as the family huddled together, the room quiet except for their shallow breaths and the occasional groan of the structure as it settled under the stress.

Finally, the oppressive charge in the air seemed to ease, and the trembling subsided. The flickering fire in the hearth steadied, casting dancing shadows across the room?"

"Is it over?" Lindsay asked softly.

Steve nodded, though he kept his gaze trained on the windows. "For now. I've seen this happen far too many times in Austria with Oliver. At least he's safe now."

The family began to emerge from their hiding spots, their movements cautious. Plates lay scattered on the floor, bread rolls under the table, and the once-welcoming pot of fondue sat abandoned in the center of the table, the cheese cooled and untouched.

"Is everyone okay?" Steve yelled. He turned to Matt and Rachel. "Mom, Dad, are you okay?"

"Yes honey," Rachel said. "We're fine. Now I understand how your plane crashed in the mountains."

CHAPTER 41

The next morning, when Steve opened the front door, he was surprised to see Sarah, accompanied by Dr. Tachikawa, Dr. Crehan, and the Mayor of Dornthal, Klaus Bärnhofer.

"Good morning Steve," Sarah said. "I hope you're all alright after the solar flare last night."

"Yeah," Steve replied. "That was one for the ages."

Dr. Tachikawa held out a sheet of paper filled with readings. "This one was unprecedented. I'm relieved the town wasn't shut down. It's becoming critical. We truly need your first-hand account on this."

Dr. Crehan turned to Owen. "Could you assist in developing an app? Your tracking application has been invaluable."

Owen rushed to join the group and said, "Really? My app was that helpful?"

"Helpful?" Sarah said. "Contractors are bidding to acquire your tracking application. It was instrumental in locating Steve, and many of our current tools and technologies for finding missing persons are outdated."

Owen froze, a sudden jolt surging through his chest. "Thank you, Sarah. It's an honor to have my app recognized, especially just before graduation."

Steve raised an eyebrow at Owen. "Speaking of college, shouldn't you be attending classes at Georgia Tech instead of being here in Switzerland?"

"I'm taking a break," Owen said. "Building that app has taught me more than my classes ever could."

A short while later, the chalet's cozy living room had turned into a makeshift war room. Firelight flickered across tense faces as maps and notes covered the coffee table. A whiteboard, propped against the bookshelf, was already crowded with scribbled bullet points. Around it all, voices murmured strategies, each one edged with urgency and exhaustion.

Sarah said, "I'd like to introduce Mayor Klaus Bärnhofer. He's here to brief you on the upcoming trial and help navigate Swiss court procedures."

"Pleasure to meet you, Mr. Mayor," Steve said, as Lindsay joined him, adjusting her sleeves.

Klaus, in a deep Swiss accent, replied, "Steve, your survival story has made headlines throughout Dornthal and across Switzerland."

"Really?" Steve asked. "Then how did I go unrecognized at the yodeling concert yesterday?"

Mayor Klaus chuckled. "They were too drunk to notice"

"So," Steve continued, "What's on the agenda for today?"

"You'll need to testify about both the crash and your immigration status. The two cases are interconnected. The judge must see you not as an outsider, but as someone who survived under extraordinary circumstances."

Dr. Crehan adjusted his glasses, flipping through a stack of documents. "For the immigration case, we'll focus on the humanitarian aspect. You brought Oliver here to save his life and acted selflessly. That kind of selflessness speaks volumes."

Dr. Tachikawa added calmly, "As for the crash, we'll need your detailed account—what happened before, during, and after. Your testimony could offer vital insights into how the solar flare disrupted navigation systems."

Steve rubbed his temples, overwhelmed. "What exactly should I say? It feels like…too much. Like no matter how much I explain, they won't understand."

Sarah leaned forward, determined. "Steve, they'll understand because you'll make them understand. This isn't just about you or Oliver. It's about showing the world what happens when people aren't prepared for the unexpected. Convincing them could lead to real change—better systems, more support, fewer victims."

The mayor nodded. "Sarah's right. And you won't be alone. We've prepared statements, evidence, and character witnesses. Denise and others have agreed to testify on your behalf. The community you've touched will speak for you, even if language is a barrier."

Steve took a deep breath, looking at the papers, diagrams of solar activity, and bullet points outlining his journey. "I'm not sure I can do this. What if I mess up? What if I make things worse?"

Lindsay gently squeezed his shoulder. "You've faced worse, Steve. You survived a plane crash, protected Oliver, and navigated all this with sheer determination. This is just one more fight. And you're not alone."

The room was silent for a moment, the crackling of the fire filling the air. Dr. Tachikawa stepped forward and said, "You're stronger than you think, Steve. Remember, this isn't just about the past. It's about the future–for you, for Oliver, and for others who might face similar challenges."

Steve nodded, a flicker of resolve in his eyes. "Alright. Let's do this. Tell me everything I need to know."

The group exchanged determined looks, and Mayor Klaus uncapped a marker, turning to the whiteboard.

"Let's start from the beginning–how the solar flare disrupted your flight."

Hours passed as the team prepared Steve, anticipating questions and rehearsing answers. The fire burned low, but the room's intensity remained.

I have to be ready. Steve glanced around the room, the quiet determination in their eyes steadying him. *They're counting on me. No turning back now.*

As the meeting wrapped up, Sarah caught Steve's eye and offered a reassuring smile. "You've got this, Steve. We're all in your corner."

Steve exhaled deeply, standing up and stretching. "Let's hope the judge sees it that way. But why are they doing both an immigration trial and a trial of the plane crash at the same time?"

"This is the trial of all trials in Switzerland. They all want to hear from you after knowing that you've survived the plane crash. Your story will be broadcasted all over."

Steve sat at the table, staring blankly at the scattered papers and notes. His shoulders were hunched, hands gripping the edges of the chair. His mind churned with questions that refused to quiet.

What if I say the wrong thing? What if the truth isn't enough? Doubts twisted through him like vines.

Was there something I missed? Should I have done more? The weight of everything—the trial, the crash, Oliver's safety, and this role he never asked for—pressed down on his chest. *They're all looking to me. God, what if I fail him again?*

Lindsay stood by the doorway, watching him with quiet concern. She walked forward, her footsteps soft on the wooden floor. "Steve," she said, her voice cutting through the storm in his head.

He didn't look up, just shook his head. "I can't do this, Lindsay. It's too much. I'm just...overwhelmed." His voice cracked, betraying the weariness he tried to hide.

She crouched down to meet his eyes, her gaze steady and calm. "Let's step away for a bit. You need a break."

"I don't have time for a break," he said, his tone edged with frustration and despair.

"You don't have time *not* to," she countered firmly, squeezing his shoulder. "Come on. Let's take a walk. Just you and me. No courts, no questions, no plans."

For a long moment, he hesitated. But then he sighed, letting the tension ease just slightly from his grip. "Alright," he whispered, pushing himself up.

❧

Stepping into the cool streets of Dornthal, the air bit gently at their clothes, but the snow-dusted village's quiet offered immediate calm.

They walked side by side through the narrow cobblestone streets, their breath visible in the cold. Shops were shuttered, and the hum of conversation from a nearby café drifted faintly through the air.

Steve buried his hands in his coat pockets, walking in silence. Lindsay stayed close, her arm grazing his—a quiet reassurance that didn't ask for words.

After a while, she broke the silence. "You know," she began, her voice gentle, "I've never had more fun in a place like this. The air is cleaner here, the streets are pristine. The only downside is that it's expensive."

'Yeah, I know," Steve said. "The crash was a blessing in disguise. Breathing Alpine air is something else compared to back home. I'd love to buy a chalet here when I become rich. Well, Owen might be a millionaire someday, with that app being purchased."

"That's not what I meant," Lindsay said. "You've got the whole family behind you in this case. Why are you so tense?"

Steve released a deep sigh. "To be honest, I've changed completely since the crash. Yes, it was difficult to navigate the solar flares and taking care of Oliver. But this is the happiest I've ever been. I'm twenty-five, but I've realized that chasing status isn't for me. I want to chase meaning. The architecture in here in Austria and Switzerland is amazing. I don't think I'd be willing to go back to the US after experiencing this level of peace."

"I've been thinking the same thing since being here," Lindsay said. "If I had to retire someplace, it would definitely be here. Anyway, you're not alone in this trial. The worst outcome is that you'll be sent back home—that's it."

"I'll miss this place a lot. That's what's been bothering me. I've never been treated this well," Steve said. "But I'm not sure what I'd do without you."

"You don't have to think about that," she replied with a small smile. "Because I'm not going anywhere."

They walked on, the soft crunch of snow beneath their boots the only sound for a while. The cool air seemed to clear Steve's head little by little. Lindsay led him toward a small bridge overlooking the frozen river, its surface glinting faintly in the moonlight.

"Sometimes," she said, leaning against the railing, "all you need is a little perspective."

CHAPTER 42

The courtroom in Zurich was a stark, imposing space. High ceilings arched over rows of wooden benches, and the air inside carried a heavy solemnity that silenced even the faintest whisperers. Steve stood near the entrance with Lindsay by his side, his fingers nervously twisting the strap of his watch. Denise, Matt, Rachel, and Owen stood behind them, their presence a comforting anchor in the sea of tension.

As they approached the front of the room, where a panel of officials sat behind a long, gleaming table, Steve's heart thudded in his chest. The Swiss flag stood tall in the corner, flanking the national emblem engraved on the wall. The sheer formality of the space pressed in on him.

"Why does this feel like the Nuremberg Trials?" Steve whispered to Lindsay as everyone took their seats.

"Mr. Stephen A Turner," announced the presiding judge, Gustav, his deep voice and heavy Swiss accent cutting cleanly through the air. "You are here today to address two matters—your status within Swiss jurisdiction and your involvement in the investigation of the plane crash tied to the solar flare events as a victim of the crash."

Steve's chest tightened. Lindsay reached over, giving his hand a reassuring squeeze.

The courtroom stiffened as the government's representative stepped forward. "Mr. Turner entered the country without clearance, under highly irregular conditions," he said, scanning the room. "There was no passport record, no customs log—only a radio call and a helicopter."

Denise, seated behind Steve, felt a surge of determination. Matt turned to her, "Mom, what are you doing? They didn't allow witnesses yet."

"It's time I fight for this family," Denise said. She stood and proceeded in front of the judges. "I'm Steve Turner's grandmother," she stated clearly. "I'm fully prepared to provide him with a stable and supportive home during the resolution of his legal matters."

Denise sat up straighter, her voice steady.

"Our family, especially Steve's parents, has always believed in standing by each other," Denise said, her tone imbued with sincerity. "In these challenging circumstances, it's imperative that we remain together, providing the necessary support to navigate the complexities ahead."

The judge listened intently, occasionally nodding as Denise spoke. Her testimony highlighted not only the humanitarian aspect of the case but also underscored the cultural and moral significance of familial support.

As she concluded her testimony, Denise's gaze briefly met Steve's offering a reassuring smile. The courtroom nodded in agreement.

The judge, after a moment of contemplation, addressed Denise, "Thank you, Ms. Turner, for your testimony. Your commitment to family unity is fully noted and will be considered in our deliberations."

Denise returned to her seat, her heart pounding yet filled with hope.

After Denise stepped down, a border agent briefly took the stand, recounting Steve's arrival at the Zurich checkpoint. Then Lea, his lawyer, stood to address the court. "We're not contesting the facts," she said evenly, "but the context surrounding his entry must be understood."

Denise sat upright in the witness chair, hands clasped tightly in her lap. Her voice trembled at first but grew steadier with each word. "Steve didn't abandon his family. He was trying to survive. We both were. He never asked to be thrown into this nightmare."

She paused. "There were nights we didn't know if we'd wake up. And yet, even then, he kept talking about getting back to his son. That hope—that obsession, really—is the only thing that kept him going."

Murmurs stirred across the courtroom. Lea gave a slight nod of approval as the judge scribbled something down.

Later, a border agent confirmed the wreckage, and the recovery of Steve's destroyed passport. Lea stood again, addressing the bench with firm clarity. "Given the circumstances, we ask the court to consider the humanitarian toll this ordeal has taken—and to recognize that my client is not a fugitive but a caretaker."

A long beat of silence passed as Gustav reviewed the last of the documents. Then, finally, he lifted the gavel.

"The verdict is that you are now free to leave Switzerland and return to the United States," he declared. "Your travel privileges have been restored, as the reason for your detainment was because of your passport being lost in the wreckage. The U.S. Embassy in Switzerland has provided the necessary details."

The gavel cracked against the block, sharp and final.

Steve's eyes wandered in confusion. "So, wait, that's it?"

"Yeah," Gustav said. "Now the real trial is about to commence. Follow me."

Gustav led Steve, Lindsay, and his family through the courthouse's labyrinthine corridors, each step echoing marble floors. As they approached the larger courtroom, the murmur of voices grew louder, accompanied by the hum of electronic equipment.

Upon entering, they were met with a flurry of activity. Cameras flashed intermittently, capturing every movement, while journalists whispered into microphones. The room was filled to capacity, with rows of seats occupied by members of various air crash investigative committees, their faces reflecting a mix of curiosity and solemnity.

Sarah said, "Now, this is where the real trial commences. The immigration trial was just a quick formality to clear you of illegal immigration charges and to restore your travel privileges. This is the real trial."

"Ah," Steve said. "Now I get what you're trying to say here."

Sarah gestured towards several Middle Eastern-looking men in suits sitting in the corner. "The actual trial is against those who established a fraudulent airline with a terrible safety record. You'll provide your account of the crash, while we'll present findings on the solar flare. Colleagues from the NTSB, Austrian Transportation Safety Board, and British Transportation Safety Board will testify against those responsible for turning air travel into a nightmare, leading to Celestine Airlines Flight 24's tragic encounter with a solar flare."

"Understood. Let's show them the resilience of survivors," Steve said. "And Judge Gustav is presiding?"

"Yes," Sarah confirmed. "The other judge is on vacation, and Gustav has extensive experience with trials of all scales. This proceeding will be broadcasted worldwide. Jim, a legal expert, will serve as the prosecutor."

Lindsay stepped forward, her heels clicking softly against the courtroom floor, flanked by Owen, Emma, Matt, and Rachel. Her eyes glistened with a mixture of pride and lingering worry.

She reached out and gently squeezed Steve's arm. "Good luck," she said, her voice low but steady. "Show the world your strength."

Owen, standing just behind her, gave Steve a firm nod, his jaw clenched as if holding back emotion. Emma offered a small smile, her fingers laced nervously in front of her. Matt hovered close to Rachel, who dabbed at the corner of her eye with a tissue, her shoulders tight with restrained emotion.

As the courtroom settled into respectful silence, Judge Gustav, presiding over the Celestine Airlines Flight 24 trial, adjusted his glasses and addressed the assembly with measured authority, the broadcast cameras capturing every moment.

"Ladies and gentlemen," he said, his voice resonating through the chamber, "we convene today to commence proceedings concerning the tragic incident involving Celestine Airlines Flight 24. This trial will explore the circumstances that led to the unfortunate loss of lives and to determine the accountability of the airline's executives in this matter."

The judge's gaze swept across the room. "It is imperative," he continued, "that we approach this case with the utmost diligence and impartiality. The gravity of the allegations necessitates a thorough examination of the evidence and testimonies presented. Our objective is to ensure that justice is served, upholding the principles of fairness and integrity that are the cornerstone of our legal system."

Steve turned to Lindsay, whispering, "There are many family members of the victims here, but I can't seem to find Barry, Mary, and Oliver."

"I presume they're relieved that Oliver is alive," Lindsay replied softly. "They probably want to avoid more of this."

Judge Gustav continued, "Before we proceed, I extend my deepest sympathies to the families and loved ones of those who perished aboard Flight 24. May these proceedings bring clarity, and ultimately, justice."

With a nod to the lead prosecutor, he signaled the commencement of the trial. "The court now calls upon the prosecution to deliver its opening statement."

CHAPTER 43

In the solemn atmosphere of the courtroom, lead prosecutor Jim Banks leaned toward Steve and whispered, "We're going to thoroughly hold this company accountable. They will answer for their negligence."

Steve nodded, his eyes firm with resolve. "Show them what you got. They're responsible for everything that happened to me."

Jim stood and approached the bench with calm authority, his presence commanding attention.

"Your Honor, esteemed members of the jury," Banks began, his voice clear and unwavering, "we are here to seek justice for the tragic loss of lives caused by the crash of Celestine Airlines Flight 24. The evidence will show that this tragedy was not a mere accident, but the foreseeable consequence of a series of negligent decisions made by the airline's leadership."

He moved deliberately to outline the prosecution's case with meticulous precision, detailing how the airline's executives prioritized profit over safety, neglecting critical challenges.

"We will hear testimony from former employees who will attest to a culture where profitability was placed above passenger safety," Jim continued. "These witnesses will describe how they were pressured to approve flights despite known issues, especially with faulty navigation software, leading to the aircraft being directed toward a solar flare."

As he spoke, a cockpit voice recording played softly in the background. Steve's voice came through, strained and urgent, cutting through static: *"We're losing altitude—no response from the controls."* The room fell silent, the tension thickening as the gravity of the moment settled over the courtroom.

"Furthermore," Jim added, his tone unwavering, "we will demonstrate that the defendants engaged in a deliberate cover-up incident, attempting to obscure their culpability by tampering with evidence and providing false statements to investigators."

Jim faced the jury squarely. "Ladies and gentlemen, the loss suffered by the victims' families is immeasurable. It is our duty to hold those responsible accountable for their actions. Through the evidence presented, we will prove beyond a reasonable doubt that the defendants' negligence and willful misconduct led to this tragedy. Justice demands nothing less. We will also give the primary survivor, Steve Turner, the opportunity to share his account."

With that, Jim returned to his seat. The defense counsel quietly rose to prepare their rebuttal.

After several poignant witness accounts, Judge Gustav said, "Mr. Turner, please approach the podium and share your experience with the court."

Steve exchanged a glance with Lindsay, Emma, his brother Owen, his parents, and his grandmother, nodding to them before approaching the front of the courtroom. He adjusted the microphone.

"Your Honor, esteemed guests, ladies and gentlemen watching worldwide, I stand before you today as one of two survivors of the catastrophic crash of Celestine Airlines Flight 24 in November 2022. It's unimaginable that I survived alongside Oliver. This is the defining moment of my life.

"Before I delve into the details of my journey, I want to express my gratitude to everyone: my family, my fiancée seated behind me, friends, air crash investigators, the media, the Austrian and Swiss people, scientists studying solar flares, and the rescue teams who braved treacherous conditions in Austria to search for us.

His voice deepened as he continued.

"I vividly recall monitoring the flight tracker and noticing our deviation from the planned course, coupled with several solar flare incidents over the Atlantic and the Alps. Within minutes, the plane veered off course into the Alps. I thought I was doomed.

"Hours later, I awoke to the icy sting of the wind cutting through the remnants of Flight 24. Surrounded by twisted metal and scattered luggage, the reality of our crash in the Austrian Alps hit me like a freight train. Every breath was a battle against the freezing air, and every movement sent jolts of pain through my body.

"Pushing through the debris, I found Oliver, a six-year-old boy from Norwich, England, crying beside his dying father, Paul. Paul implored me to take Oliver home to his grandparents in the UK. In that moment, my purpose shifted. I was determined to protect this child and ensure we both survived."

Rachel pressed a hand to her mouth, eyes glistening. Lindsay wiped at her cheek, trying to stay composed. Emma sat rigid, fists clenched in her lap. In the back, a quiet sob broke the silence as one of the victims' mothers lowered her head.

Steve continued, "Each day, I prayed for safety, comfort, and protection. The days that followed were a blur of relentless challenges. The cold was merciless, seeping into our bones. We scavenged for food, managing to find the bare minimum to sustain us. At night, I wrapped Oliver in my arms, shielding him from the biting wind, sharing stories to keep his spirits up, even as doubt gnawed at my own resolve.

"We stumbled upon a village, and hope sparked within me. But that hope was quickly extinguished by the cold stares and closed doors of the townspeople. Their fear of outsiders, especially during a crisis, left us isolated. The rejection cut deeper than the chill of the mountains. I questioned how humanity could turn its back on those in need, especially a dying child. I was told that solar flares had caused resource shortages, leading to suspicion of outsiders.

"But there were moments of unexpected beauty. One night, as Oliver and I huddled together for warmth, the sky erupted in a cascade of colors—solar flares painting the heavens with brilliant hues.

"Eventually, we reached another town, and this time, compassion greeted us. Two women, Heidi and Maria, took us in. Their kindness was overwhelming. Oliver began to smile again, becoming his true jovial self. The weight of our ordeal lifted a bit."

A sudden call came from the audience. Steve looked back, his mouth agape.

Maria waved, saying, "We came all the way from Austria for you."

Steve turned to Judge Gustav. "Your Honor, may I have a moment?"

Judge Gustav nodded with the cameras flickering, people in the audience murmuring. One of the executives from the airline stood up and laughed. "You really call this a trial? This is a joke."

Judge Gustav slammed the gavel. "It's just a few minutes. The man survived through enough hell thanks to idiots like you."

The audience chuckled as Steve embraced them. "Thank you for coming all the way here to help me through this. I'm so happy you're here."

"Wir lieben dich, Steve," Simon said. *We love you, Steve!*

Glancing at Simon and Theresa, Steve returned to the microphone with renewed focus. "These two ladies and their children were the best part of our journey. They took us in, providing warmth and care. Their kindness was overwhelming, bringing tears to my eyes. Oliver began to smile again, becoming his true jovial self. The weight of our ordeal began to lift."

Steve continued, "I've seen the good, the bad, the dark, and the ugly of life, along with the solar flares." He chuckled, looking at the Celestine Airlines executives. "The lack of action against these solar flares across Europe is disgraceful. The crash shattered my world but also revealed resilience and the profound impact of empathy. Even in the bleakest times, a single act of kindness can reignite hope and pave the way for healing. Starting today, we need to punish the executives of Celestine Airlines for their gross negligence, honor those who died, and find a way, together, to stop this threat to humanity. I rest my case, Your Honor. Thank you."

Steve left the podium and returned to his seat. Everyone, except the executives and their lawyers, stood and gave him a standing ovation, broadcasted worldwide.

Judge Gustav slammed the gavel. "Can we have Sarah, Dr. Tachikawa, and Dr. Crehan come up and make their statements about the solar flares before the executives present their case?"

CHAPTER 44

Several days later, after an intense and emotional trial, the courtroom was thick with anticipation as the jury filed back in, their expressions solemn.

The judge addressed the jury foreperson, a middle-aged woman named Reneé who clutched the verdict form tightly. "Reneé, has the jury reached a verdict?"

Reneé nodded, her voice steady yet tinged with gravity. "We have, Your Honor."

"Please read the verdict."

She cleared her throat. "In the case of the People versus the executives of Celestine Airlines, we find the defendants guilty of gross negligence in every manner leading to the wrongful deaths of the passengers aboard Flight 24."

A collective gasp echoed through the room. Tears streamed down the faces of the victims' families, a mixture of relief and sorrow. Steve, seated among them, closed his eyes, a silent prayer of gratitude for justice served.

"In light of the jury's verdict," the judge said, "Celestine Airlines is ordered to compensate each victim's family—Mr. Steve Turner included—in the amount of $1.5 million."

As Steve exited the courthouse with Lindsay, they embraced, sharing a moment of collective solace.

"I'm really proud of you, honey," Lindsay said. "You went through hell, but now you've survived."

"Yeah, I know. I only wish Oliver was here with me to celebrate. But I'm glad he and his family will be compensated as well."

Matt looked at Steve. "So, it's straight for the airport back to Atlanta?"

"I guess so," Steve said. "Right now, since I don't have my passport, I'm being put on a special flight back home. You'll have to join me back in Atlanta."

Owen rushed back with Sarah, Dr. Tachikawa, and Dr. Crehan, saying with excitement in his face, "I've got some good news to share. First, congratulations Steve."

"Thanks brother," Steve said. "So, what is the good news?"

"My trackng app is about to get acquired by the NTSB. They say the app is essential for efficient searches, making the rescue of victims much easier."

He turned to Sarah, who added, "I have a contact at the NTSB who spoke with Owen as this trial went on, and he was willing to offer a large sum of money to acquire Owen's app. Owen will be working with us to assist in future incidents that might occur due to solar flares."

"My god," Steve said. "That's incredible."

"Your father and I are so proud of you," Rachel said.

"Thanks, Mom…Dad."

Denise approached Owen and hugged him as well. "Looks like your grandpa helped raise some amazing kids and grandkids. I'm really sorry for whatever happened in the past."

"Mom, it's okay," Matt said. "It's time we move on, learn from our mistakes, and ensure they don't happen again. Dad left me a message before he passed: 'Forgive Mom for all her mistakes. She's not perfect.'"

Denise gave Matt a tight embrace.

Steve looked at the group. "We basically reunited the whole family with the help of this app in the town of Lichtersee in Austria."

"Speaking of Lichtersee, where are Maria and Heidi?" Steve asked.

Maria and Heidi approached Steve alongside Simon and Theresa and embraced him.

"Great job, Steve," Maria said. "Thank you for bringing us here."

"No, thank you," Steve replied. "You brought me back to life. Now, it's my turn to repay you. Whenever you come to the United States, come straight to my house. We'll have some nice southern cooking."

"We'll see," Maria said. "We have to manage the farmhouse back in Lichtersee, but once we can address these solar flares, then we can finally celebrate as a family."

Rachel turned to Heidi and Maria. "Thank you for taking care of my boy."

"It's no big deal," Maria said, smiling. "Come to Austria, and we'll make the world-famous schnitzel."

Steve held Simon and Theresa in his arms before signaling to the Swiss officer about heading to the airport.

"Shall we go?" the officer asked.

"Yes, sir," Steve said. He released Simon and Theresa, waved goodbye to everyone, and said to Lindsay, "We're coming back here soon for our honeymoon," before joining the officer on the way back to Atlanta.

EPILOGUE

A few months later, the newly married couple, Steve and Lindsay, landed in London Heathrow Airport on their brief honeymoon, arriving on an overnight flight from Atlanta. They planned to take a train to Norwich and then a bus to the town of Aylsham for a special visit.

As they approached the London Underground, Lindsay asked, "So which express are we supposed to take?"

Steve, glancing at his phone, said, "Take the Piccadilly line east toward Kings Cross St. Pancras, then take the Northern line to Liverpool Street. It looks like the next one is due in five minutes, so we better hurry."

Dragging their luggage, they quickly made their way to the Piccadilly line platform, boarding just before the doors closed. The train departed toward central London.

They switched the trains and proceeded to Liverpool Street Station, where they embarked on their journey from London Liverpool Street to Norwich on a crisp spring afternoon. They boarded the Greater Anglia train to Norwich, settling into their seats as the train gently pulled away from the platform.

As the train navigated beyond the outskirts of London, urban landscapes gradually gave way to the rolling countryside.

"Steve, look at those fields," she exclaimed, her voice filled with wonder. "It's absolutely breathtaking."

Steve smiled. "This is why I love the UK. I can avoid going to London, but I can't miss out on spending time in the countryside. I imagine Oliver grew up in a place like this, given his cheerful personality."

Steve leaned back into the cushioned seat, watching the British countryside blur past in streaks of green and gold. A soft mechanical hum filled the car, broken only by the occasional clink of coffee cups and the quiet chatter of nearby passengers.

Lindsay nudged him, holding up her phone. "You realize your backpack still has the tag on it, right?"

He laughed, tugging at it. "That's intentional. A fashion statement highlighting our memories surviving in the Alps."

She rolled her eyes but smiled, resting her head briefly on his shoulder.

The train began to slow, and Steve caught sight of a stone church spire rising above the rooftops. He leaned closer to the window, watching as cobbled streets and crooked chimneys came into view.

"Is that Norwich Cathedral?"

Lindsay nodded without looking up from her guidebook. "It's older than most countries."

As they stepped off the train, the cool air hit his face, brisk and clean. His legs ached from sitting too long, but there was a buzz in his chest—nervous energy, maybe, or hope.

"Aylsham's not far now," Lindsay said, slipping her hand into his.

He gave it a gentle squeeze. "Let's finish this right."

As the urban scenery began to fade, Steve spotted a weathered red tractor parked beside a stone wall, and beyond it, a row of cottages with thatched roofs and sagging chimneys.

After approximately fifty minutes, the bus arrived at Aylsham. Steve and Lindsay disembarked with Steve plugging in the address of the house where Barry and Mary lived.

"Do they know that we're coming?" Lindsay asked.

"Nope," Steve said. "I want to surprise them."

"Are you serious?" Lindsay gasped. "I don't like unexpected visits, especially showing up unannounced."

"Don't worry honey," Steve said. "We got this."

They walked for half an hour away from the center before stumbling upon a detached country home exuding timeless charm and elegance with the exterior showcasing traditional brickwork complemented by period features, reflecting the architectural heritage of the region.

"Wow," Lindsay said. "This house looks very pretty. Do you want to make sure if it's the right address?"

"Sure," Steve said, looking at his phone. "By the looks of it, this is the right one. Let's see for ourselves. What's the worst that could happen? The Brits are known for their hospitality."

As they approached, the front door swung open, revealing Barry and Mary with wide smiles. "Welcome! It's been too long," Barry exclaimed, pulling Steve into a warm embrace.

Mary hugged Lindsay tightly, her eyes glistening. "We've both missed you so much. Steve, you were outstanding during the trial against those executives."

"Thank you," Steve chuckled. "I wish both of you and Oliver were there. I could've done even better in the trial. Lindsay and I just got married and are on our honeymoon."

Barry and Mary squealed with joy, embracing Steve and Lindsay. "Congratulations to you both!"

At that moment, Oliver emerged from his room, his eyes lighting up as a broad smile spread across his face.

"Steve!" he exclaimed.

Steve knelt down, opening his arms as Oliver rushed into them. They shared a long embrace.

"I told you I'd come back," Steve said softly. "And this time, Lindsay and I are here to look after you."

Oliver beamed with joy as Steve held him close.

Mary inquired, "What's the plan?"

"Lindsay and I have discussed becoming guardians for Oliver," Steve explained. "We know there's no one else to look after him, and we've heard that if anything happens to either of you, he'd need a stable home. Grandparents should enjoy their grandchildren, not be burdened with heavy responsibilities. And after all he's been through, I don't think Oliver should be raised by strangers or the system."

Mary looked at Steve and Lindsay, her eyes filled with gratitude. "You saved Oliver and brought him back to us. It seems he truly loves being with you and could use your guidance. We'd be honored for you to look after him."

Steve nodded. "Please, take your time to decide."

Barry nodded. "I'm fine with it. I'm getting older, and I'm not sure I can keep up with Oliver."

Lindsay noticed a smell. "What's that smell?"

"We're making beef bourguignon, a hearty stew," Mary said. They proceeded to the dining room, where the aroma of a home-cooked meal filled the air. The dining table was set for a feast, showcasing the warm hospitality Barry and Mary were known for. As they gathered around the table, laughter and stories flowed, the room filled with the comforting sounds of a family reunited.

As the evening sun cast a golden hue over the countryside, Steve and Lindsay walked to the graves of Oliver's parents and sister, located in the backyard and laid flowers on top of them which Steve said, "Paul, Sophie, and Amy, I'm sorry that you had to leave Oliver behind in a tragic manner. Me and my wife will make sure he has a stable home."

Steve turned to Mary standing beside him and asked, "You buried them here?"

"Me and Barry just wanted them here with us instead of being in a cemetery. We wanted them to be close to us as possible," Mary said, tearing up. "The county was generous enough to let us do it."

"That's a noble thing," Steve said.

The skies grew dark with Steve and Oliver wrapping up playing soccer with each other, and they returned inside and sat in the living room.

"Well, it's a relief we don't have to worry about those solar flares anymore," Mary said. "We've got better protection now. "

"I'm not so sure about that, Mary," Steve replied. "It's likely to get worse. Sarah, along with Dr. Kazuo Tachikawa and Dr. Patrick Crehan, wants us to meet them in Ireland. We're planning a project to prevent future solar flares. We wanted to stop by here first to say hello and ensure Oliver is safe before heading to Ireland for the meeting. Once the meeting is done, we'll sign the papers to be legal guardians to Oliver."

"What's the project about?" Barry asked.

The doorbell suddenly rang. Mary opened the door with nothing but crickets chirping.

"Hello, is anyone there?"

A voice echoed with a thick Finnish accent, "I need to see Steve Turner, please."

Mary rushed back to see Steve with a quiver in her voice. "Steve, I think there's someone here to see you."

"Yeah, sure," Steve said. He handed Oliver to Lindsay as he walked to the front door, seemingly quiet.

"Hello," Steve called out. "Who's there?"

A masked man emerged, whacking Steve to the ground unconscious and whisking him away into his van. Mary screamed, "Call 999!"